OUR STREET

SÁNDOR
TAR

SÁNDOR TAR

OUR STREET

TRANSLATED BY

JUDITH SOLLOSY

Contra Mundum Press   New York · London · Melbourne

A mi utcánk © Legal successors of Sandor Tar, 1995.
Translation of *A mi utcánk* © 2015 Judith Sollosy. First Edition: Magvető Publishing, Hungary, 1995 Budapest.
First Contra Mundum Press Edition 2015.

Library of Congress Cataloguing-in-Publication Data

Tar, Sándor, 1941–2005

[A mi utcánk. English.]

A mi utcánk / Sándor Tar; translated from the original Hungarian by Judith Sollosy

—1st Contra Mundum Press Edition
296 pp., 5×8 in.

ISBN 9781940625119

   I. Tar, Sándor
  II. Title.
 III. Sollosy, Judith.
 IV. Translator.

2015941685

Contra Mundum Press would like to extend its gratitude to the Hungarian Books & Translations Office at the Petőfi Literary Museum for rewarding us with a subvention to aid this publication.

HUNGARIAN BOOKS AND TRANSLATIONS OFFICE

CONTENTS

SÁNDOR TAR

OUR STREET

UNCLE VIDA

The street is waiting for the mailman. His cheeks are ruddy and he has a moustache; he wears a blue uniform and a green cape with a small red ribbon pinned to it. Around here unruly horses get ribbons like this tied to the harness, so people should beware & not stroke them. The mailman does his rounds on a motorbike with a sidecar, and he doesn't have to be offered a drink anymore either, like before. Before, he did his rounds on a bicycle and people were expected to offer him a glass of pálinka or wine that he'd gulp down after a show of reluctance. And he'd take the tip, too, which came to twenty or thirty forints, a veritable fortune around here, with pensions being what they are. By noontime he couldn't sit on his bike, just push it along. Yes, ma'am, yes, sir, he'd holler when asked, tomorrow. You'll have it tomorrow! Fine, dearie, fine, but bring it in the morning before it gets as hot as it is now! If he staggered & fell he was dragged into a nearby house, rested a bit, then continued his rounds. In the afternoon he works as a hired hand, he plows the land with a horse, takes on shipments, prunes the vine. He's respected, because he's a hard worker, & nobody has ever stolen from him.

The street consists of thirty to forty houses on the village outskirts. At the upper end of the street there's a pub and a bus stop. Half the people are retired or live off of unemployment, how they manage nobody knows, least of all themselves. The houses are of varying sizes, some big, some small, each with a small garden. Some people even own a bit of land, but what's the use, Uncle Vida says, when regardless of what you grow, there are no takers. The state had the cows butchered, while those that kept theirs now have to milk them & feed them & spread the dung. As for the milk, nobody wants that either, and fattening a pig's not worth it, the fodder costs money, and then the slaughterhouse, they either take it or not, and for what? For peanuts. Besides, an animal's not like TV, you can't switch it off and go vacationing or to the movies or whatnot. The livestock's gotta be fed, Sundays & holidays included. Animals get hungry. Sunday. Every day. Several times a day. People don't think about that.

Uncle Vida is a well-read man, and sensible. He's just turned seventy. He owns five holds of land, a vineyard, a horse, a cart. He grows corn, sunflower, cabbage. He'd like to take his apples to market, too, but these days people won't eat anything but oranges & bananas, he says. He says that in the spring he buys cabbage seedlings for two or three forints a piece, and come fall, a head will fetch no more at the market than the seedling price, provided anybody wants it, of course, whereas it needs tending year round, hoeing and watering and sprinkling with insecticides, and even so it either turns out all right, or not. It's the same with everything, Uncle Vida says. I can't eat it all myself, he says, and what I don't grow, I have to buy. Like bread. And shoes. And there's the electric bill, the water, taxes. Everything. Everything costs money. But where am I to get it, Uncle Vida asks. I don't have a pension. I wouldn't mind selling things now and then, he says, but who'd buy them? People don't have money. I don't know what's to come of this, he says.

This is Crooked Street, he says. It winds around, & that's what we always called it, crooked, even when it went by other names. It's been called Ságvári,[1] and now Radnóti,[2] except nobody calls it that, not even the mailman or the chimney sweep. Nobody. When anybody comes asking for it by name, people take a good look at him, then ask who he'd be wanting. People around here don't know street numbers, Uncle Vida says, not even their own. The other day Aunt Kiss said to the doctor, doctor, dearie, what do I have to know the street number for? I can find my way home without it.

This is a hillside. It used to reach down to the stream, but there's nothing there now except a thicket. It's dried up. My father and the others used to go fishing there. Things were different back then, Uncle Vida says. As for the street, it took shape just like all the others. A cart drove along, then a second, and then a third, the tenth, the thousandth, each driving along the groove. There was plenty of mud for adobe. Today some houses have split levels. And there's even a concrete sidewalk, but only on the upper side. When it rains the water runs down to the side below, says Uncle Vida. For those that live there it's bad, he says, and there's lots of bickering, because the people living above dig grooves to divert the water and the hogs stand belly-deep in it and the rugs come floating out into the yard. But it's been some time since we've had that sort of rain, he says.

Our fathers and grandfathers could still manage to give a piece of land to each of their children, & a house, Uncle Vida says. We were expected to add to it, work hard so we could pass something on to our children, too. But that's not how it turned out. The co-op came[3] & the young people left empty handed to work in the mines or on construction sites, or at the foundry. Most of them never came back, Uncle Vida says. Then those that were born after them left, too. They went off to school, the factories, Debrecen, Pest. Wherever. And now they're trooping back, hungry and penniless. They drink and loaf about. They play cards. They live off the old folk & wait for the mailman. Some wait for their relief, others for their pension. Money. They're all waiting for money. Then when the money comes, it's payback time, oh yes, each man what he owes the other. Misi's pub, the shop, Sarkadi, Pintér. Three houses sell wine and pálinka, Uncle Vida says, on credit, otherwise they couldn't get rid of it. It's poor wine, it's bad wine. They make hedge wine from the rape and add it to the wine. By Easter it's pure mold. Then they skim the top off, add sulfur and sugar, and sell it by the glass or bottle. They ask a stiff price, but considering that people can't pay anyway, what's the harm? Strong, good looking young men stand around under this window looking out or idle about outside with nothing to do. Nobody wants to do the raking anymore, Uncle Vida says, or milk the cow, or feed the pigs. They won't sit atop a cart neither. They'd rather walk alongside or ride a bike. At home, they bicker with their wives or parents. They get divorced. There's all these handsome new houses, some with six rooms and split levels, burdened with mortgages, and the head of the household out of work, and there are children, too, they signed a contract to have them and got promised the moon,[4] and now there's nothing, just the shit hitting the fan. Then after a while the wife gets fed up and wants a divorce. That's how things stand today. And the houses, Uncle Vida says, they're up for sale. But whose gonna buy them, he says.

Uncle Vida's wife died four years ago, come Christmas. Every death and accident in the family happened on Christmas, Uncle Vida says, and he wouldn't mind if he never saw another Christmas as long as he lived. First it was his brother. He was shaving when all of a sudden he sat down & said, oh my god. But by then his head was blue, then it went black. He was gone just like that, sitting on a chair. His leg, too, got broke on Christmas. The pig pressed it against the fence & refused to budge.

Uncle Vida lives with his son, but everybody knows that it's his illness that brought him back. He used to work in Diósgyőr,[5] but after a time the fumes and the smoke ruined his lungs, but the real problem is that his wife walked out on him when he was taken ill, Uncle Vida says. His mind is sick, too, he says, it's his nerves, damn it, that's why he won't get well. They had a car & an apartment. Everything. And now he's just sitting there, Uncle Vida says, or lying in bed ill with nobody to talk to him, not so much as a handshake. He can't go out or visit people because he's got trouble with his lungs. He's not contagious, Uncle Vida says, they said so in the hospital, or they wouldn't have let him out. But even so. We took him everywhere you can think of, Uncle Vida says, before his wife left him. We paid through the nose. We gave money to them all in the hospital, even the elevator man. He can't sleep and he can't stay awake. At night he gags and coughs like the devil. I get up, go sit next to him, try to help him up. Then, half way in my lap, he dozes off like that, like a child. I took him to Doctor Szabó in the village, he's an old man, retired, to find out what's wrong. I'll give you ten thousand forints, I said, if you make him better, twenty if you tell me the truth. If you cure him, you can ask for the moon. Mr. Vida, the doctor said, don't waste your money. Your son won't ever recover. Give him whatever he wants. He hasn't got much time left. Just like that. In short, we all got our cross to bear. Mine is this. I can still work, even at my age, but this, this I can't handle, Uncle Vida says. I kept telling my wife, look, we need two or three more children, that's the real thing. But no. She may have been right, of course. For all we know, she said, we won't be able to bring even this one up properly. It was wartime and I was at the front. There was no guarantee I'd be back, Uncle Vida says. And now, this. There's no telling, ever, what the future holds.

I don't take anybody inside my house, not even into the yard, I don't want people saying it was me that made them sick, Uncle Vida says. I wash and cook & clean. My house is as neat as anybody's. Inside and out. But people won't shake hands with me anymore either, Uncle Vida says. The Harap boy says to me the other day, don't take it to heart Uncle Vida, he says, but I got my child to consider. Fine, I say to him, you go do that, but you don't know who drank from your glass or bottle in the pub before you, do you? It could've been me. Or the Dorogi boy's horse, because that's his bit of fun.

Every day, I take my boy two liters of red wine from Mrs. Sarkadi, Uncle Vida says, because she sells good wine. To me, at any rate. What would you like to eat, I ask my boy. And drink. But he won't eat. Just the wine, the wine, that he forces down. And nothing else. I'd gladly bring him more wine, but he won't drink it. Sometimes he can't even keep the two liters down.

He won't drink my wine either, just this. Doctor Szabó said, too, that red is better for him. We get on nice and quiet, who knows for how much longer. If there'd be somebody that could pass his illness on to me and my life on to him, I'd kiss his hand. But there's no such man.

When he got married, Uncle Vida built himself a house out of mud and wattle & beams. Back then, his house was the fifth on the street. Nice dry walls half a meter thick, the partitions thinner, warm in winter, cool in summer. There was an oven, too, but he dismantled it when the local shop started selling bread and it didn't have to be made at home anymore. There was nothing to make it from anyway. You can climb up to the attic from the porch, but there's nothing there. A shed with corn, a stable, pigpens, a small garden in front of the house. In summer gladiolas bloom there, and other things, too, perennials that Uncle Vida's wife had planted. They come up by themselves every year. Outside, by the fence, there's a small bench. It's nice to sit there & smoke & watch the world go by. Everything's just fine, considering.

JANCSI HESZ

I'm an Antall boy.[6] I used to work at the Bearings Plant, Jancsi Hesz says when the mood's on him. Sitting at a table at Misi's place, he sweeps the money into his palm and when it's his turn, he deals. The pub's got a proper name, but people on our street just call it Misi's, after the proprietor, who usually sits at one of the tables himself and is everybody's friend. His wife behind the counter gets aggravated sometimes. Misi! Misi, my pet! she yells, May the Good Lord slam the fuckin' graveyard door in your face. I asked you for five cases of beer. Who do you think you are? The guest of honor?

The pub doesn't get a lot of customers, but at least they're steady. The cassette player is blaring upstairs, the Misi boy is testing the volume. The pub, the garage, and the storeroom are on the ground floor. Up front there's a small patch of a garden with grass and a tall willow with tables under it. But Misi's customers don't sit outside, even in summer, because they don't want people to see. Jancsi Hesz is one of the regulars. Each time he comes in it's just for a quick drink, then he ends up staying, either because he spots somebody he knows, or hopes to. He waits and sips his drink. Sometimes he orders another round, or maybe a beer as a chaser. He chats with Misi's wife. At this time in the morning, Misi is busy slagging the furnace or packing stuff into cases in the storeroom.

He takes a swig or two from a well-hidden bottle. He's fuming mad. He hates the fact that it's morning again and would give his right arm to be out of a job, like Jancsi Hesz, who has nothing to do all day but wait for the mailman.

Jancsi Hesz is always short on time, but then he always ends up staying. I'll just win this one last game, he says, then I'm off. They're expecting me. He's short on time in the shop where he pockets a small bottle of pálinka, & he's short on time at Mrs. Sarkadi's, where he has his own glass, because he won't drink after just anybody, there's a consumptive in the street, though he won't say who, he wouldn't do a thing like that. Still, you never know… He's short on time at Pintér's, too; he's just dropped by for a quick drink, he says, it tastes like cod liver oil, but never mind, I'll have another. Let's see if it's any better. By then he's taken a seat, though, but just for a minute, he says, because of the heat. Then he goes back to Mrs. Sarkadi. She's a good listener, you can unburden yourself to her. But only when nobody else is around. If there's anybody around, he stops by the door, waiting, drinking wine, hoping they'll go away & then maybe he can ask her for a loan of two hundred forints. Or a thousand. Jancsi Hesz won't drink on credit. He won't have anybody put his name down in some damn book. He'd rather break in someplace. Whenever he stands in the door drinking his wine and smoking and not talking to anybody, Aunt Piroska knows that something's weighing on his mind. If the others don't leave, he'll leave, then come back later and get it off his chest. I didn't want to, not in front of the others, he says, excusing himself, and his cheeks are on fire. Once he told Aunt Piroska that he loves her more than his own mother.

Jancsi Hesz has a grownup son and daughter, both married, two small grandchildren, a wife and a mother-in-law that lives on the same plot with them, though in a separate house with a room & a kitchen. But given half a chance, she's over at their place sticking her nose into everything, even how often Jancsi Hesz should sleep with his wife, because their little boy could use some mothering, too, now and then, she says. Jancsi Hesz's wife works in the co-op office, but what she does he couldn't say for sure. Only that they steal and embezzle. This is what he tells Aunt Piroska, but only when nobody's around to hear. Don't tell anybody, he says, but I'm ashamed. Ashamed of the goings on here. Now that the co-op is falling apart at the seams,[7] they're selling everything. They've turned half the countryside into a sand mine. They felled the trees, cleared the woods, sold the stables, even, for construction timber. Whatever they could get their hands on. They picked out the best machines from the equipment park and sold them to the engineer Kásás & three others, dirt cheap. Anyway, that's what the people in the village say. They also picked out two-hundred hectares of land. They're going to turn it into a private enterprise to grow melon. Also, now that it's got an owner, it can't be given away as compensation land anymore.[8] Jancsi Hesz thinks that Kásás and the others are screwing his wife. What did you say, Aunt Piroska asks. She's not familiar with such words. They sleep with her, Jancsi Hesz says, his face burning with shame. Your wife, she's not that type, Aunt Piroska says by way of comfort, but she doesn't add what everybody knows, that Évike is so fat & ugly, Kásás wouldn't want her. Nor the others. Their daughter is another matter. She's a sight better looking, and younger, too, & she's working in the greenhouse, to be on hand. When they learned about her condition, they quickly married her off to a tractor driver, and the baby was born premature. But only compared to the wedding, of course.

Jancsi Hesz started working at the Bearings Plant as an unskilled laborer, but he was good with his hands, they tried him out here and there, and were satisfied. He became a locksmith, then he was transferred to machine maintenance, then he mastered engine mechanics. He was at the top of the heap. When he got laid off, they promised to take him back first thing. He shouldn't bother looking for work, they'll call him. He can hold steady till then. Jancsi Hesz hasn't taken off his work clothes since. He's still wearing them, as if he'd just popped out of the plant on a quick errand. When there's anything tricky, they always send for me, he tells Aunt Piroska, because she believes him. He doesn't socialize much with the people here. He's not like them.

When they play cards, he usually wins. It takes brains. He filled up somebody's engine with a hundred percent anti-freeze and by spring the stuff corroded the cooler, or so people say, but he says that that wasn't the problem, except he's not gonna explain, they wouldn't understand. Sometimes he hops on the bus to Debrecen. I gotta go, he says to Aunt Piroska, they sent for me because they're in deep shit. Then he adds, it's the diesel. Aunt Piroska nods. Sure, sure. Then she pours him another drink. Now go, she says, drink it & go. Just don't write it down, he says, I'll be back with the money. I won't, Aunt Piroska nods, then closes the door. Then she takes out her small notebook and writes, J. Hesz 2 x 3 decis. That's around two thousand forints, including the loans. Aunt Piroska sighs.

Over at Misi's, Jancsi Hesz gulps down a shot of pálinka. He's short on time, he says, the bus'll be here any minute. They're stuck, so they sent for him. I'll drop in on the way back, he says, & pay for everything. Behind the counter Esztike grimaces and says, I hope so, János, I certainly hope so. You owe us for yesterday, too. Don't worry, I'll be back, he says, and hurries off, because he's always short on time. Who could've come up with the rumor about him and Esztike, he's thinking. He helped her on the bus because there's an iron rail above the steps and Esztike's behind got stuck & he pushed from below so she could squeeze through. Some half-wit saw and told everybody he petted Esztike's behind on the bus. That's what people here are like. His wife gave him hell and moved her stuff to the office, and for two months Jancsi Hesz lived on scrambled eggs. He didn't know how to make anything else. And to make matters worse, his neighbor Béres saw him over the fence one night go to his mother-in-law, who squealed like a stuck pig when she saw him approach in his underpants. Béres thought he'd go over to help him out in case he couldn't manage the old hag by himself, but he couldn't move because he was standing in the pigsty just then, and his boots were stuck in the manure. It was a good story and people had a good laugh over it at Misi's, and also at Aunt Piroska's and the shop, too, not that anybody believed it. You dreamed it up, Aunt Piroska told Béres. By that time of the night you're as drunk as my arse. Which was true.

In Debrecen, the bus stopped at the railroad crossing to let Jancsi Hesz off. From there the Bearings Plant was just a couple of minutes' walk. At the plant Jancsi Hesz always tries to get the janitor to let him in. He should call maintenance if he doesn't believe him, he says. He got an urgent call in the morning, because the diesels are his responsibility, he says. Or something similar. Go on, call Kulcsár. He's in charge. When that doesn't work, he says, fine, but somebody's gonna have to take the responsibility, because there's gonna be trouble. He's going home, he says, it's no skin off his back, but they better put it in writing that he showed up. And they'd better remember to put down the exact time, too, because somebody around here is gonna be sorry. Then back home he tells Aunt Piroska it was nothing, just the feeder, it got clogged up. They don't know what they're doing. It barely took five minutes, so naturally, I wouldn't take the money. Then he asks her for two hundred forints, sometimes a thousand. Tomorrow they're bringing me a car to fix, he says. It's a big job. It's gonna pay well. Now that they know where to find me, they'll be coming and I'll break even, you'll see. Just don't tell the others.

Sometimes his mother-in-law Terka sneaks over in her rubber boots, darting looks right and left, making sure nobody sees. Their house is practically across the street, and Jancsi Hesz is always sitting by the window. Don't give him anymore to drink, she tells Aunt Piroska. He just smashed the glass door with his fist. He also tried to scratch my eye out just because I put kindling in the furnace. It's getting so I can't do anything. I have to sneak into the house to see my own daughter and grandchild. Well, don't meddle, Aunt Piroska says, why stoke up the furnace? You got a decent place of your own. Leave them be. They're young. Let them live their own lives. Sure, sure, Terka says, except they'll freeze to death. If I don't feed the furnace, nobody does, and that little boy needs to do his homework, if only he could. When she comes home from work, Évike also likes a warm house.

Lean and slightly stooped, Terka sneaks along the street like a thief, as if expecting to be yelled at. She tries not to make any noise, but her outsized boots flap against her thin calves, and she smiles and nods right and left, because she knows that the others are sitting by their window, watching. Then there's only the yard to cross. She's hoping Jancsi Hesz won't spot her. Her small house is in the back of the yard, but when her son-in-law has one of his crazy fits, that short stretch of yard is the longest in the world. The dog leaps up at her. He's happy and wants to play, and it leaves big muddy lines down her dress. Get away, she whispers, get away from me, you goddamn dog, may the devil take you, with all the rest of them.

IT'S MORNING

Aunt Piroska is a good soul, she knows how to portion out the early-morning wine. She gets up at the crack of dawn, which is another good thing about her; by five she's tending to the chickens out in the yard. Béres is waiting outside the front door, shivering with cold. You're up already, the old, gray-haired woman comments, then lets him in. I've been up for hours, the tall, bony man says. His face is heavy with stubble, but he hasn't shaved for weeks and won't until the trembling stops. Aunt Piroska takes out a three-deci glass and pours him two decis of wine. Béres usually drinks three decis and takes a liter home with him. But in the morning that's not how things work. Aunt Piroska turns her back, puts kindling on the fire, or goes to the pantry, while Béres gets hold of his glass with both hands, and tries to bring it to his lips. These are difficult moments; he has to lean down to it. Even his legs are trembling. Aunt Piroska pretends she doesn't see. She keeps busy, tells him things, pours the dirty water out of the washbowl, then fills up the bottle for him. Meanwhile, Béres manages to drink his wine, and he doesn't even spill much. He gets two more decis in his glass, and this time has less difficulty drinking it. Hesz is standing around outside in front of the door. He won't go inside with a cigarette, he'd rather smoke it first. Nobody else would be this thoughtful.

Sudák is approaching from the lower end of the street. He's wearing a leather coat with a two-liter bottle hidden under it. This makes him hold his hand in an odd way, as if people didn't know he was going for wine, and on credit, too. Jancsi Hesz waits for Béres to finish his business inside, but it takes time, so Aunt Piroska calls out to him to come in and not wait outside. This early in the morning, the choreography is tight. Béres out, Jancsi Hesz in, Aunt Piroska sizes him up, then pours, filling his glass either all the way or halfway, depending. Sometimes Jancsi Hesz also needs both hands to bring the glass to his lips. By the time Sudák comes in with a resounding hello, Jancsi Hesz is on his way out. He's got no time to spare, but he lights up again outside, telling Sudák not to go in with his.

Sudák tries to keep up with the fast pace of events. He knows that people have things to do in the morning. His hand to his heart, he apologizes for his presence right, left, and center. At one time he was a folk dancer. Nobody around here has ever seen him dance, but that's neither here nor there. There may be something to it, though, because he's let his hair grow, and he even has a mustache. Getting ready for Parliament?,[9] Dorogi asked him once, your hair's like a toilet brush. Sudák snaps his heels together & has a refined way of talking. He never swears, he just says things like "I'll be darn doodled," or "Beelzebub take you!", then hastens to apologize. He's occupied, not busy, like the rest of the people around here. I was in Pest, he explains, with the troupe. We danced in front of ministers and generals. They must've been fuckin' shit drunk, Dorogi once said, 'cause they haven't seen you dance neither. Dorogi always had a big mouth on him. You got a big mouth on you, Sudák has said many a time. If you don't mind my saying. You mustn't talk like that in front of Aunt Pirike. A brother, he says at other times, you're like a brother to me, and he puts his hand to his heart. I swear. Isn't that so, Aunt Pirike?, he asks. She couldn't say why, but Aunt Piroska doesn't like being called Pirike. Still, she says nothing. Go on, get out, she says when she's had enough of her customers, finish your drinks and go. It's late, and I'm sleepy. Time to disband.

In the morning, though, it's not a problem. They just drop in and are gone. The small shop next door opens at seven. Aunt Piroska is the first one in. She buys bread and milk and gets rid of all her change. She charges twenty forints for a glass of wine. Pintér charges twenty-five, but he fills each glass to the brim, and that comes to more than three decis. Still, nobody goes to him in the morning. Who could lift a full glass to his lips so early in the day? Pintér serves pálinka, too, but there's no knowing what's in it. He's got no fruit trees & no grapevines, or barely any; still, he's never short of wine. That's what's making all of you sick, Aunt Piroska tells her customers, that damned pálinka. Pintér also sells salt sticks & you can play cards and chess, but he often cheats on the bill because he drinks along with his customers and gets muddled about how much people drank, so he rounds it off. He's dull-witted, Jancsi Hesz commented once, that's his problem. And also, he drinks.

At home, Sudák rehearses in front of the mirror. He raises a glass of water to his lips and practices, even though wine, that's different, of course. He holds out his arm. Good. But when he takes one sip at Aunt Piroska's, his hand shakes so bad, he practically drops the glass. Also, the shaking won't stop, so he's got to steady the glass with the other hand. That helps. He's grateful the old woman isn't looking. I can't drink it all at once, he says, putting his hand to his heart. I'm sorry. Something got caught in my throat. Meanwhile, Uncle Vida is waiting outside. He wants to take wine home for his son, but he won't drink any himself, it's too early in the day for that. Also, he's not about to drink out of a glass, he won't have people saying he's come to infect them with his son's disease. He's got his own wine. Still, he wouldn't mind having a drink someplace now and then, and chat and smoke a cigarette and pour his heart out. He's got plenty to complain about. Once Sudák is gone, he tells the others that his son is so helpless, he's got to be bathed and scrubbed down. All over. And also, he had no idea till now what tuberculosis is like. When he gives his son a rubdown with warm water, it stands up straight as a pole, poor boy, when there's hardly any life left in him! He barely touches him with the washcloth, and it stands right up. Aunt Piroska's stomach turns at hearing such things, and she says so. Please don't say things like that. It's awful. Just like that? Just from the warm water? Uncle Vida could tell her a thing or two about that, and other things, too, but Aunt Piroska won't have it. It's disgusting. They're more or less the same age, not that it makes any difference at their time of life. Aunt Piroska is hoping he'll leave soon because Dorogi's coming, and so is Veres, and it's best if they don't find him here. Sudák is standing outside the shop with a cigarette, waiting for it to open.

Aunt Piroska's house stands on one corner, the shop on the other, and between them a narrow dirt path leads down to the stream. The stream is dried up. Even in rainy weather there's nothing in it but mud and frogs. This time Uncle Vida leaves through the front door just as Dorogi enters through the back. A great big hulk of a man with a thick voice and a red face, he starts by asking, was that Vida? Yes, Aunt Piroska says, why do you ask? Why is he sneaking around like that? Isn't the door other people use good enough for him? Aunt Piroska says nothing, she just wipes the door handle instead, so they can see. All right, come on in everybody, she says. His son's got cancer, not tuberculosis, Dorogi announces after a while, then sits down. Except these retards think it's tuberculosis. Lungs! Lungs! Veres says nothing, he remains standing, & he drinks. I wouldn't know about that, Aunt Piroska says. Still, I told him it'd be best if he didn't come. I give him a bottle, but never a glass. People won't drink after him, and if I'm not careful, they'll stop coming. Dorogi says he's told everybody the truth, but people are like Aunt Piroska says. As if that weren't enough for him. He's gotta be bathed, like a child. Is that so, Aunt Piroska says, as if she was hearing it for the first time. And when I think how bullish he was when he was young, Dorogi goes on, he'd do it to a fly in mid-flight! In mid-flight! And now, just look at him. His father holds him in his arm and strokes it with his soapy hand. But I better not say anymore, though I see everything from next door, through the back window. They fall silent for a while, what's there to say? Then Veres also asks for two glasses of wine and says, that's life. From the outside, all houses look alike. A fence, a yard, and so on. But what's inside the fence, you don't know unless you live there. Then they finish their drinks and Dorogi says, okay, let's get moving. Time waits for no man. For some reason, they're all in a sour mood. Just outside the door, Sudák lets out short brief coughs. The shop isn't open yet, he explains. I thought I'd come back for another round. Don't drink so much, Józsi, Aunt Piroska says, you'll end up kicking your wife again. And slapping her around. Aren't you ashamed of yourself? Who? Me? Sudák asks innocently. Aunt Pirike, you have no idea what she does! She empties the washbowl in front of the house, when I keep telling her not to. I swear. All right, drink & have

done with it, Aunt Piroska says. Don't play the gentleman with me. Wait until you're home.

Outside, a boy is herding a sow down the road.
Where're you takin' that sow, Laci, Dorogi calls out to
him. To the boar, the boy says. Why're you pestering
that poor animal for, herding her down this bad road,
Dorogi says, can't you help her out yourself? The men
laugh, & so does the boy, though he says nothing. Then
the shopkeeper shows up with his cart and opens the
lock. Jancsi Hesz is beating the side of the boiler with
his fist, you can hear it all the way to the pub. Aunt Kiss
opens the gate and her husband drives through it with
two horses, some young people are coming from the bus
stop, then when Sudák leaves, Aunt Piroska closes the
door. So much for the first contingent. Now it's the shop,
to buy pálinka. They'll drink that, too, then eat something, provided they have anything to eat. Then they'll
lie down and sleep till noon. Then in the afternoon, it'll
start all over again. There'll be five or six men bickering
at Aunt Piroska's, making fun at each other's expense,
or they'll pick on Béres or Sudák. Each one will repeat,
for the hundredth time, what a good hand he was at the
factory, and still, he got laid off. Aunt Piroska feeds the
chickens, then the dog, then washes up and boils water
for tea.

There's a small patch in front of the shop. From time
to time a car stops, then the Csige boy blasts off with the
big Ifa, people shout at him, Sudák and the others drink

pálinka by the glass, then chase it down with beer. Béres goes up to them timidly, and somebody buys him a beer. He'll soon be asking for wine, too. Aunt Piroska has a bite to eat, then looks through the small glass insert in the door. They're still out there, leaning against the wall. Dear, dear, they're not gonna be of much use to anybody today, she thinks with a shake of the head. Then the youngsters start off to school, but first they stop in front of Aunt Piroska's place for a bit, some of them go inside the shop to buy rolls or bread or chocolate, then off they go. Béres will be the first to open the garden gate, Aunt Piroska thinks, then Jancsi Hesz, and then the rest of them. And so it goes.

JÓZSEF SUDÁK, FOREMAN

Attila is the best looking boy on the street, and everybody knows it. He's an adolescent now, he's in eighth grade, but when he was little, everybody wanted to eat him all up. In summer he wore tiny shorts, and he went from house to house, and if the gate wasn't open, he'd bang on it and shout. Wherever he went, they picked him up, pinched his cheeks, & stuffed him with candy and cake. Sudák did, too. Once he sat on the ground in front of the boy and kept gazing intently at him for a long, long time. Then he asked the child, tell me. How in God's name did you turn out so well? Hm? That's when something must've gone off in his head, because something definitely went off, except it didn't show at the time. He was living with a tall woman back then, an alcoholic, and it's a good thing he didn't marry her, he later said, just shacked up, because he'd have been fleeced, with the woman taking half of everything. What that everything might have been he didn't say. He pushed her out the gate, bolted the door, and good riddance. She tried to move back in two weeks later, but the new woman poured dirty water on her, just like that, from a washbowl, over the gate. Jolán Árva stood there in her suit, with a cigarette, necklace, wristwatch, and the sudsy water running down her. I can't believe it, she said, aghast. That deaf bitch poured water on me! Because the new woman was a deaf-mute.

A thing like that can be kept under wraps for a while, of course. Sudák had brought her from a ways off. She had a pleasant face and a fine figure, except people noticed she wouldn't go out, not even to the shop. Sudák said she's not the gossiping kind & prefers to keep her council, and others would do well to follow her example. If anybody went past her, she gave a nod and smiled and muttered something as if in greeting, then moved on. She wore pretty dresses, smelled nice, had rings on her fingers, & at Misi's Dorogi even said once how he'd like to doodle her, out of curiosity, if nothing else. Then after two or three weeks he said, boys, that woman is deaf. You're kidding, they said. She can't be. Deaf as a post, Dorogi said. There I was outside the gate shouting to her to send Józsi out, but she went on hanging the wash, her back to me. I was shouting so loud, half the neighborhood came to see what was up, but she kept throwing the wet clothes on the line, I swear.

Sudák once said he's the overseer at the Plastic Works, but the card players at Misi's countered it out of hand. Hey Sudák, they said, don't push your luck. So it's foreman, Sudák said, and stuck to it. Jancsi Hesz looked into it and said, you're nobody there, Józsi. You're a janitor in the yard. Sudák didn't answer him. As far as he was concerned, he'd put an end to the discussion the other day. Besides, he'd made up his mind that he'd have a child and let their jaws drop in amazement, the whole lot of them! He was already dismantling the old house, planning to put up a new one in its place. He'd knocked together a small room and kitchen at the back of the yard, that'll do till then. The yard was gradually filling up with gravel, bricks, and beams, and it didn't matter anymore that the new woman was a deaf-mute, the street had taken a liking to her. She was neat & clean, and Sudák had changed for the better, too, thanks to her. He didn't drink in the shop anymore and stopped going to Misi's, except for an occasional shot of pálinka, then he went on his way. He preferred to buy his wine from Mrs. Sarkadi now and drink it at home with his new woman.

He'd originally come from Debrecen, & people said he was divorced. He got off the bus, saw Misi's, went inside and asked for a small glass of Unicum bitters, at which the pub fell silent. What was that, Esztike asked, Unicum? Can't a fine gentleman like you make do with nothing else? The fine gentleman took the hint. Sudák's hair came down to his shoulder even back then, and his moustache drooped to his chin. He gulped down a shot of pálinka, then asked if there was a house up for sale. There was. Even back then, the regulars at Misi's knew everything. There's old man Koda's, they said, he just died, and his son doesn't want it. They even said who he should talk to, he's right here, except he'd gone outside to the loo. It's got everything, they told Sudák, furniture, bed sheets, flowers in the window, flypaper. Even a dog lying in front of the door, because it won't leave the house as long as there's chicken to catch.

Then the Koda boy came back. He was drunk as a skunk, but manageable. The others helped steady him while he signed the bill of sale, and Sudák laid out the two-hundred thousand forints. He didn't even go see the house. He'd be seeing it plenty now that it was his, he said, and why don't they have another round of drinks? But he'd like the key, please, because he's not going back to town. What key? There's no key. The door's secured with a piece of wire. In these parts, people don't go around thieving.

It was a real bargain, the talk of the street. Sudák paid for everybody because Esztike took the Koda boy's money away. You shouldn't walk around with all that cash, not in your state, she said. Come back tomorrow. I'm putting it on the shelf behind the peach brandy. In front of everybody. You can fetch it tomorrow. And now, go on home. In the meanwhile, Sudák let everybody know that he's a gentleman. He never lived in a village, only in town. He also told them how he'd sunk so low. It was a sentimental story, so nobody liked it very much. Then came his adventures, by which time Misi, the proprietor, had appeared with three cases of beer. Sudák was showing them dance steps, how you need to bend your knee at every step, it's not easy, springing up and down like that. He said that his cap was like the cap of the Spanish volunteers. Nobody argued, as the people of the street had never seen a Spanish volunteer. Still, Misi commented that he thought it was just like the beret he kept in the cellar, except it's on crooked.

That man lies through his teeth, he said to his wife Esztike, but he can't be all bad if he's got money. Later Jolán Árva also showed up, and she could also do folk dances, and by closing time Sudák asked for her hand, and she gave it. What celebration! After the pub closed, the people trooped over to the house with a case of beer. This guy doesn't fool around, Misi said to his wife. He came with the four-thirty bus. Now it's eleven, and he's got himself a house and a wife. As for Dorogi, the following day he said he couldn't remember who slept with whom in that rumpus, but in the morning the dog climbed out from under Sudák and it was growling something awful.

People could've gotten used to Sudák's flights of fancy and his strange manner of speaking and dressing, if only his money hadn't run out. Jolán Árva was a great help to him in this, because she took it into her head that she'd have to put on airs and wear nice dresses now that she's hooked up with this handsome man with the dancing feet. She stopped being on a first name basis with people, and started smoking like a chimney. They didn't get married. It was so old fashioned. We love each other just as is, she told people. They went to a dentist in town, but only when they needed a tooth pulled, that's all they could afford. Consequently, Sudák's lips shifted on his face, while Jolán's stretched. This may have also played a part in their relationship turning sour, but the main reason was that Jolán Árva took to the bottle and refused to have children. Except by then Sudák was hell bent on having a child. There was Attila to remind him. He wanted a child as pretty as Attila, except a girl with long, curly locks, and dark blue eyes.

It hadn't even occurred to him before that he didn't have a child. Before, his entire life was taken up with various culture groups, dancing, and pranks. He worked in Barcika, then Pest, then Debrecen, where he began to suspect that he'd never become a professional folk dancer. His ex-wife had changed, too; she got old, kept breaking her legs, then gave up dancing altogether, whereas you should've seen the two of them dancing to the song that went, on a starry, starry night in spring. In Palkonya the prison warden even made a special point of congratulating them. He said it's not even dance, it's art! You can practically see those stars sparkle, I swear! Jolán Árva was a far cry herself from sparkling, and she didn't want children either, that was the source of all their troubles. She said she couldn't. Sudák took her to see a doctor. I took her to the bee farm, he told the men at Misi's, and they gave her a physical from head to foot. Then they couldn't stop laughing. What's so funny, I ask the doctors. Nothing much, they say. Except, half of your wife's lungs have got to go. Her lungs? I ask. What for? To make room for her liver! Just like that. It may not have been true, but everybody had a good laugh over it. Sudák had shacked up with the new woman by then and was planning a new house, a garden, and a family in earnest. There's gonna be palm trees growing in the yard, he announced, the likes of which this place has never seen. And then some. A swimming pool! A glass roof! And monkeys, somebody said. Two at the very least.

In 1989 he was waiting for the change in regime like spring rain. The Magyars, their time has come, he announced. At last! Magyar music, Magyar dance, Magyar bread! In 1990 he was laid off, because almost always it was the morning shift that woke him. He was a night watchman and they got fed up. For months he got no money, and bit by bit he sold the gravel, the bricks, and the beams from the yard. Also, Katóka still didn't bear him a child. At times he thought it might be too late. Meanwhile, next door, Attila was growing into a handsome adolescent. As time passed, Katóka divided off a part of the room with a curtain, because when Sudák was drunk, he was unaccountable. He'd dance & sing in front of the mirror, then slap Katóka around, or kick her in the shin.

Sudák had wanted to be many things in his life. A dancer, a partisan, an actor. When they started broadcasting ice skating shows on TV, he even took up ice skating, and in his dreams he was the happy father of little Attila and a beautiful baby girl. Now he took it into his head that he's going to be the mayor. But only a couple of people know about it, just Jancsi Hesz, Dorogi, and Aunt Piroska. He stands in front of the mirror, practicing his acceptance speech. He is fifty-five years old, and his hair has turned gray. Just you wait & see, he says to the mirror, just you wait & see.

THE RETURN

Old man Veres's son is dark and lean, and he can fix just about anything. He's got the tallest house on the new row, because the old row across the way is higher up, and he didn't want the rain to flood him. And besides. Jancsi Hesz just laughs it off, he's from the mountains, these people reckon everybody there lives on top, he keeps saying. What's wrong with one house being higher up than another? Nobody cares, except here, on the Great Plain. It's an ugly house, no plaster, no fence, the barren yard runs down to the field and the wind sweeps garbage over it. It's the best Laci Veres could do before his money ran out, all of it, and his strength and will-power with it. Down in the cellar two piglets squeal all day long from hunger, but at least the kitchen upstairs is fit to be lived in, and that's where the Veres boy eats, drinks, and sleeps. The rest of the house has gone un-finished, and his wife, too, left and took their child with her. She said she's had it. Laci Veres was a welder in the factory before he became redundant, but that's where he got all his know-how, because there was all sorts of work there, plumbing, gas fitting, machine repair. Any-thing to do with ironwork was right up his alley. But he could fix anything, as long as they gave him the tools. There was nothing he couldn't fix. Except the money, the money's the problem. The only money he's getting now is what the mailman brings, and that's precious little.

He got married in Debrecen. He married a woman from town, but he soon came to regret it. Everything about Laci Veres is oversize, his nose, his ears, his feet, his hands. If he stands in front of them, the women look right past him. Angéla was the exception. She figured she'd get used to it. They lived in a rented room in an old house, it was damp and chilly, and then the baby came, whereas they didn't want one yet. But since it came they had to do something, and so Laci Veres joined the Party, except it didn't help. Six months later he joined the Workers' Militia,[10] where they were glad to have him, there were hardly any workingmen in the detail, just department heads, engineers, chief accountants; they were on a first name basis, hi there, hi there; during drills and in the lecture hall they ate and drank, they sang, then the men got in their cars, while he and three comrades were left behind to wait for the bus. The others called them the physicals, though only behind their back, of course, but they were on to them. They didn't much care, though Laci Veres once said, I'm gonna fling a hand grenade right in their midst, and then we'll see who's a physical. I hate every one of them like my own shit, he said to his wife back home. But what can I do? Maybe something will happen. On the other hand, when he had a hangover or some business to attend to, he called up the platoon commander who promptly wrote out a temporary transfer request and he stayed home from work. But apart from that, nothing.

He then tried to organize the welders into a brigade, something nobody had managed before him, but he managed it. Welders are a different bunch in every factory, but he convinced them that the brigade would bring in some money, and they didn't have to do anything to get it, so why not? He became the head of the brigade. He gave speeches and participated in debates, made sure to talk big everywhere, & took personal charge of the brigade diary;[II] they got recognition after recognition and the money that went with it, and as a matter of fact, they didn't have to do anything for it, and they liked that. You're not half as dumb as you look, they told him, so keep up the good work! In return, the men in the brigade taught him welding, adjusted the voltage on the converter for him, handed him the proper stick, and as for the rest, it took care of itself. It was smooth sailing all the way. The brigade became socialist, which was no small matter. Laci Veres requisitioned the factory bus and they went on an excursion to celebrate. Before they set off they got so drunk in the pub next door to the factory, they hardly had to replenish at all and were well disposed all the way, and later he wrote in the brigade diary, "After the breathtaking beauty of the countryside, we arrived in Tokaj." Truth is, nobody could remember, but it must've been true. At this point Laci Veres was sure that the time had come and they'd give him an apartment, but he thought wrong. The apartment was not forthcoming. No problem, he said to his wife,

I'll wait a bit longer. But then there's gonna be hell to pay. They were sitting on the side of the bed & had run out of anything else to talk about.

When he slept on the couch, he poked his legs between the bars of his son's playpen, which lay at the foot of the bed, and the little boy kept grabbing and biting his toes, and it felt good, and they laughed a lot. Once he had a bad dream, or something happened to him, & around midnight he kicked the playpen with the child in it all the way to the wall, and he said he's had it. What's the matter, his wife asked a hundred times, if one, but he said nothing, just sat on the side of the bed, his back to her, drinking his beer. He later swung his huge paddle hand behind him and flicked his wife off the bed, as if she were some bug. Come morning, Angéla packed up, and taking the child with her, went back to her mother, but he didn't particularly mind, she'd done it before, & she always came back. Laci Veres didn't say anything now either. Let her go if she wants to. In the morning he called his detail commander and said he's got something to see to and asked him to write out a transfer request for two days, then drank beer with vodka. He found a bag of frozen chicken wings in the freezer, he thought he'd cook it on the stove but must've done something wrong, because the wings got stuck together, they burned on the outside but remained frozen on the inside, cold, inedible. Still, he ate some of it, sprinkled it with salt and pepper, then threw the rest in the garbage.

He remembers everything clear as day, he says when he tells his story, even that he pulled on his Workers' Militia uniform, gun & all, then he went five houses down the street to threaten that scumbag Molnár, because he's perpetually drunk and beats his family and carouses. He said that unless he mends his ways, he's gonna shoot him. They just stared, nobody spoke, even the dog forgot to bark, then he put the gun away and walked out. He visited four families that morning and told all of them that from here on in things are gonna be different. He's gonna come check up on them. Every day. He said the same in the pub, and also to the cashier at the shop. There's gonna be trouble, he said, if they try and shortchange their customers. Also, three beers and two small bottles of pálinka, that's as much as they can give anybody. Who are you, the manager asked cautiously. Workers' Militia, Laci Veres said. In case you haven't noticed. But now you have. Yes? Yes. Good.

Then seeing how he was into it anyhow, he figured he might as well go to the factory, too, to the Party secretary's office, place the gun on the table and ask what the fuck else is he supposed to do before he's taken seriously? That's when Halász, the Party secretary, decided that he'd have a hidden alarm button installed on his desk for just such eventualities, and at home, too, because this is crazy. He said something encouraging, then sent word that Veres should be demobilized without delay because he's threatening people with a gun, and he ended up in neurology, then the psychiatric ward, and later, on the street. He might've been thrown out of the Party, too, he can't remember. But he remembers that while he was in the hospital, his wife Angéla gathered up her things again, canceled the lease, took their son, and moved back to her mother. Later his father came for him and he was discharged, because psychiatry, you can't just walk out of there on your own.

They went home in silence, got off the bus, then headed for Misi's, where they came to a decision. Laci must move back to the village, because it's no good the way it's been. You belong here, the others said, too. Dorogi gave him pálinka, Béres repeatedly tried to shake his hand, but couldn't quite manage it, while Sudák said, your place is here with us, Sanyi boy! Laci Veres drank his beer and pálinka in a daze and was soon drunk, because he was still weak. Then after a while he went up to the counter & kissed Esztike's hand, just when Jolán Árva showed up. Her eminence, my wife, Sudák said, introducing her. I say it like it is. Isn't that right, Esztike? Then Misi, the proprietor, also made an appearance, patted Laci Veres on the shoulder repeatedly, then showed him the house, the cellar, the storeroom, the garage, the pub, the apartment upstairs, the garden, everything. Out on the balcony Laci Veres felt a bit dizzy, but as soon as he'd relieved himself of the mixture of beer, Lithium, Noveril, and Andaxin, he felt a lot better and decided he'd build a house just like Misi's, & he'd build it here,

among friends. With these two hands, he said to Jolán
Árva that night in bed, because they'd all been drinking, and afterwards everything got all confused. Sudák
danced some sort of folk dance with Jancsi Hesz, then
without Jancsi Hesz, then ended up sleeping on an old
cot in Misi's cellar. They must've locked me in, he concluded when he started awake in the middle of the night.
I can't get out, he said out loud, and wet his pants. He
felt better by the morning and he saw cases and more
cases of beer in the gloom and couldn't stop drinking
from sheer amazement.

In the morning his father took Laci Veres home so
people wouldn't see him in this state. At home he ate
something and talked a pack of nonsense, he was in a
grand mood and said he'd build a house bigger than anybody's on the street. He's gonna show them! He drank
pálinka, but he gave his medicines to his mother to lock
away. He didn't even want to see them, he said. Then
he went to bed but couldn't sleep from anticipation, his
brain spinning like a wheel. He even remembered that
he'd slept in the same bed as a child, right here under
the window, with a big down comforter to cover him
against the cold of the unheated room, and he used to
pee in bed. There was nothing wrong with him, he just
didn't feel like climbing out from under the warm comforter and going to the back of the yard, and he waited
and waited until it was too late. And then it was morning already, there were people stirring outside, & when

he looked out the window he saw the same thing he'd seen back then, the pump well in front of their house that rarely drew any water, but people kept pumping it just the same, tinkling the empty tin cans, and further off an old locust tree and the large pothole in the road. I'm back, he sighed as a nice, familiar warmth flooded his body down there, just like in the good old days.

MRS. DOROGI, MANCIKA

Three generations live side-by-side on this street, or all together, but everybody knows that if a train passes around noontime, it's eleven-thirty or three-ten in the afternoon, or five-fifteen. The railroad's nearby, the station, too, is just down the end of the street, but hardly anybody takes the train these days, the bus is less trouble. The people here learned the real story behind Mrs. Dorogi when around six o'clock one evening somebody spotted her lying on the tracks. She was nicely dressed, with a watch on her wrist, a necklace, a knitted cap. Terka Papp, Jancsi Hesz's mother-in-law, sneaked up, thinking maybe she's asleep; she even called her, then went back home, changed into another housedress, splashed some water on her face, and even washed off the rubber boots she had on. Then she headed for Mrs. Sarkadi, Aunt Piroska. She sells wine, so there's bound to be somebody around. Piroska, she said quietly to the gray haired old woman, because this time there was nobody around, just Piroska, Mancika is lying on the tracks all dolled up. Can you believe it? What, Aunt Piroska asked aghast, what is she doing? She's not doing anything, Terka said, just lying there. Well, didn't you ask her what she's doing there? No, Terka said, I just called her, Mancika! Mancika! But she didn't answer me. I thought I'd better tell somebody, because she can't stay on the tracks.

You mean you left her there? Didn't you even pull her off, Aunt Piroska asked, the train's gonna run her over! The train's been and gone already, that's why I thought there was something wrong with her, but I was afraid to touch her, what if the five-fifteen ran her over? What do you think? Well then, go tell her husband, Aunt Piroska said. Or somebody. Quick. She might still be alive. Besides, freight trains run on these tracks, too. It's not safe. I can't go myself, you know that! Go tell your daughter or son-in-law. You live with them. But we haven't spoken to each other for the past two months. Just imagine, not so much as a word! I'd rather take it all back.

Nobody knows anymore how long Mancika lay on those tracks in her Sunday best. Terka must have alerted somebody, or maybe Aunt Piroska, and then the news reached Misi's, where the men have plenty of time on their hands, and where they'll listen to what anybody's got to say. As luck would have it, Dorogi happened to be there, too; he was just giving his horse a drink of beer from a bottle. He listened to the big news, then asked for another shot of pálinka, then told Jancsi Hesz he'd better come along, because if he goes on his own, he won't take responsibility for his actions. It was getting dark, this is when people feed the livestock, provided they have any, but now, as Dorogi drove past on his way to the railroad tracks, everybody was out on the sidewalk, or looking over the fence. He had some fresh hay in the back, so they threw Mancika on top; she was too drunk to get in on her own. Then as night fell, people went about their business as usual.

Mancika dressed well, she even bragged to anybody willing to listen how well she was doing, she bought a new dress, and not from the ragman either, but real fabric that Aunt Kiss made up for her, with ruffles & lace. She found the pattern in a fashion magazine, and also shoes, a hat, a knitted cap. And gloves, too. In summer, too. She even told Aunt Piroska that her husband is not like the rest of them here because he's a toolmaker, he makes medical equipment in the factory, and as everybody knows, that's just a step away from being a doctor himself. And he's handsome, and a good man, too. He likes kissing her, and some nights he's got to have her twice. Building the house, too, had been off to a good start; she had a bit of money put aside, and so did Pista, and the walls were soon up, and they'd already moved in on the ground floor when the others were still digging the foundation for theirs. Also, they were the only ones with a cement mixer, the one the others are using to this day. Aunt Piroska liked what Mancika had to say, it's so rare nowadays to hear about a couple who get on so well, just that she didn't believe everything, but that's neither here nor there, seeing how Aunt Piroska's got some quaint ideas. For instance, she looks to see if a chimney is smoking, because where it's not, whereas the people are home, they didn't light a fire that day.

And if they didn't light a fire, they didn't cook, and so on. Of course, it's possible that they're cooking with gas, except there's no gas on the street, and as for gas tanks, nobody buys them off of Feri Hamar, who comes by on his small pickup every day and blows his horn, on his first round for gas, on the second for soda water. And come summer, for watermelon.

Dorogi is not bad looking, he's got ruddy cheeks, he smiles a lot, and is cheerful, too, he's got a high school diploma, and he won't drink on credit at Aunt Piroska's. Everybody here is his friend, young and old, especially the children. When he had time, he took them around on his small Simson, one on his lap, another in the back. When it's pig-killing time, he's everywhere. He's strong as an ox, and people ask him over in the morning to catch and hold down the pig. Once he slaughtered Béres's piglet on his own. He hoisted it under his armpit and stabbed it, then put it down, here, take it! It's all yours! He used to work in Debrecen, where he was a trained polisher along with about twenty others. He stood his ground there, too, but they laid him off all the same, and a good thing, too, Mancika had said, because he was going to leave anyhow, and this way he got six months' severance, enough for a car, they'll hardly need to add anything to it. Besides, given his profession, he can find a job anytime he wants. Except, it's best he rested for a month or two. We're not so hard up, she said, that he should go running after a job.

And he didn't. In a matter of days, Mancika says, her Pişta changed completely. He used the severance money to buy a horse, a harness, a dray wagon to go behind the horse, and also boots, a hat, a quilted jacket. Mancika didn't leave the house for days, then went to the doctor & asked for tranquillizers, or anything that'll make her husband come to his senses. When she walked down the street she quickened her pace and wouldn't stop to chat with anybody and wouldn't get on the dray for anything in the world. Fine. So walk, Dorogi said, flicking her with the whip when she couldn't keep up with the horse. Then after a while he snapped the horse's backside with the harness and as they galloped, Mancika had to break into a run alongside, because Pişta kept beating her calves with the whip. Few people saw them, but those that did didn't believe their eyes, they thought the two of them were having their bit of fun. That Dorogi, he never fails to come up with some prank, then the two of them end up having a good laugh over it, like they always do. When they got to Misi's, they stopped. Dorogi had some pálinka, and he said to Mancika, you have something, too, but Mancika was in such a bad way, she said she didn't want anything. Not even beer? Not even beer. Fine. I'll give it to Palkó, Dorogi said, and went outside. Hey you, he yelled at the horse, then forced its mouth open and poured the beer down its throat.

Lots of time has passed since Dorogi turned into a peasant again, and as for Mancika, she appears on the street now & then, like before, and she still dresses nice, though not as nice as she used to. Also, she'd gladly talk to people again, except they'd rather not hear, they've got troubles of their own. From time to time Aunt Piroska gives her three decis of wine, but no more, and she listens and listens and listens. About how everything's different now. The mortgage costs an arm and a leg, nearly twenty-thousand forints a month, but they haven't got it, they've already fallen behind with the payments. My Pista doesn't sleep with me anymore either, he'd rather pick some woman up on the dray. Then they go out to the garden and make love. He goes through the young women on the street one by one, he even said so at Misi's, and she happens to know that most of them can't wait for their turn. In the meantime she's working at the laundry, in the steam, the heat, ironing sheets all day, and folding them, her arms and back often feel like she's bound on a wheel of fire. At other times she also confesses that her Pista wants to drive her from the house, whereas half of it belongs to her. She's taken to sleeping in the attic now, by the chimney, where it's warmer, and she won't come down as long as Dorogi's at home, because she's scared. He's knocked out the rungs of the ladder so she can't climb up, but she manages anyway. Yes. Luckily, he's still sleeping in the morning when she leaves for work. He's making gurgling sounds on the big bed inside, and likely as not, there's a woman with him. And he won't go look for a job either. He pinned his high school diploma to the stable wall with a large nail, whereas he was an excellent student. He wants me to go away. Or die, she says amid tears. The other night he held me down and poured two glasses of pálinka down my throat, then pushed me out on the street, see everybody? Drunk as a skunk! Just like that.

Later Mancika started going from house to house, practically, to complain. She says she's afraid the time's not far off when she won't be able to take it anymore & she'll kill herself, because it's too hot up in the attic this time of the year. She relieves herself into a bucket, and she's got to bring that down, too, every day, and as she talks her mind sometimes wanders, her face takes on a curious expression, then she asks, where was I? She tells Aunt Piroska that when this happens, it's as if she'd lost consciousness. She has no idea what she's been saying and she has no idea what she's supposed to do next. Aunt Piroska doesn't know either, & suggests that she should see a doctor and tell him everything. Also, she & her husband should sit down and mull things over, she'd like to say this, too, but she knows it's no use. At this point, the Good Lord himself couldn't help. They have no children. They wanted to wait until the house was up, though probably that wouldn't have solved anything either. Uncle Vida says that the government is to blame for the plight of these two unfortunate people because it only allowed split-level houses, that was the condition for getting a building permit, and now the present government is punishing them with the interest, as if they were to blame. No wonder if everything and everybody goes to the dogs.

Later Mancika also says she can't remember how she ended up on the rails, only that she's lying in the ambulance, & that she got passed around in the hospital, one doctor handing her over to the next. She got examined, jabbed, cut up, then they took her out to the waiting room for somebody to come pick her up. But nobody did, so she dragged herself out to the bus stop, and from there home, up to the attic. Then she stops for a moment & asks Aunt Piroska, what was my face like just now? And what was I saying? Just as I thought.

SÁNDOR TAR

NEIGHBOR BÉRES

Our street is a dirt road barely a kilometer long. It swerves off the high road leading to the village. At one time that was a dirt road, too, then they faced it with stone, then with asphalt, but not this. This could've been the main street of the village if it weren't inhabited by poor people who made adobe bricks and mud clay on the former watery pasture that once stretched alongside for their houses. Later the whole village discovered it, people hauled water from the stream, the adobe dried in big stacks, and come spring and fall, the rain turned the whole pasture into a lake. This mussed up, pitted field separates the street from the village, says the local Protestant minister who is unmarried and who's been wandering around the dried out adobe pits in the summer for the past thirty-two years researching the village's history, but he can't find anything, just cast away cigarette stubs, paper hankies, torn condoms, candy wrappers. But the reverend is convinced that there are Avar graves hidden here, and Roman Age relics, and when people plow the land he walks along the furrows for hours on end, though the plow never turns up anything, at most frogs, grub, & mouse nests. The reverend, who is practically bald, is a knowledgeable man. For instance, he knows that neighbor Béres will die soon, because he drinks like an animal. Then he quickly brings a hand to

49

his lips and apologizes. He mustn't talk like that, but what can you do? Now that it's out, it's out. He's even told Mrs. Sarkadi, Aunt Piroska, who sells her wine to people indiscriminately, that she mustn't let Béres drink on credit, because she'll never see the money. That was about six years ago, and Béres has been drinking on credit ever since. He pays once a month, and gets three decis for free. His daughter comes running to the minister every other month, come quick, my father's dying. So what, the clergyman says, he was dying the other day, too. And the day before that. I've lost count of the number of times he's had one foot in the grave. You should go to the doctor is my advice. The Good Lord himself couldn't help your father anymore. You don't even attend church, he reprimands her in his Trabant. Neither you, nor your father. Your mother never attended either. Ever. In which case, what do you expect from me? But he told me himself to bring a priest, the little girl shrieks, because he's going to die! No doubt, the reverend says. No doubt. But that's not my fault. Or the Lord's. He drinks too much.

Neighbor Béres's house is unassuming. The fence is almost gone, and at night the little girl secures the gate with a piece of wire, though not during the day, there's nothing in the yard except rag grass & weeds, so why bother? So what is it this time, the minister shouts from the yard. He's got on a sweat suit; after all, he's not in church. The large kitchen has a stove, a table, chairs, two beds. Béres's wife Magdika is sitting on one in her pink nightgown, her husband's lying on the other, moaning. Sanyi old man, Béres says after a spell of silence, I want to confess. I want to confess everything. The old reverend is a patient man, but some things curl up his lip, if, for instance, somebody wants to confess. To him of all people! In that case, he says with infinite patience, kindly call a Catholic priest. We don't go in for such things. Well, he's not Sanyi either, he's Géza. And I'm Márton. So now what? You're not Sanyi, Béres asks after a while, trying to get the words out. Where's Sanyi? The reverend opens the small black book he's holding. Look. Since I'm here, we might as well say a prayer. Unwashed dishes on the stove, steam rising from a red pot in the middle, on the wall to the left a broken mirror, next to it an old embroidered sampler. The little girl is standing by the door. Her shoulders are stooped. She's a hundred and eighty centimeters, she's twenty-four, and she's the spitting image of her father. The other door leads to the inner room. It's dark inside. Say it after me, the minister says. Béres's wife, a bucket & a box of medicine at her feet, is laughing softly to herself. Our Father, who art in Heaven, hallowed be Thy name, the minister mumbles. What religion are you anyway? I'll be damned if I know, Bishop, the lean man says. What's it to you? I thought there was only one god? Or have I been misinformed?

Béres is tall and bony, he's got a big nose and stooped shoulders worn ragged by the years. In the morning, he starts off the day with two decis of pálinka, that's so he can shave, he explains, then he goes over to Aunt Piroska, who pours him two-and-a-half liters of wine into a plastic bottle, and also twice three deciliters into a glass. Then she enters three liters into her small black notebook, which means a full deci of clear profit for Béres. If there are others around, somebody always pays for another glass for him. Stop that hollering, drink up, and go on home! Béres speaks so loud that the whole street hears him, the dogs bark, back home the pig scurries into the sty, frightened sparrows take to flight from the boughs, & sooner or later Jancsi Hesz from next door yells, will you shut the fuck up. What're you hollering for? Are you, deaf? Still, it's a good thing that Jancsi Hesz lives next door, because at least he can spot Béres, help him up off the ground, drag him in from the street, several times a day, if need be, then he sets him down in front of the door and leaves him there. The little girl can't cope with that big, bony body on her own. She's even stopped shaving him because she can't do it; her father won't stop yelling, he's constantly moving his face and head, and he hiccups, & sometimes he even vomits.

Béres worked as a hired hand all his life. He was a pick and shovel man, he made adobe, cut the soil, then went to work on the big busy constructions in Palkonya, Pentele, and Barcika. He also worked in a mine, digging for coal and uranium ore, but it never amounted to anything. Then he got married, stopped traipsing around the country, and went to work in Debrecen. From then on, after their regular shifts and on Sunday, the two of them, he and his wife, worked as hired hands. Some bacon and bread in a small sack, and water in a five-liter tin, and two hoes. If need be, every day. In the morning they each drank a deci of pálinka, then for the rest of the day they drank the five liters of water, & also wine, if the farmer gave them some, but nothing more. During the day they made do with the bacon. They ate a hot meal only in the evening, but not always. Magdika gave birth to a daughter on schedule, but then stopped. She's enough, they said, but this one, she's gonna get an education. She's not gonna be a hired hand. They lived with Magdika's mother in the room and kitchen attached to the small thatch-roofed house. The two of them slept in one bed, the child in a wooden tub, then later they stood two chairs facing each other, and on that, for the night. When she was still tiny and got sick, she lay next to her mother, and Béres would then sleep in the lean-to, and in the summer in the corn shed. If it was very cold, he kicked the pig aside and lay down in the hay next to it. We say our prayers before going to sleep, he'd holler when people asked what the two of them were up to in there. What do you do, the minister also asked once, let's hear it! What? Béres countered, you really want to know? No, don't, the clergyman yelled at him, you should be ashamed of yourself! It's things like this that bring the Lord's wrath down on your head!

But Béres was not ashamed. On our street, things like this were nothing to be ashamed of. Once the children got older, someone would end up in the stable, the bake house, the shed, the attic, or the stack. As I see it, Béres once said, it's the Lord that should be ashamed of himself if he allows such things. We'll have the world on a string, he later told all and sundry, as soon as the old hag is dead everything will be ours, because we're looking after her. And then we'll live in the back, & the little girl up front, like a princess. Except the old woman refused to die. At eighty she still swept the yard and chased the chicken with a knife, and she made chicken soup for their Sunday meal, the feathers floating on top, and there was vinegar in it as well, and soap, and the occasional hair pin, now one thing, now another. The old woman was not in her right mind anymore. Then she was bedridden and things got a bit better, because she didn't have to be watched all the time. Béres fed her twice a day, washed her down once, changed the plastic sheet under her, but that was all. At first this was his wife's job, but it proved too much for her, and their daughter was busy with her homework, and so Béres was left with all the chores. Leave her to me, he said to Magdika, and get out of here! He picked up the old woman, set her in the washbowl, then flung her on the bed so it creaked. He finished with her in no time, cut her nails, and pulled the dentures from her mouth so she shouldn't swallow them, and gave them back only when she was eating. Then he clipped some of her hair off as well. You won't be needing that bun anymore. You can't braid it anyway. He also cut off what was hanging in her eye. She'd be better off dead, his wife kept saying. Let's move her out to the shed. She doesn't know where she is anyway. But Béres said, let's not. If a person's born, they might as well live.

People in the street say Béres started drinking in earnest when his wife was taken ill as well. She couldn't get up one morning, she fell back in bed, and her head just hung from her neck and she laughed. Then the ambulance came. By evening Béres was soused out of his mind and Jancsi Hesz had to drag him in off the street. Go call the doctor, he told the little girl. Hurry! I don't need a doctor, Béres yelled, call the priest, I'm going to die! And the gravedigger! Everybody. The little girl called both, but the gravedigger she couldn't find. But Béres was feeling better by then. He'd brought a bottle of wine from Mrs. Sarkadi, and he was drinking it and singing old songs. Two weeks later his wife was back, and a month later his mother-in-law died. Time for a change, Béres announced when he saw the cold body, then he lay the old woman on the floor and went to fetch Magdika. You're the princess now, goddam it, he said to her, and not the little girl in the front room. We're starting all over again! I love my wife, he told the men at Misi's, I swear. Now that she's sick, more than ever. She's like a child. I take her wine, let her drink. Then we sing.

If I wake up at night, I go out to the yard and start talking. Loud. Except, I can't get it out. I can't get the pain out. The reverend isn't interested, nobody's interested. Whereas even the Danube would overflow its banks if I were to pour it into her. So I'm left with this yelling. At least the yelling, that everybody hears.

THE WIND, TOO, IT JUST STIRS

The trouble is I can't get it out, can't get out what I want, when it's right here in my chest and in my mouth, Béres keeps saying, and he beats a hand against his torn, filthy shirt. He even sticks his tongue out. It's right here. Read it if you can. For some reason the tall, lean man is affectionately called Oszi. It might have been Dorogi that gave him the name, or possibly Jancsi Hesz, or maybe somebody else. His proper name is Bálint, but Oszi, Oszkár, that sounds better. Stop sticking your tongue out, people tell him, or it'll dry out! Don't you believe me, Béres asks at such times, and he grabs somebody with his huge hands, but won't hurt him. He's got to walk his wife to the outhouse in the back of the yard like a child, supporting her by the waist on both sides as she hobbles along with a cane, one foot dragging behind the other, and the urine running down her thigh, and by the time they're there, she doesn't need to go anymore, she says. Fine, Béres says. But sit on it anyway. Try. I'll be right back. Then he stops in the forsaken yard and stares into space. When his wife gets bored sitting out there, she starts yelling. Nothing's gonna come out of her anyway, not until she's inside, where it's warm, and sitting out here is bad, her naked bottom is cold, the cold's rising from the hole below, but by this time Béres is over at Mrs. Sarkadi's complaining and drinking red wine on credit, or at Misi's, yelling, then he remembers, half an hour, an hour later, or sometime in the course of the afternoon or the evening that his wife's in the outhouse. Magdika can't start off on her own because she'll fall and won't be able to get up. She waits patiently for a while, then starts beating the outhouse wall with her stick, hoping somebody will hear. If the little girl is at home she'll go fetch her, but she's awkward herself and keeps tripping and stumbling at every turn, dragging her mother down with her. Her father's better, she needs to wait.

For a while a masseuse came to see Magdika once a week. She pounded and stretched and tortured every limb, and Magdika groaned, sweated, and cried, but she can stand up now, if with difficulty, and she can even take a couple of steps with the stick, which is a big deal, considering the state she was in before. She can even eat with her hands and wipe her bottom. Only her urination is still a problem. They paid her five hundred forints a week that Béres hollered out of the village council, until somebody said he needs to bring a paper from the doctor. The doctor demurred. Fine, Béres said at the end of the argument, you'll whistle a different tune soon enough. The next day he told Dorogi to bring his dray around, then the two of them bundled Magdika on top and drove her to Town Hall. There are two leather armchairs in front of the office, and they put her in one, despite her protests that she doesn't have to go now. Just

sit there, Béres yelled. Try. I'll be right back. So Magdika
sat there. It was better than the outhouse, her bottom
wasn't cold. Then as people began showing up she had a
kind word or two for them all, about floods, Tito's par-
tisans, the bran that was left outside, whereas the dog's
out there, too, & to a child she said bleach, though she
also likes peas, there'll be plenty of peas come harvest
time. Then she wetted herself and wanted to light up,
and she laughed softly, except she couldn't understand
what all the rumpus was about, and where are they taking her, and in a car, well, well! She even got to show
them that she can wipe her bottom in her nightdress,
but that was back home already, because it's better for
her there. Béres was given early retirement and a small
supplement to go with it for tending to his sick wife,
and they got to keep the armchair, too. The masseuse,
on the other hand, stopped coming.

   Béres was close to thirty when he met Magdika somewhere around the threshing machine. Magdika was a
chaff gatherer and he a sheaf heaver; the thresher was
running from dawn till late in the evening, then the
group washed up from a barrel, ate, drank, and went to
sleep in the hay. The two women chaff gatherers slept
separately. Béres tried both of them out, and concluded
that the one with the black hair was the better match,
and also stronger, and by the time the threshing was
done, this was somewhere in Martinka or Aradvány,
they agreed that he'd marry her. Magdika was a found-

ling. A widow took her in when she was a child, and when she got older, she became a hired hand. In summer she worked with various threshing teams. They liked her because she was a hard worker and put up with the tremendous dust, the heat, & the machine noise. She had to run with the chaff piled atop a wire mesh, stack it up, then go back on the run and with a pitchfork pull from under the thresher what it had spewed out in the meanwhile and dump it on the wire mesh. Her head was bound and her neck & face, too, and her light summer dress was drenched in sweat and buttoned to the neck, because the tiny bits from the sheaves found their way into the smallest crevice and pricked and itched like the devil. From the earliest times this work has been done by a pair of women, and always for the smallest threshing share. The rest of the group is composed of men. It's the way it's always been.

There was no big wedding. Béres's parents had passed away, and the few relatives he had were in Romania, if they were among the living at all. Magdika didn't have many guests either, but lots of people from the street attended, & they even brought presents. Mrs. Sarkadi lent her her old wedding gown and brought a can of wine, Béres put on a suit, a white shirt & tie, which he took off at midnight & hung in the wardrobe, where it has remained ever since. The wedding guests stumbled home in the early morning over Béres's protests, who didn't want the festivities to come to such an abrupt end,

& who was dancing alone in the yard now, singing, the whorehouse bells are ringing for me & my gal, the birds are shitting for me and my gal, and Magdika laughed, and then they lay down together in the old woman's bed as man and wife, while the widow did the dishes and cleaned up, slammed the door, and went out to the shed for the night. That was her wedding present. Then the next day they changed places.

At night our street is quiet, only the dogs bark now & then. There's no lighting, and when the wind's up, it, too, just stirs. Béres always starts awake around dawn, and he's haunted with fear & drenched in sweat, whereas he'd kicked the cover off. Magdika is softly breathing by his side, and sometimes in jest, sometimes in anger, he shakes her, hey! Wake up! You hear? Time to go! At first Magdika tried to get out of bed like before when they set off in the dew or the freezing cold, and then he'd pin her down, where do you think you're going? You're a sicko. An invalid. Get it? Sure, sure, his wife said, like always, a sicko, and went back to sleep. Now, too, she's sleeping, though she smells down there. But that's not Béres's concern now, there'll be plenty of time for that later. He staggers out to the yard just as he is, he throws a blanket over his shoulder against the bitter cold, and that's it. He knows that he's going to have a nasty time waiting for the morning, because the mash, as Dorogi would say, is gone out of his system, and there's nothing to drink around the house. It's like somebody's shooting a gun off inside my head, he says to Mrs. Sarkadi, Aunt Piroska. I hear a horrendous bang inside my skull, and it scares me. I wake up. What's causing it? It's a veritable explosion. Could it be an artery?

Aunt Sarkadi wouldn't know, whereas it's the one thing Béres dreads in earnest, because if he suffers a seizure, like Magdika, what's to become of them? It's bad enough as is. Béres won't go any further than next door, or maybe to Misi's, because his head is spinning; he's afraid out on the street, he wouldn't climb stairs for anything because he'd fall; he walks along the street as if he were negotiating a tightrope, holding his hands away from his body so if he falls, he'll be able to grab hold of something, hopefully. And the doctor, he wants to put Magdika in the hospital, a hospice of some sort to die, because she refuses to take her medicine, she'd rather drink. So what? He gives it to her himself, she's his wife, he can do with her as he damn pleases! At least this way I know why she's got a screw loose, he tells the nurse who comes once a week to give Magdika her shot, and she also brings prescriptions that won't get redeemed. What else has my Magdika to live for, nurse, can you tell me that? What has she got to live for? What? he asks the dark night after night. And what have I got to live for? First her mother, and now her! First all that work, and now nothing! Everything would have turned out just fine, he tells Uncle Vida, if only this illness hadn't come. Believe me. We'd have put a little something aside.

We'd have had some peace & quiet in our old age. And now this! I don't know what to do. I haven't got the brains.

Uncle Vida understands. He's got a sick son with bad lungs, he's got a miserable life, too, but he doesn't know what to say either, just that one must bear it. One must. That's all that's left. I know I'm an animal, Béres yells, go ahead, say it, but Uncle Vida says nothing of the sort, he just sits on the bench under the open window and smokes. Heavy belabored breathing issues from inside. His son is still alive. What possibly could he say to others? He'd like to drink, too, but there isn't enough money in the world for the amount of drink he'd need, he'd rather work as long as he can. As for Béres, he can't even walk anymore, he's wound down like a clock, this big, strong man shrinking in front of everybody's eyes, and provided that anything's left of him to put in a coffin, it won't take more than one man to carry it out to the grave.

Béres stands around in the yard for a while. Sometimes he doesn't go back to bed at all but heads for the lean-to and hustles up something to lie on, hoping the fear won't follow him there. But it does, tugging and straining at him so his teeth chatter, even when it's warm, and his brain whirls like an engine, it veritably creaks and grinds like a mill, but what? Who knows what? I love her anyway, my wife and the wine, too, he groans into the hay, and it's none of anybody's damn business, not even the good Lord's! It's my life! Sometimes he starts shouting, and then it's better, he beats his head against the boards, will morning never come? A dog howls outside, and then the others join in, and as for Béres, he just talks *&* talks behind the boards, wanting to say it, struggling, stammering, wanting to get it out, but all he does is curse, and by now they all hear, ours is a bad street, plagued by frenzied dreams.

BÉRES'S LITTLE GIRL

Béres has one daughter, she's twenty-four, a hundred and eighty centimeters tall, lean, with a long face, like her father. At home she's the little girl. She was fifteen when she first noticed that people couldn't take their eyes off her. She went to high school in Debrecen, and if the seat was empty, she sat facing the back of the bus, or else by the window in the single seat, so people couldn't get in next to her. Barring that, she stood all the way. Seated like this, she could take out one of her textbooks or a novel and pretend to read, and she'd keep her eyes glued to the page until they reached the Kossuth Street bus stop. Once there, she was the last to get off. She waited until the bus had left and the people who got off had gone their way, then she crossed the road, and she was in front of the school. It took some time until she worked out this routine. Before that she'd sit wherever she could, and often somebody would sit beside her, even if they could've taken another seat. It even happened that they would start talking to her and would then look at her as if expecting an answer, even though she was holding a book in her hand. Anybody could see she was reading! If the bus was crowded and she had to stand, she'd go to the window in the back, where she'd look out with her back to the other passengers. At such times she'd push one leg slightly forward and bent the other just so; this way she was more or less the same height as the others, she didn't stand out as much. On the other hand, by the time she got off, her knees were shaking. But even so.

When the little girl was born, Béres was so happy, he paid for drinks all around and didn't go work in the fields for two whole days, he just drank and laughed. The little girl was beautiful, with rosy cheeks, and so she was given the name Rose, which soon caused a problem, because the registrar said that that's no name, and put down Rozália instead. Later, the little girl found out that a cow on the street had the same name, and she began hating both Rose and Rozália, and wouldn't tell people her name unless she couldn't help it. When the time came, she tasted her own stool and urine, like the other kids, & she told her mother that they didn't taste good. For a minute or two Magdika was in a state of shock, then she slapped her and washed her mouth out, phew! she yelled, then she poured water over her and gave her a bath. Vomit it out, she ordered and poked her finger in the little girl's mouth, but nothing happened. Magdika, on the other hand, threw up everything that was in her, and in the evening she told her husband what had happened. Béres didn't make a big deal out of it, he just asked, was it good, little Rózsi? No, the child said. Well and have you eaten dog shit yet, her father asked, and cow's dung, and spit? Stuff like that? The little girl said no, but her father wasn't so sure, so he explained that it's the stuff that comes out of here! And here!

And also from here, he said, pointing. None of it is any good. It's poison. Understand? Yes, the child said, thinking that now she knows everything, but she's not going to tell the other children. Let them eat what they want. Nobody told her either.

Later curiosity got the better of her and she tasted the hog's and the cow's, and the black dirt from between her toes. She ate ants, a clipped off nail, and once even half of a Gillette blade, but she didn't tell her mother about these, there was no need, because she now knew that she shouldn't be eating them. And then, when it was time, out on the goose patch a boy, a stranger, pulled down his pants in front of her, and in turn she pulled up her dress to the waist. She also pulled down her panties, but then her dress fell back down, so she took it off. Back home she told her mother all about it, and also what the boy said, and that a goose was missing. Once again, Magdika was in a state of shock, so she slapped her and yelled at her, then she quickly examined the child inside & out and bathed her in the big washbowl. Better safe than sorry. In the evening after dinner she told her husband. Béres, who was a bit worse for drink, for a while just stared, mouth agape, where should I begin, he said over and over again, then they sent the child out. The little girl stood by the door but couldn't hear anything, then they called her in. And once again, everything started with her being told that she mustn't. She should've guessed, she thought, but now at least she really does know everything, now that her father has told her that boys have weenies. He even wanted to show her, but her mother wouldn't let him, she kept slapping his shoulder, and laughed. As for the goose, they forgot all about it.

The next day or the day after that the little girl saw the boy again, and now they could do whatever they liked, because she knew that she mustn't. The boy even showed her what her father couldn't, and so now she really did know everything for real, and also that the boy had taken the goose the other day, and he took one now, too. But she didn't tell them back home, there was no need, because she knew that stealing is bad, too. Also, they didn't catch on. Later on everything was much easier because the boy told her beforehand that what they're doing is wrong, and also about the goose. But the other boys who eventually had their turn with her said the same thing, and it got around what a nice girl she was. It was summer and the geese were all over the pasture & the sun was shining and it was good in the adobe pit and they liked her, they even said how pretty she was. But she knew that already. She didn't care what the boys looked like. To her they were all the same. When they started to stroke her, she shut her eyes, and if she stroked them, she shut them then, too. It's all the good she had in her life. She was nine, the boys older or younger; in August, on Constitution Day, the school bus took them on an outing to Debrecen, to the flower

SÁNDOR TAR

show, but she didn't see much of the whole thing, all she could remember was that the strange boy, Jóska Ács, called her a colossal whore.

The little girl always wore flower printed or polka dot dresses, or else she was all in white. Her mother let her hair down over her shoulder, let it grow, she said, and it'll be like that singer's on TV, but that was not to be, because when she didn't want to do that thing, Jóska Ács set a match to it. She didn't cry. At home, although she knew she mustn't lie, she said that somebody in the crowd accidentally scorched it with a match. Only the ends were burnt a little, and they could be cut off. All the same, her hair remained short, which is how she finished school, & meanwhile she grew like hemp, her arms and legs like sticks, her neck like a gander's, even though she'd pull it way in inside her collar. Also, the boys didn't ask her to go to the adobe pit anymore, and she also knew now that they had lied to her. And so had her father and mother. Because she wasn't pretty. Also, they didn't love her. So now she really did know everything there was to know. At school celebrations she was made to stand in the back of the line because she was too tall, and nobody would dance with her in the disco. She also knew that they were poor, and that her father and mother were illiterate. The whole street knew, though it's worse than sin, it's something to be ashamed of. Now and again her father said to her, go have some fun, little girl. Go. Enjoy yourself while you can!

69

Once when he was drunk, he wanted to show her on her mother what married life was like, but Magdika poured a pail of water over him & shoved him out into the yard.

Her grandmother was sick by then, and then her mother, and her father was on disability, but he said, never you mind, little girl, you just attend to your studies. I'll see to the rest. Don't you worry about anything. There's your grandmother's room. Use that. We'll bring your mother out here to lie on the cot. What do you say? Béres did the cooking and cleaning best he could, turned Magdika on the bed, helped her urinate, brought the bedpan, gave her something to eat. Then he started drinking. One time he got so drunk he couldn't walk and his neighbor had to carry him home. Next day he apologized to the little girl, but by evening he had to be brought home from off the street again, and from then on, practically every day. Once he said to his daughter that he can't take it anymore unless he drinks. On another occasion he accidentally lay down next to her, but she pushed him off, and the next day he apologized again. He was nearly sober and he said to her, get married. It doesn't matter who just so long as you get out of here. If you can't get married, at least get yourself knocked up. Then he'll have to marry you. He cried and said this is not how he had envisioned their lives, but there's nothing he can do about it now. Which was the last time anybody could talk to him properly.

She failed school twice, but graduated all the same. At home everyone was happy, except for her. For weeks she just loafed around, then she told her father the good news. She was pregnant. At long last. Who was it, her father asked, Jóska Ács? Of course not, the little girl said. Dorogi. Twice. Her father held his head in despair and said, girl, you're a moron. Then he went and got drunk. In the evening the little girl grabbed all her mother's medicine, but the water she washed it down with smelled like urine, and she threw up. Meanwhile, her father was singing old songs to her mother next door so loud that the neighbor, Jancsi Hesz, yelled, stop that racket or I'll burn the house down, and good riddance! They yelled back and forth for a while, but eventually they quieted down. By morning the piglet had died of hunger. Béres shed some tears over it, then dug a pit in the yard. Magdika watched from the door and laughed. Later the little girl went to the shop for milk and rolls and ate them in the yard by the well. Her father would be going to the shop himself soon for two decis of pálinka, then he'll bring wine from Aunt Sarkadi, & they'll drink that, too. Then the others will follow in his tracks, Sudák, Hesz, Uncle Vida, Veres, and then Dorogi, on the dray, and then all the rest of them, one by one. And they'll drink. It occurred to her that she should try it, too, maybe it'd help, Mrs. Dorogi drinks, too, and Jolán Árva, and the others as well, for all she knew. But then she remembered that her whole life is still ahead of her, and that's enough to drive anybody mad.

THEY'RE BRINGING THE WATER

A while back somebody got it into his head that Radnó-ti Street should have running water. The young people are moving in from town, they'll want to put up houses, they'll want comfort, the village is developing. Hardly anybody lives on the odd side of the street, and given public utilities, the vacant lots would sell. Just one question remained: which is Radnóti Street? Well, Crooked Street, what else? And where's that? Where so and so from the council lives, and he deserves running water, he's a good man, with a family. Besides, it was his idea in the first place. That's different, everybody said. In that case, let's do it.

Then they started collecting the ten thousand forints, which took the wind out of everybody's sails. That wasn't part of the deal! There were two pump wells in the street already, and besides, everybody's got their own well, so why should they pay? Terka Papp, Jancsi Hesz's mother-in-law said she doesn't need running water, what water she needs she'll fetch from next door. Forget it, Jancsi Hesz, who also happens to be her neighbor said, you dump your garbage in my yard when I'm not looking because you're too cheap to pay the hundred forints. But if you mean to drown yourself in it, be my guest, he later told her as he locked his mother-in-law out of the yard with the help of a clever device. Except, in our village,

that's not how democracy works. The doctor went from
house to house with an assistant in tow, and they put
up a NOT DRINKING WATER sign over each well
and they also had the pump wells dismantled, saying
that the water pipe's coming. Besides, those wells are out
of commission anyway. And if anybody was reluctant to
pay, they added the ten thousand forints to their taxes.
There's order in our part of the world. And eventually
an excavator appeared, and also a small shack, inside it
a lazy, obese man with black hair, Tarcsai, the engineer.

It was no big deal, really. Tarcsai didn't even come out
of the shack for days, he just shouted to the machine
operator from inside, start over here, or over there, the
rest you know! The trench wasn't deep, the children
clambered about in it, and also the Protestant minister,
who has been intent for the past thirty years, at least, on
compiling the history of the village, hoping that thanks
to a sensational find, the unimpressive story will take a
dramatic turn. It didn't. On the other hand, the bottom
of the dugout yielded fine yellow sand, which is a great
treasure around these parts, and people hauled it to
their yards to sprinkle the bottom of the eaves, or shovel
under the chickens and the pigs, or use inside the houses that had pounded floors, and for the mortar, too, of
course, for those that were building a house, while others carted it away for later use. It would surely come in
handy sometime. And so after the pipes were laid, there
was nothing to fill the dugout with, which was awkward,

to say the least. Also, it came to light that Tarcsai wasn't an engineer at all, just a foreman, though by that time nobody cared, Tarcsai least of all. He just sat in his shack where Misi's place is standing now and drank beer, and when he had to answer the call of nature he got up, went behind the shack, and took a leak. If he had to, he also squatted. All in all, he felt just fine in that shack.

The work progressed as best it could, and the reverend Márton Végső showed up every day with a small shovel and a spade, he even brought a brush to clean off the bones he was sure to find, and once he even warned the machine operator to go slow who, for his part, dumped half a cubic meter of earth at his feet. Watch out! he shouted after the fact, because by then the clergyman was struggling, hand and foot, to free himself. I told you, shouted the machine operator, and he may have even laughed an ugly laugh. Work's not gonna stop just because you're standing where you got no calling to, Tarcsai remarked when he came out of the shack. Shit! Who the hell are you anyway? Then he went round the back to answer the call of nature.

The shack was just big enough to hold a small bed, a fold-down table for the paper work, an iron cabinet, and of course Tarcsai, who spent most of the day lying on the bed, keeping an eye on the goings on outside through the open door. There wasn't much to see, though, just the minister and a bunch of bratty kids horsing around in the trench; in the morning the peasants passed by on their way somewhere, probably the fields, others were off to catch the bus, and then for the rest of the day, only a handful of people loitered outside on the street, their movements more and more uncertain as they went into one house and out the other. They're drinking, Tarcsai concluded. The livelong day. A nice, quiet place. Then he decided to take charge. One boy returned the empty beer bottles to the shop, the other ran off after the machine operator to see where he was, and they brought him wine, too, from home, without being asked; they stole money for him, and sausages, whatever he needed, though what's the use, he asked himself, if none of them has an older sister or a neglected mother, whereas they'd have sold him even the street by then, lock, stock, and barrel. The older boys, too, had left the minister in the dugout to fend for himself and switched their loyalties to the sluggard Tarcsai. They loved his filthy mouth and that he didn't do anything except scratch his balls. They began aping his walk, and after a while they went to the back of the shack, too, whether they had to or not. They even tried to get women for him, but then things took care of themselves, as they usually do.

At one time, our street was the Romanian border, but only the minister knows when that was. A couple of the old locals remember having to fly the Hungarian and then the Romanian flag in front of their houses, back and forth. That's how we knew if we're Romanian or Hungarian, Uncle Kocsis said into the minister's tape recorder, but that's as much as he could recall. And that there was a man among them who looked just like this Tarcsai, but whether he was Hungarian or Romanian, he couldn't say. He might have been Russian, he reflected another time. Or German. They've all been through here. Uncle Kocsis's son died young, and he left behind a wife and a child, Esztike. I thought a lot about what to do so things would turn out all right and the little we have shouldn't disappear, Uncle Kocsis told the clergyman, but then everything turned out just fine, he explained, because his wife died. How's that, the minister asked, appalled, because for the life of him he couldn't see what was so fine about it. But Uncle Kocsis pointed out the advantages, first & foremost the fact that his son's wife took his wife's place, though unofficially, of course, he added. We never got hitched. Aranka's not family, just an outsider, so everything will go to Esztike. The clergyman had heard hearsay about the strange life of the Kocsis family, a den of iniquity, he thought, shocked, & for a second, lost his firm grip on the world.

Esztike grew into a lively, playful girl, if a bit on the plump side, and when she was fourteen, she announced one Friday that she was going to get married the following Sunday. And also, that she was going to have children. Her father, who saw things differently, took the razor strap off the hook, but come Sunday, Erzsike snuck off with the boy, only to appear a week later, saying she was hungry. Later she made friends with another boy, then a third, then God knows how many more.

Kocsis didn't approve of any of them. Sometimes she'd be gone for days, then she'd come back, tired and hungry, & sleep for days, and then it started all over again. Uncle Kocsis beat the living daylights out of her, but he eventually realized that he was helpless against her nature. So he set to thinking again, wracking his brains for days, only to conclude that he was too old to take her on himself. Not because of my age, mind you, he told the minister, who was listening with mounting consternation, but because her mother's alive, and what am I supposed to say to her?

Though Esztike finished a postal service school, which was almost a high school, she ended up working at the Tools Factory for the sake of a boy. She got fired during the first wave of layoffs, due to some disciplinary action, it seems, because the expediter caught her going at it during the night shift. Jancsi Hesz even knows the details. He said that Esztike was painting with Rilsan, which means that the heated iron has to be dipped into the paint powder floating on top of a tub. Jancsi Hesz even illustrated, in minute detail, how Eszter had to bend over the tub to do it, and some guy got behind her which, in wrestling, means two points, but this time, it meant disciplinary action. The guy, who couldn't control himself, made a clean breast of it, but Esztike was relentless in her denial. In the end they closed the records by concluding that when Esztike bent over the tub something happened, but she wasn't aware of it.

Despite his years, Uncle Kocsis has his wits about him and he takes things in stride. The minute they pulled Tarcsai's shack down in front of his house and fence, he knew that sooner or later it would be payback time. He didn't mind. His dug well had sixteen rings, but ever since his wife died in it, they didn't drink from it, just the animals. No, he didn't mind. A couple of days later he saw that the man from the shack came to pee by the foot of his garden. He also crapped there. He put up with it for a time, then he had an idea. He called Esztike, come with me! Esztike went with him to the bottom of the garden with no inkling of what Kocsis was about, but then her jaw dropped. Tarcsai was just taking a leak behind the shack, his face to them, while further off the clergyman was digging in the ditch with the help of some boys, and about twenty meters further off the excavator was roaring. Tarcsai saw nothing because of the bushes. Besides, at such times one's eyes tend to fill with tears. He thought only what one tends to think at a time like this, then he shook it, as if he were waving to someone, then tucked it away. The old man said nothing, just let Esztike take everything in. Then he said, chose. Either the minister, or this man here. What you just saw. The sun was shining and at such times it's eternal summer, the birds are singing, & as for Esztike, she was struck dumb, because she was just making up her mind.

THE SHACK

There used to be an inn at the top of the street, but those days are now lost to memory. The village clergyman, familiar with the history of the village, insists that the inn lay behind the big carriage stand with partial eaves that had stood where the bus stop stands today and that it was the hideout of brigands and highwaymen. Thieves and burglars. Just like now, he'd add if only he dared, a hint that Misi's, which was put up in its place, is also a den of iniquity, and Tarcsai, the proprietor, is no better than he should be. The former building kept burning down, so after a while they didn't put it up again. The owners may have died or were killed, which wouldn't surprise him in the least. Around here, anything is possible. As for the debris, the people carted it off and the large plot was eventually overgrown with wild lilac bushes, which is why the Volán bus people came to call it the Lilac stop. For lack of concrete evidence, the minister has come to some foolhardy conclusions. For instance, he insists that our street grew into a street when somebody went looking for the inn but couldn't find it, because of course it was gone by then, so he went where his horse or ox took him in the dark, and they eventually left the main road, and then later the rest of them followed in his tracks, and that was that, the clergyman concludes with a dismayed shake of the head, because people around here will leave the true path for a shot of pálinka at the drop of a hat! Just like that! And he snaps his fingers.

People say that when the waterworks showed up at the head of the street with the excavator & the wooden shack and announced that they were going to lay the water mains, they distinctly remember that Tarcsai was inside the battered wooden contraption when it was still on top of the truck. Be that as it may, they first laid eyes on him when he came out and told the clergyman to fuck off, but this happened only after the dozer had already dug a trench about twenty meters in length and three days had passed. The clergyman was dismayed, the children laughed. You should be looking out for the children, he said, his voice trembling with suppressed emotion. It was summer vacation, and left to their own devices, a bunch of school children from the village came to see the goings on, though after a while only a handful remained, the rest lost interest. Tarcsai paid no heed to the children loafing around the site, though he paid no heed to the grownups either, for that matter. He just said to the boys in front of the shack, boys, any of you step in here & I'll rip your fucking face off. Get it? Good. Now scat!

In those days the minister was a constant presence; taking advantage of the fact that they were digging a trench for the water mains down the length of the street, he showed up every day, because the minister always showed up where there was digging to be done, when, for instance, they excavated the foundations for a house or dug a cellar, and he pottered about the furrows, too, when they tilled the soil, on the lookout for finds. Meanwhile he'd engage whoever was around in conversation; at first he even brought prayer books and Bibles with him, though he desisted when the excavator turned up a psalm book just like the one he'd given somebody the other day. One of the children dropped it, he thought aghast as he brushed it off, no, no, it can't be anything else. He also found a dead hen, an old pan, potato peels, and domestic trash of all sorts, and that's when he realized that people dumped everything in the ditch, piled some dirt over it, and good riddance. An abomination, he concluded that night as he got into bed, and the next day he made up his mind to tell Tarcsai, whom the people called engineer, whereas he was just a foreman. Engineer, sir, the people are throwing their garbage in the ditch. Is that so, Tarcsai, who liked being addressed as engineer, asked without the least sign of interest. And what's wrong with that if you don't mind me asking? The clergyman didn't understand. But it's been dug out for the mains! The big black man just glared at him. So? I'm a traitor, the clergyman thought shamefacedly, a Judas. But he felt defiant all the same. You snapped my head off the other day, he said, his voice trembling, his lip twitching. I did no such thing, Tarcsai said. I just told you to fuck off. Remember? I remember, the old clergyman said. Well, Tarcsai said and smiled. You want me to repeat it?

Uncle Kocsis's daughter, Esztike, first lay eyes on Tarcsai on a cloudless afternoon in the manner familiar from hearsay, and promptly fell in love with him. It never takes her more than a minute. She'd seen the big, black, thirtyish man before, but never paid him any heed. There was nothing special about him. Also, she was still going with Zsolti, the car mechanic's son, and at such times she barely looked at anybody else. Except, Zsolti had suggested just then that she go sleep at home because he's had enough. Esztike couldn't understand how anyone could have enough of this thing, especially since they're both out of a job & have plenty of time on their hands, but if he doesn't want to, he doesn't want to. Truth to tell, from time to time Esztike would do a little favor for the car mechanic himself when his son wasn't around and his wife was busy in the back office cheating on their taxes, but she didn't have to undress for him. She also felt sorry for his assistant. If he wants it so bad, why shouldn't he have it? So after the car mechanic's wife put the garage off limits to her, she suddenly had a lot of free time on her hands. She'd sometimes do it with Dorogi, too, and she visited Laci Veres and Pintér as well. On the other hand, she didn't get to do it with Sudák, because Uncle Kocsis, her paternal grandfather, got fed up & said, okay, girl, that's enough! Squeeze them together, because you're not leaving the house for some time.

Uncle Kocsis had a plan. First and foremost, he wouldn't let the girl out of the house. Some say he locked her up, others say he tied her to a cow chain, but one thing is certainly true, Esztike wasn't seen on the street for weeks, to the regret of many. Uncle Kocsis himself didn't go further than the foot of the garden, behind the bushes lining the fence, from where he studied the people going about their business, always pretty much the same, a bunch of loitering drunks with bad lives, which of course was nothing new to him. Which left Tarcsai and the clergyman. The old man didn't care if the clergyman was married or not, just as he didn't care about Tarcsai's family life either. He knew that one way or another, such things could always be patched up. Then one evening he showed the foreman to his daughter & said to her, off you go. The rest is up to you. The foreman, who was just taking a leak behind the shack at the foot of Kocsis's garden, had no inkling that his future had just been decided, but even if he had, he wouldn't have cared; there were few things he cared about in the world. On the other hand, perfumed & all dolled up, the very next day Esztike sauntered out to the bus stop as if to check the schedule, then on her way back she went to the shack, as it were, on a sudden whim, where instead of saying hello, she just said, my father wants me to tell you not to use the back of our garden for an outhouse. The foreman was sitting on the side of the bed, drinking beer. Well, well, he said after a bit, and who the hell are you?

Esztike told him. She also said that actually, her father is her grandfather, because her father, her grandfather's son died, and her grandfather's living with her mother. Tarcsai mulled it over, then he said he's not sure he understands, and that he's got a Zaporozhets,[12] and he'd like somebody to steal it, & then the insurance people would pay for it, so he left it out on the street, and why don't you sit down, Esztike? Esztike tried explaining everything to him once again, but Tarcsai just went on talking, saying he'd left the car door open on purpose, just a jot, mind you, so somebody would notice, and he even placed a storage battery on the back seat, but nobody stole it. Can you understand that? Esztike couldn't. Well, said Tarcsai, I'm the same way with your family. And close the door. It's gonna be too hot, Esztike said. It won't, Tarcsai countered. Not once we're undressed. And he was right.

Esztike soon learned that when it comes to love, Tarcsai doesn't beat about the bush, and also that he's not a foreman, just some sort of guard, but since he's here, he might as well do the bit of required paperwork. And also that he's a bachelor and he used to live in a sublet in Debrecen, but gave it up because of the pipe laying, and so basically, the shack is his home. He was a real foreman once, but they came vexing him with all sorts of dumb problems, so he turned his back on the whole thing. For her part, Esztike told him that that's not the way he should have gone about that business with the car.

She had a friend in insurance and he told her that the best way is for the owner to steal the car himself and bury it deep in a ditch. It was around midnight by then, and Tarcsai pushed the door open a bit to let in some fresh air. Bury it? he asked the girl, don't you need a big hole for that? Besides, where? Esztike just laughed. Then she told him that she's fed up living at home because her grandfather keeps molesting her sexually, but because she won't let him do it to her, he wants to take revenge by forcing her to marry the clergyman. Tarcsai commented that that would be a big mistake, but then reverted to talking about the Zaporozhets. At dawn they went to the back of the shed to pee, where the girl told him that the kind of big holes she's thinking of are dug when they build a house and that Tarcsai's got no idea the number of cars that are worked into the foundation without anybody being the wiser, except for the owner, the insurance guy, and possibly the policeman, who can't find it.

By then Tarcsai's head was reeling from the beer and all the love that Esztike and he made together, and so the next day he had only vague recollections of what came next, for instance, that they would build a house right there, the plot is no problem, it's her father's, and they will open a nice pub, and the Zaporozhets will also be in a safe place, and the insurance people will pay. So that was settled. On the other hand, the door remained open, with the two of them all tangled up, naked, sleeping. The first person to pass by closed the door. The next one opened it. And then somebody closed it again. And then somebody else opened it again. Later the wind rose, and also a small commotion, but eventually that died down, too.

THE REVEREND MÁRTON VÉGSŐ

These people? God? In His own image? Resting by the side of the ditch, the clergyman was watching Sudák by the bus stop who, for the good part of the last hour, was busy wrestling with the long pole, trying to let go, and when he finally managed and pulled a rag from his pocket and raised it to his nose, he ended up flat on his back. Just before, Jancsi Hesz had come by with a neat heart shaped shovel, telling the clergyman not to make a laughing stock of himself with the plastic shit he's using. And just before that, Béres had staggered by, wobbly on his feet, have you found it?, he asked grinning, because when the digging began, he knew the clergyman would sooner or later lose something in all the commotion. Then the other day Jolán Árva had found him on the sand hill with two cream puffs she'd dropped, then wiped clean on her dress, have one, she urged the clergyman intimately, then added that the two of them had much in common. Sudák, too, had shown up a couple of days ago, telling him that there were once Roman ruins here, he can be trusted, he'd seen them with his own eyes. They all had a word or two to say to him. Sometimes they stopped just so they could hold on to the fence, or take a leak on the sly when no one was looking. It took the clergyman a couple of days before it dawned on him that basically, around here, everybody's perpetually drunk. Later he learned that that wasn't the case, but by then he didn't care. The moony machine operator dug the ditch for the mains along the line of the old houses, along the path worn down into the semblance of a sidewalk, and piled the earth he'd dug up in the middle of road. Late at night some of the men found their way home only by walking along inside the ditch because you could lean against the sides; also, strange sounds issued from below, singing, snoring, whispered exchanges; dogs went at it in silence down there, and in the daytime the geese that had lost their way gaggled the silence to shreds. Also, a hen went there to lay her eggs.

The clergyman next turned his attention to the boys, who guffawed as they looked askance at him and engaged in brief whispered exchanges, and he was convinced that they were secretly planning to push him into the ditch. These, too? In His own image? He shook his head to be rid of these heretical thoughts and tried to occupy his mind with the splendid finds that would soon come into the light of day, and then eager scientists and archeologists would descend on the spot, followed by radio and television, and the street would be cordoned off, the waterworks' shed would be spirited away, along with Tarcsai, and they would make everybody move out and a great big bulldozer would make short shrift of all the houses, in which case there'll be no need for archeological finds. The reverend had no liking for our street. It was poor and drab, with bare, dirty, untidy yards, flies, stinking piles of manure, outhouses without doors, and the new houses flaunting themselves on top of junk heaps, most of them lacking plaster, & the windows filled in with brick. Furthermore, nobody went to church. In the reverend's dreams the residents even got slapped around before they were shipped off to the Great Plain, where they got slapped around some more, depending on his mood that day. For instance, Tarcsai was regularly whipped with a leather strap in a sheepfold, and they didn't want to stop even when he woke up in the morning. The reverend was an intense dreamer.

He'd noted in his diary ages ago that a certain sluggish depravity characterized the street, where the people are even too lazy to commit the unholy act of being swallowed up by the earth. But drinking, that they don't mind, cheating on each other, cursing, pulling knives, corrupting children, & bickering, that they don't mind, though after a while they get bored with that, too, and are reconciled. Also, they steal things. And should a stranger happen to come by, they corrupt him as well. Tarcsai, for one. When he first came here, he just drank like an animal, but then he met that slut, and what's going on in the waterworks' shack now, before the eyes of the world, why, it's an abomination. And to make things worse, the boys told him, and this was typical of the street, that the girl's father lassoed the foreman for his daughter by his you know what. For a while the elderly reverend didn't understand what these adolescent boys were chuckling about, but then one of them explained, which made him turn as red as a house on fire. The boys laughed and showed him with their hands. He grabbed one of them & smacked him on the neck, then tried to change the subject, but the boys wouldn't let him. Okay, I'm off, he said, and walked away, the way he always did at such times, but they ran after him and pulling and shoving, tugged at his clothes, or bit his hand.

Some of the boys had hung around the excavator from the very beginning and wanted to know what the clergyman was up to, but they soon realized that basically, he wasn't up to anything, and then they turned their attention to Tarcsai. The foreman offered more interesting prospects, except Esztike showed up, and from then on they weren't allowed anywhere near the shack. Don't go there, the reverend told them, he's a bad lot. Why? Just because. Why just because? Had the clergyman children of his own, he'd have never walked into this trap, but things being the way they were, he answered them in earnest and in the end they got him thoroughly confused & made a laughing stock of him. Later they pelted him with clumps of earth, then tried to push him into the ditch. Which was the last straw. The minister smiled meekly in self-defense, but when they threw sand at him he grabbed one of the boys by the arm, what's your name, he yelled, angry as hell, who's your father? He then turned on another, then a third, but then the bear-sized Dorogi showed up and with a loud howl pulled the whole entangled screaming bunch into the ditch along with himself. They rested a bit, then he peeled the boys off the clergyman and flung them up on the sand heap. He said something while he took a leak, but what that might have been the reverend didn't hear because he was wheezing too much. Then Dorogi laughed & walked off with the boys looking after him as if he were god.

The reverend had no children and had no idea how to handle them, he was awkward and lame, and he could read it in their eyes. Sometimes they even told him so to his face. He'd had a girlfriend once for nine years. He regarded her as his bride, but she kept putting it off until the young clergyman lost his patience. Then at last they agreed and it seemed that everything would go smoothly, but during their first idyllic encounter Irmus spat in his mouth and fought him off like a wildcat with a pack of wolves in pursuit, intent on raping her. The second time around she jerked her knee up at the worst possible moment but apologized, saying it was a reflex, she couldn't help it. Finally, when almost everything went according to plan, her retina got detached, and then they fell off the bed. The problem is, there's no knowing when, how, and why the Lord takes it into His head to punish you, that's what this seven generation thing is all about, the clergyman has concluded many times since. He was lonely, though strangely enough, after so many years he felt a sense of relief when he thought about it.

Irmus had eye surgery, & it turned out that nothing got detached, just that the reverend had injured it, though how he could have done so, seeing how both hands were down there, remains a mystery. Anyway, after what happened, marrying the girl was out, and as for him, he officiated at weddings, preached, and administered the Sacrament, while some officious busybodies, dressed in black, their faces as despondent as the hereafter, busied themselves ringing the church bell, taking notes, keeping records, and counting the revenues. Afterwards the reverend had a couple of adventures, but mostly in his dreams. Irmus was a plump, soft-bodied woman, feminine, attractive, and in his dreams things happened that hadn't happened back then. Repeatedly. With others, too. At such times his hands wandered to the place where two dark spots betrayed all too frequent use.

It was hot. The clergyman clambered to his feet and began digging the soil with the small shovel he used to tidy graves, and when it got stuck, he checked to see what it was that caused it, but it never was. Just an iron nail, a piece of tin, some wire, a pebble. The boys were in attendance, because Dorogi had told them that he was looking for gold. That can't be, they laughed excitedly, you're kidding! But from then on, whenever the clergyman showed up, they were already on the spot, offering to help, and after a while they were even courteous to him, which made him feel uneasy. What did they have up their sleeve? Then unease gave way to fear.

When the clergyman bent down for something, the boys would bump their heads, because they bent down as well. Then, rubbing their heads, they laughed. They laughed all the time. They laughed easily, full heartedly, and they laughed at everything, flashing their teeth, a bit of saliva gleaming on the tip of their tongues and in the corner of their lips, and he even caught some of them panting right into his face. Even their breathing was lively, brisk, & warm. They now stopped and asked, are you really looking for gold, reverend? Treasure? Like on TV? The clergyman laughed. What an idea! He then tried to explain, but saw such animosity in their eyes, he stopped. Why don't you admit it, one of the boys said. He was disappointed & broke down in tears. You can't even play along, you old donkey! They said something else as well, but by then they were walking away, leaving him high and dry. They ran to the mud pits, and as for the clergyman, he felt like he'd been slapped in the face.

Then he resumed digging in earnest, as if relieved of a heavy burden, when an unsettling thought assailed him, namely, that he's doing all this for nothing. Good Lord, there's nothing here but dust! They were already on the pasture, Dezső, Attila, & Jóska Ács, maybe he should go join them. He could see them even with his eyes closed, Attila's beetle-brown eyes, Dezső's dirty shock of hair, perched on top of his head like a hen's nest, and Jóska Ács, who was the wildest of them all, his frame tall, sinewy like a serpent's, each one covered in grime, their knees & elbows marked with wounds, their nails black, their cheeks grimy, and they blew their noses between two fingers. He even knew by now how far each one could spit and how far each could pee, and he knew, too, that he could never tell what they were concocting in their sneaky, shifty little heads. He could even see them in his dreams as he's about to buy one of them off their father, or even all of them, except they're not for sale. What mad dreams, frail, humiliating, unworthy. He? Buying boys for money? Especially this lot? When this happened, he woke up in a sweat, his sheets drenched and rumpled, because in his dream he'd done it, he beat them to a pulp, then told them to fuck off. He stood in the road like Tarcsai and said he'd rip their fucking faces off. Then he got out of bed & reflected how nobody loved him.

They'll be back, he thought with trepidation. (May God grant that they be back.)

LAJOS MÉRŐ

Some people fly in their dreams, or fall, others are pursued, and though they'd like to get away, their feet are rooted to the ground. In his dreams Lajos Mérő hears shouting and wakes up to find that it's him. What is it? Lack of sexual overindulgence, Dorogi said at once in Misi's place, where the usual group gathers whenever it rains, and also when it doesn't. There are three tables in the small place, at one they're playing cards, Misi, the proprietor, stacks the other with beer, then sits down with the card players. Dorogi never sits down. Lajos Mérő will eventually sit at the third table, but he's got to drink first; in the meantime he moves about, listening to all the senseless banter. Dorogi goes on to say that Lajos's problem is that he's repulsive, why not say it like it is, he, for one, wouldn't lie down next to him for all the money in the world. Lajos still says nothing, just smiles, it's the same old tune. He stands gazing through the open door, from time to time taking a sip of his beer. Dorogi sticks to hard liqueur, though later he'll be asking for a bottle of beer for his horse. He now tells Mérő he should talk to Jancsi Hesz if he's got a problem, but Jancsi Hesz is busy at cards, he hasn't got the time, but we'll see to it later, Lajos, he calls to the dark, spunky, balding little man. Just strip to the waist. From above, he adds.

Later he asks Esztike for pencil and paper and three beers, & they calculate that Lajos Mérő hasn't bopped anybody in six-thousand three-hundred & forty hours. Dorogi double checks. That's correct. Enough to open a sperm bank, Misi, the proprietor, observes. Lajos continues smiling. He doesn't mind in the least being the center of attention. In the morning he drinks two raw eggs, then puts on his deadpan expression in front of the mirror to last him the day. He removes his dentures, combs his hair, then goes looking for them for about twenty minutes, replaces them, then brushes his teeth. Well, not always.

While she was around, his wife hated this, too. It was always her that found it and she never missed an opportunity to ask, why the fuck must you remove them to comb your hair? And what the fuck must you comb your hair for? Those half a dozen strands? But Lajos Mérő just smiled at that, too, then replaced his dentures in front of the mirror and set about brushing his teeth. His wife said he's doing it on purpose to put her nerves on edge and why can't he brush his teeth when they're out of his mouth? Lajos couldn't have said either, but once when he accidentally switched the order around, his wife Ibolya went ballistic while he just laughed, then he figured he might as well have Ibolya laugh along, so whenever his wife was around, he did it this way, and after a while, also when she wasn't. Except, Ibolya lacked a sense of humor, even though he tried everything to raise her spirits, he swears. Needless to say, he knew what was up. Ibolya had somebody. He knew because he smelled her in the place where a man gets cheated on & he could feel the other's smell down there.

Lajos was a maintenance man at the Tools Factory; he did odd jobs for the painters, then gradually he learned all there was to learn of the trade and was soon regarded as a bona fide house painter, and eventually he was even given major assignments. For instance, he painted the manager's office apple green. He'd get an idea as he worked. He drew a big rose, cut it out, pasted it on the wall, and sprayed it with color. When he removed the stencil, the flower was there on the wall. The manager was so taken with it, he had the company car drive him to his own home and he had to put a rose on every wall. He later made other pictures as well; he painted rabbits & butterflies, too, for children's rooms, and once even tried his hand at Lenin, who turned out so well, you'd think the gold was radiating from right inside him. But if asked, he made more complicated things, too; as far as he was concerned, nothing was impossible; he even painted the yellowish image of a couple making love for above their own bed that even Ibolya had liked back then; indeed, after a time he did almost nothing in the factory, he just drew designs on large cardboard sheets, some of which he cut out from inside, others from outside, and he got married, he had the money now, he made as much as any of the skilled workers, & he even started building a house.

And that's when it all went wrong, because the foundation was barely dug and the first floor up to the cross beams, when they showed him a royal flush and he couldn't better it. At least, this is how he put it to his wife in the basement back home & laughed. Ibolya, though, was not in a laughing mood. So what's next, she asked with a sour expression. Freedom, Lajos announced, & laughed over this, too. His wife was on maternity leave at the time and the child in their only bed. At night they put him somewhere for the short time it took, then his wife took him into bed with her. There were also two kitchen stools and a wardrobe and also a TV on the floor, on top of it a video; for the time being that's all they need, they said, the furniture can wait till the house is up. They've already picked out a leather sofa and chairs and a set of colonial-style living room furniture with twisted baroque legs, and they were planning to buy other things as well, provided they needed them. There had been enough money, though, only to make a room habitable for his wife and the child upstairs, where Lajos was soon not welcome. There was also a bathroom and a kitchen and a toilet, though the sewage drained out to the yard for now, and from there it ran down to the pasture. But the others did it the same way.

When he got fired, Lajos Mérő didn't despair. He took on whatever job came his way. He painted huge industrial tanks on the outside & on the inside, too, & also bridges, & pylons. Sometimes when he got home he looked as if he'd been drinking, he was cross-eyed from the paint fumes, and he stuttered. Then his teeth started falling out, and also his hair, and in Lenintown he fell off a pillar, and his spine & shoulder have been hurting him ever since, so he can't paint ceilings anymore. He still had the old Zhiguli back then, he loaded it with paint, foil, this & that, and set off. If there was no work, he talked the owner into painting and making repairs, it really can't wait, don't they agree, and he's the cheapest. Also, he won't be needing an invoice. Then once he rolled up his sleeves, one thing followed another, some wood paneling here, a false ceiling there, he did it even if they didn't ask. He gave people the shivers. They couldn't wait to be rid of him. Except, by that time, his wife felt the same way.

The fact is, Lajos Mérő was never too tired to come up with some prank. When he saw that Ibolya wasn't as devoted as she used to be, he did his best to sweeten her to him again. On winter nights, he turned off the oil stove to make her come down to the basement, and in the summer he let the mosquitoes in on her; once he even filled a foil bag halfway with water and leaned it against his wife's door. But there was also a big bang when he filled the oven with gas. Why all these idiotic things, Aunt Sarkadi once asked, it's enough to drive a person mad. No it's not, Lajos Mérő said, I'm just having a little fun! A little fun. Since she's cheating on me. How do you know, Aunt Sarkadi asked. How do I know, how do I know, Lajos stammered & began to cry. Aunt Piroska, he said, I just want to make her laugh. Would it be better if I beat her up? Have you any idea how much I worked for that house? What am I supposed to do? Can anybody tell me? When I took home fifty or even a hundred-thousand forints, I was good enough? We rolled about on the bed naked, right on top of all that money. She even kissed my you know what. But then she didn't want to, even when I smeared it with Hubertus liqueur! If she'd laughed just once, I wouldn't have done those things anymore, I swear. Oh yes, you would've, Aunt Sarkadi said. You, Lajos, are like a mischievous child.

Things didn't go smoothly in court either. The wife's attorney pushed for mental cruelty, citing Lajos Mérő's nerve-wracking practical jokes. At first this brought some chuckles in the courtroom, then outright laughter. The regular divorce hearings crowd appreciated Mérő's type of humor. Lajos looked around with a satisfied smile, but the judge called for silence. When was the last time you had sex, she asked the couple. Ibolya said four months. Come on, countered Lajos, we did it last Tuesday! That doesn't count, his wife said. You raped me. What do you mean, said Lajos with pride, & launched into an explanation. You know, ma'am, it was like this, he began, but the judge cut him short & asked him to call her judge. Fine, said Lajos, and from then on he didn't call her anything. On the other hand he said that Ibolya and him, they have this game. If she, meaning Ibolya, wants it, there's a small bottle of Hubertus on the shelf above the bed. They drink it, and then she runs away from him. Who? the judge asked. Ibolya, who else? And where? Nowhere. She just pretends. Then I catch her. It's just a game, judge ma'am. See? Well, was the Hubertus there this time? It wasn't. I just figured. You figured what? He caught me under the table, Ibolya said. He pinned me down! You figured what, the judge asked again, and this time she laughed, too, but she didn't get an answer. You see, Lajos Mérő said after a while, the two of us, we don't go vacationing or to the casino, and I can't remember the last time we went to the theater or the movies. I'd like to go away, like other people. Far away. Just once. But I've never been farther than Pest, and now I never will. All we do is work. We work like animals. We have to. And now, there's not even the work. Believe me. Please. A poor man's got only what recreation he can find in the other. If you separate us now, she'll be left with nothing, and I'll be left with nothing. Can you understand? Fine. Now go & laugh.

Lajos is forty-five years old. He insulated the rafters with Isolyth padding in the part of the house that's fit to live in. It makes it easier to heat. A small house inside a big house, he explained to Aunt Piroska. When I walk out the door, it's like I'm in the yard, when it's just the hall. One is real, the other a dream. In which I shout. There's lots of pigeons under the big roof. That's what I eat. I'm perfectly alright. If only what little time remains would pass.

THE DAY BEGINS AT NIGHT

Pintér gets up at the crack of dawn. He turns on the light above the front door so people can see he's up. He'll climb back in bed soon, but first he takes out a bottle of pálinka, & a glass. None of the glasses are clean, but he knows who drank out of which one the previous day, or thinks he knows. Then he drinks right out of the bottle, not much, just a sip. It goes down his throat so he can almost feel it burn and sting, and then he needs to sit down because he breaks out in a sweat and must wait for it to pass. It only takes a minute or two. Then he wipes himself dry and drinks some more. And then it's better. When the nausea comes, he takes deep breaths. He sleeps in the kitchen, his wife in the back room. If they don't want to, they don't see each other for days. There's another door from the hall to the yard, & a good thing, too, because his wife doesn't like the customers, only the money. But the money she loves. Except, what's the use? She hasn't got a life anymore. Or her health. She keeps the money in that small iron box. She doesn't even know how much she's got anymore. She buys bread and milk and sometimes dry noodles. Pintér can't remember the last time he's had a proper lunch. Ilonka is ill. She's got high blood pressure. She can't cook, & she doesn't like to cook. She's sixty years old. Pintér has repeatedly said to her, look, why don't we order lunch, like other people? You don't need to bother. But no. It costs money. Before he went to work in the factory, Pintér had a bad stomach, sometimes he had to diet, sometimes not, but the factory food patched it up. He's told his wife a thousand times, listen, just cook like them. Just some soup, then something else, potatoes or rice or egg barley, a bit of meat, gravy, that's all. But his wife gives him a look that, if looks could kill, he'd be a gonner by now, and she says she remembers how when he got home, he couldn't get enough of her cooking, so what is he talking about? And she continues to make those heavy soups with roux in a five-liter pot, with smoked pork, then it's bean soup for three days and dry pork, and she's off the hook for a while. Then it's five liters of potato soup with smoked meat, & so on. On Sunday, it's five liters of clear soup with pork. The smoked pork serves them for breakfast, too, and dinner, and meanwhile up in the attic the sausage goes bad, but he's got to eat it all the same. There's also the three-year-old lard, about fifty liters' worth. And smoked meat from previous years. It's as dry and black as the sole of his boot. His wife can't climb up the ladder anymore, so he's got to bring it down for her, but even so, she knows exactly how much is left. She won't let the dog have it, though. She won't hear of it.

And to think what a pretty young woman she was! Pintér reaches for the bottle again & takes a sip, thinking how he barely remembers those years, just the com-

fortable feeling that everything was good, just the way
it was. For instance, he can't remember if Ilonka could
cook back then, but back then it didn't matter. Maybe
they ate smoked pork all the time then, too, & five liters of soup. If there's no leftover cooked pork, they have
eggs for breakfast, so that by now Pintér hates the hen
as much as the egg! Ilonka whips three up, then a bit of
bread on top so it'll do for the two of them. They eat out
of the pan, his wife pushing it toward him as if she didn't
want it, and he back to her. It's proper courtesy, isn't it?
Then his wife puts down her fork, and then he does, too.
Something is always left in the pan as if nobody wanted it, whereas he could've eaten the whole thing all by
himself. Don't you want some more, his wife asks. Have
you had enough? Sure. He's been saying this for forty
years now, whereas he can't recall the last time he got up
from the table with a full stomach. Sometimes he's so
hungry, he could chew a piece of iron. Anything but
the smoked meat, the bean soup, and the potato soup.
And also, the clear soup with smoked pork.

Pintér takes another swig from the bottle, then he
tries to remember if he'd opened the front door, because if he hasn't, nobody's gonna come in even though
the light's on outside. They'll think he'd forgotten to
switch it off the night before. It's cool out in the yard,
but it feels good. Pintér thinks he can hear Béres shouting in the distance, in the first flush of the morning.
There's somebody at the gate, Laci Veres or Lajos Mérő,

they're the early risers, Pintér thinks, but it's the reverend, his back to him. I was at the bus stop, he explains, to see when it leaves, but somebody tore off the schedule. Pintér knows that it gets torn off the day after it's put up, & that was a long time ago, but he doesn't say anything. Also, he's surprised, but then remembers his manners, won't you come in, he asks. What's the use, the clergyman is thinking as they walk along the narrow path leading to the house, & what is he doing here anyway? But by then it's too late to turn back. Pintér takes out a tray, on it glasses that Dorogi may have drank from the previous day, or Jancsi Hesz, and the clergyman looks on in silence. You think I should, he asks sheepishly, but Pintér isn't thinking anything, he just clinks glasses and throws back his drink. The reverend shudders at the sight, but then he gulps down his drink, too. That's life, Pintér says after a while, then refills their glasses. Then they lapse into silence. Nice weather, Pintér says just as the clergyman is about to comment that it's chilly, so he says nothing. Then after a while he says, somebody's talking. Pintér nods. This early in the day it's Béres, he says. This time of the day, they're all a bit unhinged. Drunk? No, of course not. The trouble is they're not. As if he were having it out with God, the clergyman is thinking. Around here, Pintér says, God is our greatest enemy. The complaint, it's pouring out of everybody, the clergyman says and takes another sip of pálinka, the bitterness, it comes pouring out. Like a flood, he adds and throws Pintér a sideways glance to see if he understands. I know, says Pintér, I vomited a chamber pot nearly to the brim myself last night. But it's a joke. Though maybe not. Yes and no, both. So. How do you like the pálinka?

In our street, everybody knows the reverend even though he doesn't live here, but in the rectory next door to the church. When they laid the water mains he used to come around all the time. Pintér even remembers how the children made fun of him, and the old fool putting up with it. A man like that, people don't respect him, but they don't hate him either, they take him in stride, like drunkenness and love. When Pintér saw the clergyman in front of his door he was surprised, but now he also suspected that he's a strange sort. Or he's got some other problem. As for the clergyman, who was sitting by the table, he still couldn't figure out what he was doing here. Pintér was on the side of the bed, about to lie back down, with the bottle on the floor next to him; the sun was coming up, the clergyman was talking, but Pintér knew that he was talking besides the point. He'll get around to it, though. Given time, they all do. The clergyman was just talking about the Bible, taking small sips of the pálinka as he spoke. Read it, he said, as if talking to a congregation, or for a moment he might have really thought he was in the pulpit. It will bring you peace. How about you, Pintér asked. Because I've never seen a clergyman traipsing through the street in the middle of the night, if you don't mind me saying so. The clergyman didn't answer right away, so Pintér got up and refilled their glasses. There's a woman involved, yes?, he asked in the meantime, patted the old man on the back, & laughed. The reverend blushed to the roots of his hair and tried to make a reply, but Pintér clinked glasses. To your health. And in fact, it really did feel good. We'll know tomorrow anyway, Pintér said when he put down his glass. What I mean is today, because the day has already begun. This time you're wrong, the clergyman said. You're not a stupid man, but this time, you're wrong. How much schooling have you had? Not much, Pintér said. Except, you see, for years I lived in a workers' hostel, and we had all sorts there, even doctors. Also, around here nobody's stupid. Except it's more comfortable, not letting on.

Then he remembered that he should offer the clergyman, who was even laughing occasionally by now, something to eat. He found smoked pork in the fridge, and put out some bread, green peppers, knives, & two small plates. Later, they also had something to wash it down with, and the clergyman said he hasn't eaten anything with such relish in a long time. Pintér admitted that he felt the same way. The clergyman told him that he hasn't got a wife and that the desiccated Mrs. Hüse does his laundry and cooks for him, but her major preoccupation consists of spying on him. For instance, every morning she checks the sheets. Slightly the worse

for drink, the clergyman also mentioned that he tried
to teach the local children the Lord's Prayer when they
were bringing the water, but they always said our fart
that art in Heaven, and not our Father, though it took
him a while before he was on to them, because they
laughed when they said it. These kids, they're fit for
the gallows, Pintér offered. What you need, reverend,
is children of your own. The reverend very nearly said,
yes, exactly, but thought better of it, this was not the
place. He also very nearly confessed that he hasn't had
a good night's sleep in ages & prefers to get up, but it's
no better when he sleeps, because he's plagued by bad
dreams. By morning he forgets, but the fatigue of the
night lingers, along with the dejection. He didn't say
anything about the aimless early morning wanderings
either, he just looked at the man in front of him with
warmth and affection, then asked, very softly, what
about you? What's missing from your life? Ah, Pintér
said quietly, you're not a stupid man either, reverend.
Because I got three of my own, except they're gone
and I don't even know where they are. I got nothing
but my wife, & she's sick, so what good are they to me?
Still, I suppose we're better off than those that get a leg
cut off by the train. Right? They snickered at this for a
while, then they drank in silence. Okay, it's time to go,
the minister then said as he got to his feet, thanks for
everything, and if you happen by, but Pintér cut him

short. I don't go that way very much. Why don't you come here instead? Others that can't sleep do the same. My friend, the clergyman said from the bottom of his heart as he propped himself against the wall, you do know everything. This way, please, said Pintér, then helped the clergyman out of the larder and along the fence. It was safer that way. I won't write down what you had to drink. You'll bring it next time you come.

BIRD'S EYE VIEW

If anybody turns off the main road into our street, he'll find himself smack up against a pub, but who'd bother turning into our street? Officially it's the Café Lilac, but people just call it Misi's, after the proprietor. The massive two-story building is supported by reinforced concrete, rough-hewn stone, and a red Zaporozhets to the end of time. The Zaporozhets, it's part of the building, though how this came about is anybody's guess. People say all sorts of things, but that's neither here nor there. Dorogi, for instance, says that on quiet nights he can hear the purr of a car's engine, a muffled, muted sound, and that the plaintive wail of a car's horn echoes in his ear, & if he's had a shot of pálinka, it's more plaintive still. There's also a general store & a provender supplies place down in a basement, as well as three watering holes to serve twenty to twenty-five idle men with hunted eyes, plus two locust trees. A skinny cop, two pairs of firemen, as well as a timid prison warden also live along the old side of the street, and also the old people. The rest are poorly dressed half-peasant, half-workingman types, the kind you'll find all over the country. There are also two public tap wells from which you can't draw water, but nobody minds, because there's regular piped water in the street now. They'd even removed the casings, but later replaced them, because they look better that way.

There's fighting in the pub once a week, but the anger or resentment don't last, just as love, joy, or happiness don't last either. Our street is bleak and dreary, like a row of gypsy shacks. In summer it is scorching hot and depopulated, the dust is practically on fire, while in winter a chill wind tears at the fences, and the months' old snow turns to ice.

The boys start smoking at fourteen or fifteen, then a couple of years later they start drinking, too. They get through school as best they can, then they work at a couple of plants and factories in town, but few have the strength to leave the place for good. With its busy constructions and large factories, at one time the nearby town siphoned off half the male population. They discarded their spades and shovels to work as slaves, commuting or living for years, even decades, in workers' hostels or shacks on wheels. Then most of them came back home just as they'd left, drunk and empty handed. Meanwhile they got married, multiplied, & died. Most of them can't say I love you their entire lives, though nobody said it to them either. Finding a mate is quick & to the point, the district physician says, it starts with come on, let's do it, knowledge about sex is superficial & inadequate, eulogies are brief. Caring for children is practically nonexistent. They get fed & they get clothes on their backs, but that's just about it. The greatest adventure in their lives is serving in the army, and in almost all the houses hand-colored photographs hang on the walls as reminders, & also some ungainly knick-knacks, watch towers made of match sticks, a cigarette lighter inside an empty shell, images painted on glass, date, place, in memory of my service days. In a couple of the houses there are also colored reproductions, mountains, waterfalls, and in two new houses even posters with palm trees & the sea.

The old houses were built long & narrow, with one end backing the street, the rest of the building stretching well into the yard, and up front mulberry trees, barns, and a shed. The kitchen is in the middle, the one clean room faces the street, the pantry is in the back. But people continue to live in the kitchen, though come summer, they move to the summer kitchen outside, because of the flies. They used to whitewash the walls and paint the bottom black with Vienna soot, but now they use sandstone powder, even on the old houses, red, yellow, blue, and around the bottom, imitation ashlar scratched by hand into the mortar & red jointing. There are also some houses from the sixties with pitch roofs, as well as six new split-level homes with basements, a garage, & a mansard, but these have largely gone unfinished, and nobody feels at home in them. The armchair prevents you from opening the door of the cheap assembly line wall unit, the water flows in from the porch, and those unfamiliar with the house keep bumping into stairs, pipes, & bricks at every turn. Fortunately, there's a temporary summer kitchen of sorts everywhere that's fit to live in.

They were originally intended for the parents, who put up the money for the house, but who where somehow left, forgotten, in their old homes.

There's been a death every year lately, and births, too, but there aren't enough young people. Visits are frequent & informal. People hang the key to their front gate on a nail just inside or place it in the open mailbox. In the new houses it's left in the lock so the visitor can reach it if he slips his hand through the iron bars or the boards. There are five street lamps, but at night only one gives off light. The rest serve as dove's nests. On the official local map the road is supposed to be a concrete road with asphalt topping, but something must have come up at some point, because it's still very much a dirt road. Most of the people owe back taxes or can't pay their electric bills or owe the state for one thing or another. A civil servant would say that in our street, civil discipline leaves something to be desired. From time to time a car equipped with a loudspeaker bumps and grinds along the road making an announcement, and the children take off after it. It announces the circus, a town meeting, elections, chicken for sale, used clothes to be had cheap, by the bundle, but nobody pays much attention. The melon man and the gas man come round, too, honking their horn, even though business is almost nonexistent; merchandise brought to your door is suspect, and it costs more, too. Regardless of what's on them, posters get ripped off almost before they're up.

If anybody's got anything to sell, they secure a head of corn to the fence with the help of a sharp stick, or a small bunch of hay, or apples, or potatœs, or they just let the word get around, but everybody knows to begin with that Uncle Vida, for instance, always has potatœs and maize for sale, and Aunt Sarkadi has wine, and also apples & eggs, and in an emergency, she'll even sell you a bunch of soup greens. The Kocsises have chickens & hens.

Every other week a pig is slaughtered at one of the houses and it's sold piecemeal. A couple of days before the pig-killing the owner, but more likely his wife, goes from house to house to take the orders, but whether people will get what they ordered remains to be seen. Everybody wants the fatty cuts because they're suited for making lard, and they're cheaper, too. The flank is harder to sell. Once in a while the Csige boy slaughters a calf or a sheep, but people don't stand on line for that, it's poor meat, a pig is more economical. You can make soup from it that'll last for days, then the cooked meat is roasted in lard and consumed with potatœs, rice, or egg barley while it lasts. Animals are kept mostly by the old folk, out of habit; the young people make calculations and conclude that it's just not worth it, fodder is expensive, and besides, you can't even sell the milk anymore. At one time lots of people grew apples, gooseberry, raspberry, and sour cherries. They kept chickens, hens, and goats, fattened pigs, milked cows, tried making money from nutria, rented sows and heifers from the co-op for fattening, & worked the soil. That's when the houses with the pitched roofs were put up, with big yards and stables. Then their world collapsed. The state paid people to slaughter their cows and kill the laying hens. In fact, they were paying you to do nothing. One could put up with that, people say, but whose gonna bother farming again here for the next one hundred years? The privatization of the land they'd nationalized after the war didn't make much of a stir either. A couple of old people took back theirs, but they know as well as anybody that it's no good, sooner or later the state's gonna take it back again, or slam taxes on them they can't afford. Jancsi Hesz says that when the layoffs were announced at a workers' meeting at the plant, the others started shouting, demanding that the workers from the countryside be laid off first. And they were. Okay. So what am I supposed to do now? They had no use for me when I was a factory hand, and they had no use for me as a peasant, and as for ministers, how many ministers does a government need? What do they expect me to do? Lie down and die?

The best land in the neighborhood was bought up or rented by new money, former co-op leaders, well trained, ruthless, cunning professionals, fifty & a hundred hectare fields are lying fallow, but the work machines are already in place, there's gonna be plenty of work, Uncle Vida says, we can work by the day or the week, like in the old times. For a pittance. But even so. Or part of the yield. The large pasture below the street now belongs to a man from Debrecen, he's going to fill it up with sand & turn it into a service station. The used car lot is already up. Then he'll bring in water and electricity and sell the whole thing to a developer. Except, how did these people get hold of so much money in just four years?[13] And to make matters worse, seasonal workers come trooping to the neighborhood from Romania. They're cheap, they don't care how they live, and they'll take on anything. At night they sleep in deserted barns and sheds, & then work from sun up to sunset, like animals. They don't even go out on the street. What's going on here?

What's going on here, Sudák asks in the early morning light. He thinks he sees Lajos Mérő prowling around Aunt Sarkadi's house, then Béres, then the Veres boy, and even others, sometimes. The irregulars, Dorogi once called them. He doesn't stand around outside at this ungodly hour; he's got his own pálinka and wine, but he won't share it. The irregulars are all independent men, divorced or unemployed, some are retired, the type that have time on their hands in the early morning, though Lajos Mérő could've sworn he saw the minister the other day, if only vaguely, coming from Pintér's, and he was drunk off his ass. He didn't tell anybody, though; he thought he was imagining it. Also, what if people laughed? Faces ashen, hollow, hung over, they stand around in silence, saying nothing, but pleading inside for Mrs. Sarkadi, Aunt Piroska, to get up already and open the door. Aunt Piroska sells her own wine & she even measures it out on credit for those she knows, and around here, she knows everybody. Except, she's not been well lately and she's getting on in years. A nasty trick if she went and died on us, says Béres, his voice deep and grainy. We wouldn't have to pay back what we owe. But where would we drink? Pintér gets up early, too, but he rarely gives you anything on credit. Also, he charges more. Besides, by now they're used to standing around like this, then going about their business. Aunt Piroska gives them what they need to wake up, wash, & shave, even have breakfast, if that's your game, and then you can go out on the street, though not too far, and look like anybody else. What she gives you is enough to tend to the livestock, provided you got any, to make up the bed or lie back down and sleep again, sleep as long as you can. To sleep would be nice, a long, long sleep, and then to wake up as if this whole thing here were nothing but a dream.

SANYI HARAP

If you're planning to hang yourself but first you can't find the rope and then you can't find a handy hook, that's a nuisance, but Sanyi Harap is a jack of all trades, he's not about to be daunted by such things. He has no intention of hanging himself, but you never know, in which case it's best to have everything on hand. Take Mrs. Dorogi, Mancika, for instance. She lay down on the tracks at the lower end of the street, and the train had long gone. People laughed for months. He's got time, he thought, he's gonna make sure. He's not gonna have people laugh at him. He had two hospital bags on hand, locked in the chest; in case one of them should have to go unexpectedly, they shouldn't have to rush. They also have the stones for their two grave markers carefully laid out on two braces in the shed, so only their names will have to be carved on them. He's even got the gravesite picked out, except he hasn't got the money yet, because where a person's laid to rest, in a prime place up front, by the roadside, or somewhere in the back, by the ditch, like a tramp, that's not indifferent. Sanyi Harap is thirty years old, and he sees to everything in good time. There was no rope, but it's no wonder, he never had a dog, a cow, or a horse, and there's never been a hanging in the family either. He was sitting in the kitchen watching the flies on the dirty dishes that had been piling up for days, then he gazed out the cracked window into the yard, where the heat throbbed above the two shriveled pear trees, the assorted trash, & the trampled down weeds.

Before he knew it, he worked himself into a state, like he always did, so that his head turned pale from all the thinking, just like on a certain May First once, when he spit in the manager's eye. Then he went looking for string to make rope; after all, the rope you buy in a shop is also made out of string, except he couldn't find string either, though come to think of it, why should there be string, of all things, when so much else was also missing from the house. Curtains, for one. And fly paper. Plates, beds, a desk, and the like. Sanyi Harap wanted a desk more than anything, because when they were discarding things at the Leather Factory he nearly got his hands on one for a hundred forints, but in the end somebody else took it. One desk is like another, but this desk was special. It was nearly his. He even knew where he'd put it. Few men in the street could boast of a writing desk. People at the factory liked Sanyi Harap because he's a funny little man, as the secretary called him when he went to see the manager about the desk. That funny little man Harap from the locksmiths, she said into the phone and smiled. But that's not when Sanyi Harap spit in the manager's eye, because he didn't get to see him. It happened later, at the May Day festivities in the Great Woods, because of an empty iron drum, while the gypsy band was playing.

Because he didn't get to take that home either when it got discarded.

He didn't particularly need that drum either, but there was a drum or two standing by the well or the faucet in almost every yard in the street, and he had room for it as well, and it was real despicable, the manager not letting him in to see him that time either, he just called outside to the secretary that all the drums were taken. That afternoon, Sanyi Harap stood by the gate & made a mental note of the people taking the drums home. It was just as he thought. They were all rich men, clerks, engineers, and the like. They had the drums carried to the front gate by the unskilled workers. Their names were written on them with crayon, & they took them home in their cars, some as many as three. They cost only fifty forints. Why couldn't they let him have just one? So many bad things were happening to Sanyi Harap around this time that he'd have liked to cry his heart out. He sat on the bus so people couldn't see his face; he didn't speak to anybody, & he kept wiping his nose with a handkerchief so if he should start crying, it shouldn't come as a surprise. Eventually, the matter of the drum got solved, though, because Sanyi Harap had his wits about him and he more or less knew where each of the men were taking them, then he settled on Járai, whose plot in Martinka was closest to home. They're the ones, he nodded, and that very night he rolled both drums home from a distance of six kilometers.

He even remembered to sweep the dirt behind him with a broom. People in Misi's place are still saying that the street had never been as clean as when Sanyi Harap pinched those two iron drums.

They became famous, the manager and he, after that spitting in the eye, because the following day the big ram-headed man went up to him in the shop and asked, well, little man, have you sobered up, then they shook hands, but he was scared shitless and couldn't get a word out; still, he pulled himself up so the others could see, the manager and he, well, well! What do you say to that? The other day when they were washing up, the manager threatened to kick his ass and fire him, and just you wait, you little skunk, if I lay you flat, they'll use you for a doormat, you little nobody, but nothing came of it. Wow, the men who had stood around them said, so they didn't dare! Anyway, that's when they must've come up with the idea that he was drunk and didn't know what he was doing, whereas he knew perfectly well. If he had known that nothing would happen to him, he'd have even kicked the ugly shovel-faced man in the balls. But now he just squeezed his hand tight and wouldn't let go, let them all see! The other tried to withdraw it, and there was even a security man standing nearby, and so he was the hero once again, he, the funny little man who was the shortest in the shop and also at home and on the street, too, not counting the children. Then he released his grip and said, goodbye.

Good and loud. On his way home people kept pointing at him as he sat on the bus, there, there! That's the man! The little gypsy that spit in the manager's eye, and he just smiled and pulled himself up in his seat, but then he remembered that he should've mentioned the matter of the desk while he was at it, and this got him so mad, he practically exploded. The excitement kept him awake all night and the next day he tried to see the secretary, but this time they wouldn't even let him through the door. A shame, because he'd have liked to show off, he'd have hauled that desk back on a small hand cart all the way from Debrecen, and once home, he'd have slowed his pace so people could see that he even has a desk, & that he pushed it home all by himself.

Sanyi Harap had to have everything that other people had, as well as what they didn't, and to prove, day in and day out, that he's as good a man as the next, and he's worth as much as they. That's why he's got three iron drums standing in the yard now, & that's why he's got a two-wheeled hand cart he never uses for anything, and a bench clamp in the cellar, and a pig scorcher, a saw blade, and a machine drill that's out of commission, but so is the washing machine, the centrifuge, and the TV. He's got six children, because there's somebody in the street with four, but nobody's got six. Boys! All of them! And his wife's pregnant again! Isn't that something? Around here, if you're not married after your turn in the military, people say you're a homo, and if you don't have a child a year later, they say you can't hack it. Well, he wanted a guarantee before the wedding. He told Joli, his present wife, he'll marry her, but only if he's sure. Otherwise, why bother? Even three months pregnant, she was a lovely bride. Her height was just right, not too short. They had the wedding picture taken with Sanyi Harap standing one step up so their heads were level, though later he had it out with the photographer, because he should've been two steps up, and he, the photographer, should've known.

Still, it's a good picture. Joli looks good in it, and so does he. They look like a pair of pretty, innocent children dressed in wedding garb for fun. They were eighteen, but even back then Sanyi Harap was thinking ahead and he decided to tie the knot before his stint in the army, because if he's declared unfit for service, he could always say it's because he's married. But he was accepted. He pulled himself up until he was the required height. It wasn't easy, but he did it. He drove a tank, and he drove it like a maniac, they screamed into his headset, stay in line! in line!, but he always maneuvered his tank just ahead of the others, and he wouldn't have even minded a real war so he could show them! He'd have driven a wedge through everything like a tornado and not stop till he reached Berlin. When he was awarded a star as lance corporal he was elated, and on the way home, he added two more on the train for good measure, and he wouldn't have taken his uniform off for anything in the world. Only the shoes were a problem, because there was nothing smaller than a size seven.

He can hold his own in the factory, too, as well as anybody, in fact, better, and they can't fire him, because he spit in the manager's eye and then everybody would say that that's why. Of course, that happened a long time ago and there's a new manager now, but they all know not to get on the wrong side of him because he's like spitfire, he goes for the eyes, he bites, he works himself into a state, but then they grab him, throw him on top of a table, and tickle him until he nearly passes out. That's because they like him, everybody likes him here at home as well. Uncle Kocsis dumped half a cart of potatoes in his yard, and they bring the sick animals for him to eat. Still, one of these days somebody's gonna draw the short end of the stick, he says, because they don't all know the size pants he wears. They better remember that when he works himself into a state and turns white he'd better be left alone, else there'll be hell to pay. His neighbors like him, too, even if they went and built themselves bigger houses than his. Every one of them. Of course, he'd bought an old house, and they come smaller. But never you mind, because he's gonna pull up an extra story, a tower, except he hasn't told anybody yet except Aunt Sarkadi & Jancsi Hesz, and he's gonna have an elevator and floor heating, even in the outhouse and the pigsty, just you wait and see! He can hold his own. Let them do what they want, he's gonna keep an eye out and do it bigger & better than any of them. Right now he's filling the well with water from the tap in the yard because it dried out, though nobody's on to why he's doing it. And he's also dug the base for the new house in four places, on all four sides, and last year he opened the roof where the tower will go. People are curious about that, too, but he's not telling. He'd like to tell Joli, but she's gone off with the children again, it's been nearly a month now.

ABOUT A LOCUST TREE

Sanyi Harap took it into his head one evening that little Zoli Zeke is his son, because there are two locust
trees in our street, one by the shop, the other by Misi's
place, and that's where people take all sorts of things
into their heads. He, too, was standing right there when
the thought struck him. Sanyi Harap's got a wife and
six sons, his wife's pregnant with the seventh, they're
expecting a girl, but if it's a boy, so much the better, because having six boys is something, but seven's even better, there's probably nobody that's got seven sons in the
entire nation. He might even go for eight. After all, why
not eight? Around her fifth pregnancy the doctor with
the weary eyes gingerly asked Sanyi's wife, ma'am, are you
protecting yourself? Don't you think you should? Joli
didn't understand the first time, and she didn't understand the second. Why would I protect myself against
my husband, she asked in all innocence, he never hurts
me. He loves me. I can see that, the doctor said patiently,
then he talked to Sanyi Harap as well, you just pull it on,
he said lovingly, on what, Sanyi asked, his guard up, then
when things had reached a certain point, he burst out
crying like a child and jumped out the dressing station
window just as he was, with his pants round his knees.

The tree by Misi's has seen many things in its time.
There's hardly any bark left on its trunk. Customers

from Misi's intent on reaching home find their support here, and this is where people tie their horses if there's no place left in front of the pub. Neighbor Béres likes to scratch his back against it as he rests a bit and yells. Dried up saw and ax marks indicate that on crisp, snowy nights when the wind, too, is up and it's as dark as a mine, from time to time somebody tries to cut it down, but luckily, there's always somebody else to sound the alarm. It's not that anybody's worried about the tree, but why this tree? It's common property, Dorogi says, and if he finds out that anybody makes off with it, he's gonna burn their house down with them inside it. He's tough as nails, so people take him at his word. Also, he's got a high school diploma, he gives his horse beer to drink, and he uses words like rational and evident. But anyone with half a heart wouldn't dream of felling the locust anyway, because it's even got a name, because once at dusk, when a man suffers from night blindness as he comes out of Misi's, Béres bumped into it and said, hi there, Béla old buddy, you're the decentest man around here, did you know that? And me. Béla's lower branches can't be reached anymore, which is lucky for Béla; they got snapped off a hundred years ago, at least, and Béla didn't say anything then, and it most assuredly didn't say anything now either; but ever since the Béres episode, Sudák says hello, too, and also Jancsi Hesz, if he's in the mood. Laci Veres kicks it, Lajos Mérő leans his bald head against it and chuckles. From where it stands there's a fine view of the sloping pasture all the way down to the village, and also the adobe pits where as a young boy you first try cigarettes, pálinka, and skinny little girls, and think nobody sees. Then you grow up and from time to time you stop by the tree and watch today's kids and their shenanigans & shake your head and scratch your back against the bark and you seem to see your whole life, the years of your youth, but that's more than a body can take, so you gotta go back to Misi's, may the devil take this whole thing!

Sanyi Harap used to go there, too, but the pits had water in them back then and you could bathe, and meanwhile lots of things came to light. The boys had to mind their clothes and splashed around in the water naked, so when they started changing, the older boys wouldn't go in, or they slipped in from the side, their back to the others. The water was so muddy and black, you couldn't see anything in it. Little Sanyi was a sweet boy and he was always laughing. The others tickled him and touched him, and they were surprised, but that's because he didn't let on that he's fifteen, and that's why. Because he was like all the other ten or twelve-year-old boys in every other respect, playful, plucky, tireless, & also, he liked everybody, too. His voice, too, it's acquiring a velvety depth, it sounds like an organ, the tremulous Mrs. Zeke told him when she realized the truth. Sanyi didn't realize anything at the time, only that it's good, but especially the doughnut with jam, & that he'd like to go back to the others, but he can't, not yet, and then he can't stop. He later ran down to the pit to tell the others all about it, & boy, were they amazed, is that so, you don't say, but they didn't believe a word of it. And besides, Mari Csősz thought she'd give it a try, but nothing happened, see, she confronted him, cheeks burning, you lied!

From time to time the locust's branches dried out, then a year or two later it turned green again, bringing flowers, but no seeds, it's too old, people said, & that's why. Dorogi could still recall the time when it burst into bloom every year & had seeds. Jancsi Hesz says it's all the vomiting certain people do at its base that's causing it. Sanyi never vomits, he can't drink that much, he hasn't got the money. But when he goes to Misi's, they always offer him a drink, drink it and get out, you smell like an outhouse! Sanyi Harap works in the Leather Factory, it smells bad and the smell eats itself into a man's skin. But even so, they shouldn't say. He feels like crying, but laughs instead. His tears can wait till he's outside with Béla. I could use another drink, he says with pretend gaiety, and Esztike slams a beer down in front of him with a resounding bang. Sanyika, she says with ominous calm, drink this one outside, will you? Sure, says Sanyi, and meanwhile he's thinking how he'd like to dick her like nobody's business, but takes his beer and heads outside to the tree, where he looks out over the pasture and is free to cry at last, if that's what he feels like.

All sorts of things come into one's head by Béla. Neighbor Béres, for instance, remembers that his wife's been sitting on the boards in the outhouse ever since the morning. It's no big deal, she's paralyzed, she can't walk away on her own, except she might be hungry, or she's hot, in winter she's cold, in which case he better get going. Jancsi Hesz is also in a rush, he hasn't got time like the rest of them, but then he turns around because he's forgotten something, or he's left his key on the table, & then he might as well have another shot of pálinka, and then, wouldn't you know, finds it in his pocket. Lajos Mérő chuckles, he's thinking up new ways to make his wife laugh when she comes back to him, or some way to get her gander up so she'll beat him over the head and the back and he'll grab her and drag her down to the basement and give her what she wants. And Józsi Sudák's hernia got strangulated here because his stomach heaved so bad that they had to call an ambulance, and they poured cold water on him while they waited, to prevent an infection. If several of them troop out of Misi's together, they stop here because they have to take a leak, the urge always comes after you stand up; each man waits his turn, then they argue about something until they work themselves into a state and have to go back inside, but just for a shot of pálinka or a beer, mind you, & then they declare that that's enough for the day. Cross my heart and hope to die. Meanwhile, if it's still light outside, they watch, aghast, what these modern kids are up to down there in the pasture, my my, aren't they ashamed of themselves, then they go on their way.

Sanyi, too, remembered about him and Mrs. Zeke by the tree, though only because the Zeke boy was passing by; the boy even greeted him, kiss your hand, and he felt sorry for him. Everybody felt a little sorry for the Zeke boy because his parents were divorced and for a while it looked like nobody would want him until his mother got married again in town, and Mrs. Tót from the village shacked up with his father, but the next day she told everybody that from here on in she's Mrs. Zeke. Just so they know. Ever since he finished elementary school, that boy's been wandering the street, with no father and no mother to look after him, Terka Papp laments. It's a disgrace! Which is not true, because they feed and clothe the boy properly, and he works with his father driving horses, or hoeing. He even has money for cigarettes and beer, he goes to the disco and drinks and gets into fights, like the others. But it feels good saying it and feeling sorry for him and hating his mother and his father, who has everything, no less, everything, a truck, a big house, there's not that much wealth in the whole street put together, & just look!

But Sanyi Harap has his own way of feeling sorry for the boy. Something veritably grabs his heart, holds it in a vice, it hurts so bad he wants to cry out, he can't breathe, and he'd like to burst into tears, because he's now sure that the boy is his, except there's nothing he can do about it. Also, nobody believes him. What makes you think he's yours, they ask. And Aunt Sarkadi, she said, don't you go mentally harm that boy at his age. What're you nuts? How can you make up such a thing? Don't you have enough of your own? People don't understand that that's not the point, the point is that he'd be the hero again, the little man with seven sons, if not eight, who got a married woman with child when he was fifteen, and who will now take that poor abandoned orphan under his wing. Dorogi, too, he said that the boy's got everything he needs, why would he go live with all those ragged, hungry gypsy raklo. Did you put your brains on ice? He might even slug you if you suggest it. Only Sudák is on his side. He says he'd gladly take him in himself, if only his wife would die, and that they gotta take blood samples from his father and mother, and you, too, that'll clinch it. Sanyi Harap was terrified at the idea of having his blood taken, but when he heard that they also take bone marrow and samples from the base of the skull and the nerves and the eyeground, and sweat from his balls, to which Dorogi added anthropology and mesentery, that was the last straw. He never even got around to hearing about the spinal tap, because he ran out to Béla and threw up from sheer panic. I'm sorry, I'm so sorry, my darling little son, he groaned into the tree, but it's more than I can take. We'll just have to love each other as best we can.

The question is how? The boy's there now, too, fiddling with his bicycle in front of Misi's, Sanyi Harap's leaning against Béla, the locust tree, swallowing his beer and the lumps in his throat when it suddenly slips out, Zoli! My son, he adds in a whisper, so soft he can hardly hear it himself, & yet the child stops what he's doing, and with that funny little smile of his he goes up to Sanyi, except Sanyi can hardly bear to look at him, because as the boy approaches, he's the spitting image of his younger self, the boy is his, no doubt about that, his blood, his eyes, his face, even his walk! What's the matter, Uncle Sanyi, the boy asks in the velvety organ pipe tones of Sanyi's youthful years. Nothing, comes a voice from inside Sanyi Harap, just that everything is so strange today. Even the sun. Look. It can't go down. As if somebody were holding it in check.

JENŐ NAGY & SÁRIKA

When a man decides to build a house and stops in front of the empty plot for the first time, he involuntarily puts his hand on his wife's shoulder and is lost in reveries. In the course of the next fifteen, twenty years, this gesture will become less frequent, or it may stop altogether, but that's not what you think about at a time like this. No. You're gripped, if only for a fleeting moment, by the fear that you won't be able to build it after all. The dreams about the three rooms, the hall, the big tiled kitchen and the equally big, sunny bathroom seem beyond your reach. Wallpaper, chandeliers, furniture. And mountains of gravel, cement, bricks. And chaos. Your wife is thinking along the same lines, but she's also thinking about their unwashed, ill-smelling embraces. The anger and resentment. We'll be tired, sweaty, and evil-smelling, she's thinking as she smiles at you; it'll be beautiful, you'll see, she says, and you nod, what? Then they look in on the neighbors. They've launched into it already, and already they've got problems, and there's a child, too, now, and anger, and debris everywhere. They sit down someplace and drink the beer their hosts shove in front of them and try to reason first with the one, then with the other, two people who haven't spoken to each other in months. But they're proud-minded, there's nothing they can do, they're into it, it's out of their hands.

Jenő Nagy and Sárika don't have the same problems that plague a young, nervous married couple. Jenő is fifty-eight, Sárika just over sixty, but they want to build a house next door in place of the small adobe one that's there now. They just got married and have a little something set aside, so they're optimistic. The sand around the small house got carried off anyway & it's dug up all around, because Sárika needed the money. Their neighbor knows, he carried some of it away himself. Sárika would let you have a carload for a bottle of wine, so why not? There's nothing left, no garden, no yard, it's been bitten into. They all came and carried it off, Jenő says. He's ill at ease. A shame on them. His neighbor listens, nods. Sure. Well, you wanna know what I got to say about that, he now asks. If I could start all over again I'd leave good enough be & not build a new one. Tell him, his wife cuts in, he can still do that. Jenő says nothing to either of them. Nor does Sárika. And also, the husband goes on, raising his voice, anybody that gets married & knocks a woman up is a moron. What problems would I have in that small house you want to tear down? Well? In which case, the wife continues, turning to Sárika, let me ask. Who kneeled in front of me and kissed my feet when I said, no, no, no! And who wound the electric cord around his neck? Tell her, the husband cuts in, that I was naive & had no idea that a piece of trash like…. Are you off already? We're off, says Jenő gingerly.

We have so much to attend to. But we'll be seeing each other again, I'm sure. We had such a lovely chat. Goodbye. Would you like to go anywhere else, Sárika asks outside, panting heavily. No dear, let's not, Jenő says, it costs such a lot. The one we've got is good enough for us, says Sárika as she helps Jenő up on the bicycle. These people are all unhappy. We don't need that.

Jenő Nagy walked as if he were perpetually driving a ball against two teams, because he was recruited into the state security forces in '56 and was wounded.[14] In some big building where everybody was running helter-skelter — the building may have even been on fire, and the Russians were shooting — in the chaos he rolled down a bunch of stairs and a brief round of fire from his own gun landed in his own body. There was nothing terribly wrong and he wasn't worried until about ten hours later, when there was nobody left in the building. He managed to crawl out onto the street, where two reliable witnesses found him, who later swore that wounded as he was, he was the last to leave the building, along with them. He said then, and he never tired of saying, that that's not how it was, but they just patted him on the back & smiled, don't be so modest, we know what we know. When he could stand again he was decorated, he was even given a small apartment, not just the hospital bed, and a colonel shook his hand and said, you're the kind of soldier we need. Then he was discharged and a couple of years later was forced into retirement.

It was a good shot in the ſtomach, it won't kill a soldier, juſt renders him unfit for battle, though truth to tell, it injured his ſpine, too, which ruined his walk, but nothing else.

He and Sárika met in the hoſpital. Jenő was undergoing some sort of rehab and Sárika was sleeping and smiling nonſtop in a bed with bars around it. She wasn't locked up. I'm here by miſtake, she told Jenő, & Jenő said he, too, because nobody shot him, except they won't believe him. He's written everybody, even János Kádár, but his name is all over the place, they make him sit at those long red tables during celebrations, pioneers and young Communiſt Leaguers badger him, wanting to take him under their wing. It's enough to drive a man berserk. Sárika juſt laughed. At the time she was given medication that makes you laugh at everything; she even laughed at the faʄt that her husband had died only recently, she loved him very much, she loved everybody, juſt ask the people in the ſtreet, and they love her juſt as much. They consoled her and brought her pálinka and wine, they chopped up the kindling, and some even ſtayed the night so she shouldn't be afraid, because it's one of those ſtreets. They were both well into their therapy when Jenő told her that he's got his own apartment, but it's on the eighth floor, and he's renting it out because he's afraid of the elevator. Also, it's too high up. They're going to give him another one on the ground floor, but in the meanwhile he sleeps in the frisking room at the gate house of the faʄtory, & during the day he sits around in the lobby of the office building, except they warned him that when the big boss comes he better hide, and then he hides in the switch box, it's closest.

Medical science is highly advanced; there are drugs to relax you, make you almost irresponsible, your thoughts wander, your face is smoothed out. All in all, life is beautiful. By the time the patient realizes, he's asked a woman's hand in marriage, he's making plans, he's practically happy. Out in the park behind Psychiatry and the Isolation Unit, Jenő Nagy showed Sárika that except for his walk he's hale and hearty and there's no impediment to him making her his wife. For her part, Sárika saw no impediment to it either, they're both retired, their life is ahead of them. They left the hospital together, in broad daylight, so people could see, then they went to Misi's at the top of the street, where even more people saw them, and that's when Dorogi said to Jancsi Hesz that this man walks as if he were driving a ball against two teams. Sárika ordered pálinka all around and Jenő paid, then they ordered a bottle of wine to go, and Jenő slammed a thousand-forint bill down on the counter, and everybody gaped. My bridegroom, Sárika said to Mrs. Sarkadi when they went to her place for a glass of wine. We're getting married. Good, Mrs. Sarkadi, Aunt Piroska said, that's the way to do it. But you still owe me three-hundred seventy forints, Sárika. From last month. Sárika nodded, and Jenő took out the money and said, from now on it's gonna be different, isn't that right, dear!

In our street there's dust, poverty, and a bunch of unrealized dreams and lives, and there's no knowing, even, when people are helping each other. When it got around that the big mouthed, drunkard Sárika hooked herself a man from town with a funny walk who practically feeds her with a silver spoon, that they hardly ever leave the house, & sometimes people see a bicycle with Jenő sitting on the frame and Sárika pushing it, that they go to Misi's place or Mrs. Sarkadi's for wine, at first everybody just laughed. But then it also got around that Jenő's the kind of guy that sold his house in Debrecen and bought Sárika a white wedding gown to be married in. Also, that the gown cost fifty-thousand forints all told, and in today's world! Jancsi Hesz said that a funeral costs less and is just as beautiful, but Terka Papp, his mother-in-law, ran along the length of the street, it's the hand of God, and there's such a thing as true love! Not like her son-in-law and her daughter! Except it piqued her that she couldn't see into Sárika's yard properly, when little Sanyi Harap's boys come in and out as they please. All six of them. And they're always chewing something. And even the reverend cried at the wedding, there was organ music, the little Zeke boy brought a tape recorder, and from that, because the ceremony was held in the house. There was a cauldron of goulash soup, sausage, ham, drinks. And the whole street ate, whereas nobody brought anything, they just had a laugh at the sixty-year-old bride in the white gown and a myrtle wreath on her head. Yes.

Days later a huge, long awaited downpour came and people took shelter in Misi's place, where they listened agog to Dorogi, who told them that everybody better cart back the sand they carried off from Sárika's house. The rain's stopped, so get moving! They couldn't believe their ears. Jancsi Hesz, who hadn't carried off anything, seconded Dorogi, it's a disgrace, yes, and the law's the law and he's gonna be the first to go to Town Hall, if that's what it takes. Another downpour like this, Béres yelled, and it's gonna wash away that house. He didn't cart anything away either, but he's gonna cart something back! Don't make me laugh, Misi, the proprietor, said, she practically gave it away. For wine! Then they changed the subject and continued drinking, and then Misi said to Dorogi, the old graveyard in the village, it's being liquidated. Cart it from there. And rubble from the railroad bed. Bring along some beer, Dorogi said, then they went to Sárika's house to settle the matter. It was getting dark, but not that dark, you could see the small house with what was left of the tiny yard standing in the middle of a pool of rainwater, and in the yard a walnut tree and under it a table, and there they were, Jenő Nagy in shirtsleeves and pants, his feet resting on a low stool, smoking, and across from him Sárika in her white wedding gown, and she was smoking, too, the two of them sitting there as serene and quiet as if they were listening to the sound of music.

THE GETAWAY

Laci Kiss is a tall, lean, round faced boy. He's almost seventeen, his eyes are green, and once he closes them, they won't open for anything in the world. He attended trade school in Debrecen, but the first year took him two. Classes started at eight, but sometimes he wouldn't show up till twelve or after, when his head lowered, he apologized shamefacedly. I'm sorry. I overslept. For a long time they wouldn't believe him, then the principal said, okay son, go on home and don't come back until you've had your share of sleep. And he didn't, because Jóska Ács talked him into working at the Clinic where they experiment with animals, that's where he helps out. They dissect rats, rabbits, and dogs, but they gotta be caught first and the rest fed and given their shots, and there's also the cleaning up to do. He's on vacation now and Kati Sós and he agreed to meet at the bus stop in the afternoon as if by chance, as if they were going someplace separately, then they'll walk down to Uncle Kocsis's farm by the river and stay there. What would happen afterwards they didn't consider, but it didn't matter, only one thing mattered, that once they were there, there was nothing anybody could do about it. At two o'clock Laci was still sleeping, & he was still sleeping at three, when the bus had come and gone. The bus driver, who in the meantime had been to Debrecen and back, called to Kati Sós, are you coming? Also, people were watching her from Misi's across the way. Around four o'clock, when a small crowd of people were coming back from a funeral, she decided she wouldn't wait any longer, she had lipstick on, and she didn't want people to see. Also, she was crying, though not very much.

Kati Sós's eyes are also green and she's also almost seventeen, and her face is round, too, but much nicer. Her skin is as pure as snow, Aunt Sarkadi said, & also that she mustn't get addicted to anything, it would ruin her looks. She mustn't curl her hair either, it's naturally curly and as smooth as silk, and blond, and don't you cut it, these days natural hair is such a rarity. And her teeth and neck and every part of her. She must take care of herself! Aunt Sarkadi is worth listening to, she's got an education, she sells her own wine across from the general store & handles drunks like nobody else, but Kati Sós wouldn't have minded getting addicted to something, because what's the use of having beautiful blond hair when she spends half the day standing in the pigsty pitching the manure with a fork or carrying slop for the pig, feeding the chickens, sweeping the yard, and nobody sees either her eye or her neck, and as for her skin, it stinks. And her sick father, he's in the house moaning and groaning the livelong day, because he can't manage to die, though she's been telling him for two years, he just groans and complains and is a disgusting nuisance.

Well, she's really had it! About two weeks ago a woman that rubs people down with ointment came to see him and gave him such a rubdown that her father said, now that was something! Later she read his palm and said that his wife died because they weren't suited, and he's going to die, too, if he doesn't marry a short, forty-year-old black woman, but if he does, he's going to be healthy again. He might even have a son. She then took half a side of bacon and ten thousand forints from him. Her father told her about it last week, and also that he's going to marry that woman, if it's in the books, there's nothing he can do. She's just right. She's short, forty, & black. Then the day before yesterday he fell ill again and sent her to fetch the woman, but she didn't go. She told him that she couldn't find her. She didn't call the doctor either but went for a walk instead, and back home she said, don't worry, they said they'd send an ambulance tomorrow and take you to the madhouse.

She wasn't in love with Laci Kiss, she loved Attila & would love him till her dying day and beyond, except he won't notice her. They played together as children, she hugged him, called him her little field mouse; they wrestled & she always made sure that he won; he lay on top of her, shouting; they laughed, she held him close and sometimes peed in her pants from sheer delight. Then it all stopped when her mother died, whereas they were waiting for her father to die, even back then, and she was left with all the work. Attila also went to school, but they hardly ever met; most of the time he didn't even say hello. He had a bicycle, expensive clothes, even jeans, and in summer he ate ice cream and drank Coke. He's a big boy now, he palmed Tímea's tits in the disco, but not hers, even though she held them up to him, and also, hers are nicer. When she was little she wanted to become a dancer; she took her clothes off in the adobe pit, down to her panties, in front of the others, and danced for them, like on stage, and the boys beat the rhythm on their knees and the girls hummed; Attila stood above the pit with his bicycle and ate his ice cream, though by then she didn't take her clothes off to bathe or when she played spin the bottle with the others. Once she asked him to take her home on his bicycle. The boy nodded, okay, come on. He helped her on the bike. Not like that, she said. On your lap. Like that. He said he can't, the bike can't take the weight. Fine. Forget it. In the end the boy sat on the bike and she ran alongside through the grass. Another time she said to him, Attila, let me have some of your ice cream. He said he'd already licked it. That's why, she said. He then gave her the whole thing and bought himself another. She now wrote all these things down in the letter that she threw in his mailbox before she left. Also, that Attila will always be her true love, but she's going away with Laci Kiss because at least he's mad about her & is going to commit suicide if he can't marry her. And she wouldn't want anybody's death on her conscience, and besides, nobody else loves her.

She hopes that Attila will get on well with the little Tímea, who is with child by Dorogi and also Sanyi Harap, which is why she can't deliver it.

Laci Kiss was by no means on the verge of suicide; at any rate, he knew nothing about it, because he was sleeping, he'd been told at school to get plenty of sleep. As for the doctor with the weary eyes, he had asked if he gets a hard-on during the night, etc. What et cetera, the boy asked, turning slightly crimson. Ah, the doctor said impatiently, so you do, and he blushed, too. No I don't, the boy protested. I sleep alone! I see, the doctor said and wrote out a prescription, but then thought better of it. What would be the use? When Kati Sós suggested to him that they should get away, like Erzsi Simó and her friend, he agreed, his only condition being that it shouldn't be in the morning, because he's still sleeping. Is ten o'clock okay, the girl asked. Noon would be better. But that's no good for Kati, she's got to feed the animals. Two o'clock? Fine, the boy said. And what happened? He's sleeping like a log! He doesn't even hear Kati come in, whereas she's not even quiet & stops by the bed, like one who has been slapped in the face. Out on the street just a moment ago she swore she'd kick him, but now she'd rather stroke his face, those full lips, sweaty skin, flies on his forehead, thick, black hair. Like a dead man, he's hardly breathing; he's just snoring in this shameless, rumpled nest. Then she shakes him, he turns, in a daze, then sits up, what is it? What's the time? A person can wait till doomsday, Kati says, on the verge of tears, but then checks herself. So. Are you coming or not, she asks after a while. The boy yawns, he doesn't even put his hand up, he stretches his arms and legs, and gradually collects himself. Listen, he says. Do we have to go out there? My parents aren't coming home from the farm this weekend. We can do it here just as well. What do you think?

Out on the old, deserted farm, they can't get in anywhere. No problem, Laci Kiss says, there's a ladder, we'll go up to the attic. He's fully awake now, and at such times he's as lively as an electric wire, which is lucky, because for her part, the girl's enthusiasm is waning. Also, her shoe chafed her heels, even though they'd come barefoot from the gate, with rye fields to right and left. The boy started hugging her at the gate & managed to kiss her lips, and he panted nonstop. Meanwhile he told her that he can do it to a dog, too, with one firm grip, you gotta squeeze its cheeks on both sides, which makes the dog open its mouth, and then you can shove anything inside. Like this, he says and squeezes the girl's cheeks on both sides, and she cries out, oh! You see?, the boy says as he sticks his finger into the girl's mouth. They laugh, then he kisses her lips. Let's go. Meanwhile she's thinking of the boy on his bed, naked, sweet as honey, she nearly touched him but then she just covered him up, and felt sad. We should've brought something to drink, she says moodishly up in the attic. And cigarettes.

Like the grownups. Then she's thinking that she'll lie down & then the boy could watch her, like she watched him back home, and he could stroke her face and even kiss her, but so she doesn't notice. But that's no good either, she doesn't feel like lying down in the straw naked; meanwhile the boy has stripped to his underpants and maybe he's gonna do it to her, too, with one firm grip. His face is up close to hers, he's got his arms about her, he's licking her, but it's no good, she can smell the cabbage he's eaten on his breath, because he's still panting. They're sitting in the straw by the attic door, because Kati won't lie down, she felt a bug crawling on her skin just now. Where, the boy asks, & reaches for her breast and draws her closer, as if he were her mother, and she whispers, let's kill father, she breathes, the boy is devouring her breast, and she's thinking how the other day the little Zeke boy had put his finger up her in the movie house yard, and her rectum burned for days, so it's no use for the boy to fumble down there, she's not gonna let him. I'll be over tonight, she says, so you can help, and looks past him at the flock of sparrows taking to the air. Let's go, she says, it's getting dark. In a minute, the boy says. He's doing it to himself again, she thinks.

Let's come early tomorrow, all right?, she asks the boy. Fine, he says, but not too early. And let's bring drinks and cigarettes. And something to eat. And we'll never go home again. Fine, the boy says to this, too, fine. At the bus stop, they part ways. The boy stars running, but she waits a bit, though it makes no difference anymore. Back home she feeds the chickens & also throws something to the pigs, and she's done. It's dark, only the dogs are barking, Laci hasn't got any, it's safe to go over, everything's wide open. She sees the boy through the glass door, he's sitting in front of the TV in short underpants, and he's sleeping. What's up, he says when he looks up. I'm not going tomorrow, Kati Sós says, beaming, my father's dead. The boy rubs his eyes, yawns, then he holds his arms out. Come here, he says lovingly, this time you're not getting away.

IT'S HOT

Soon after the great rain, the local chapter of MDF presented Jenő Nagy with a fabulous wheelchair.[15] Nobody showed up at the presentation, so they sent it with Dorogi, who didn't know what to do with it for some time, because Jenő Nagy said he doesn't want it, and Dorogi shouldn't bother taking it off the dray, thank you very much. No way. Forget it. Dorogi didn't take it back right away, which was a mistake, because the next day they sent word that they wanted it back. Jenő Nagy was in the security forces when he was wounded, and he should thank his lucky stars that they're not taking him to court, much less a wheelchair. Defiance breeds defiance. Had Jenő Nagy accepted the clever wheelchair without a word and left it on the street, it'd have been stolen in two minutes, and everybody would've been happy. But he felt he had a case. Sárika wheeled him to Town Hall on her bike, where he explained, rationally, and for about the hundredth time in his life, the story of his wounds: he doesn't even know where, but in all the turmoil he tripped and rolled down the stairs and meanwhile his gun went off and he shot himself in his own belly and spine with his own gun, and what are they going to do about it? Which is what the clerk asked over the phone, too, in about a dozen places, while he waited, fanning himself with a sheet of paper. Later the clerk sighed and said, you know what? Take the wheelchair and do with it whatever you want. Just deny you were ever wounded, because your case is so confusing, it boggles the mind.

But seeing how he was there, Jenő Nagy thought he'd point out that the wheelchair was a used item anyway, old man Koda died out of it, & by what right does the MDF give him a wheelchair to begin with? He can walk, just slower, and he needs more room to move his legs, but he's not to be pitied, if anything he's to be envied, because this way he and Sárika could meet in the hospital, he'd have never met her otherwise. So everything's just fine with him, thank you very much. But if they're hell bent on giving things away, they should give him two, one for Sárika, because her legs hurt, too. Besides, what if it should break down? What then? He was addressing the tail end of his speech to Dorogi, out on the street, because in the meantime he'd been flung out of the office. Okay, so what's it to be, Dorogi asked, you want it or not? No, we don't, Sárika said defiantly, then she helped Jenő onto the bicycle frame. Let's go, dear. So what now, Dorogi asked in the office upstairs. He doesn't want it! Take it after them, the clerk said. At first they're all reluctant. What if he won't let me in? What then?, a question he was now addressing to his horse out on the street, and the horse, for his part, responded by making a mad dash for Misi's.

I can't make this animal stop drinking, the big, ruddy-faced man said when they reached Misi's. Which one, Misi, the proprietor, asked. There's a whole bunch of us once we congregate. Dorogi had planned to take this cripple chair home, except his horse was facing the other way, and why make him turn around? Besides, at Misi's there's always somebody to share your troubles with. Because troubles, who hasn't got troubles? His, for instance, is the wheelchair, Misi's is something else. The other day that damn horse even swallowed the bottle, Dorogi said resuming where he'd left off, that's how badly it wanted that beer. It's still inside him. A shame, Misi offered, it's got a deposit on it. Misi was out of sorts because it was early and the pub was empty, & he still had the beer to haul up from the cellar. He didn't understand why people couldn't drink it down there. He's tried it many times, and he managed just fine, and as far as he could tell, his customers wouldn't have minded either. There's even comfort in being surrounded by all that alcohol. It's like the warmth of one's home, seconded Sudák, dreamy eyed, because he'd tried it when Laci Veres slept with his wife by accident, & he was locked in the cellar with all those cases.

Our street stretches along the southern slope of a hill, the heat beats down on it all day, the sun dries everything out, parches it, the wells are practically depleted, the pocket-sized gardens languish in front of the houses, the air won't stir, sometimes for days, while at other times a mad whirlwind whips desert sand in your eyes, your mouth, and under your skin. Drop-dead heat, said the scrawny Terka Papp, who also happens to be Jancsi Hesz's mother-in-law, and she spit. She doesn't usually go to pubs, but she was out looking for Dorogi. And she found him. What is it this time, Dorogi asked after he threw back a shot of pálinka. You need help getting to the graveyard? The stooped, skinny woman who was wearing a loose housedress, a pullover, and a pair of rubber boots on her feet, just smiled. Why don't we discuss this in private? Dorogi asked for another shot of pálinka. One for you, he asked. No, Terka said, and blushed. Maybe just a sip of yours. No you don't. That's for my horse. He won't drink after just anybody.

Dorogi worked for the Mayor's Office when there was something to ship, like this chair now. He also took kindling to the retired people, & in summer, the dead to the cemetery, because in summer the hearse was in Aradvány, carting melon. So what is it this time, he asked Terka once they were outside. Terka didn't quite know how to break it to him and it took some time, but the essence of it was that she wanted the wheelchair. Sárika and Jenő Nagy don't want it. But she does. What do you want it for, Dorogi asked, you walk just fine. Sure. But for how much longer? Once she can't walk, she'll have nobody to count on. Her son-in-law and she don't get along, and neither does she and her daughter, and it's gotten so bad, she hardly dares go home anymore.

She could even use it to go to the market. She'd have gone on and on, but Jancsi Hesz was heading towards them in a blue working uniform. Oh, Terka Papp sighed, just don't say anything to that animal. We'll get back to it later. I'll pay you, of course, she added with a smile, then ambled off to the bus stop. Dorogi just stood there and stared. It wasn't her wanting that wheelchair, but that she was willing to pay for it, because it had never happened before, she'd never said any such thing, and the sky hadn't fallen!

Jancsi Hesz also had a look at the wheelchair, and Misi came outside, too, and they hauled it off the dray. Then business picked up. For instance, Béres showed up, he can't bare to look at it, he said, he sat in it plenty when they took his pancreas out of him, but his wife could use it. He'd cut a hole in the bottom and put a bucket under it. Is it for sale? Then Lajos Mérő and Laci Veres joined them, and before long wheelchair fever had reached new heights. Laci Veres, who knows everything, quickly explained how the wheelchair works, it's a fold-up, he said, but they wouldn't let him demonstrate. Two big wheels in back, two smaller ones up front. You see, it's easier to push that way, because it's like going down-hill. All the time. You gotta be kidding, the others said. If that was true, you could never let go, and the nurses would be chasing patients with a butterfly net all day long out in the yard. That's not how, the Veres boy be-gan, but had no more aces in his pocket. Jancsi Hesz explained that they could even fix an engine to it, diesel's the best, with automatic ignition. That way it would start even in winter. The frame could be reinforced. There are ways. They might even manage to get a license plate. In less than two hours, there wasn't a man on the street that didn't want that wheelchair, though the truth is, they were pretty drunk.

It was impossible to tell afterwards whose idea it was, but they wheeled the chair out to the street and got Dorogi to hitch his horse to it and do a round. Esztike was fed up with all the fuss about the chair anyway, and Sudák hadn't even shown up yet. Sudák had lost his credit with Esztike because the last time, he was reluctant to pay. He said that Esztike writes down more than what he drinks. Which was not true. Esztike never wrote anything down. She drew notches, God only knows where. Sudák joined them when they passed his yard and seeing how brilliant the moment was he ran back inside, drank what was left of his liter of wine & slapped Katóka, who tried to prevent it. Gentlemen, he said once he was outside, brilliant! And he bowed from the waist. It later turned out that he also wanted the wheelchair, but by then they were at the shop, where the more adventurous among them threw back some pálinka here as well, & swore to the women that they were just giving the chair a test drive before anybody actually used it. They even told Aunt Sarkadi to come on out & have a look, but she said, have you all gone crazy, Pista, acting like this. Aren't you ashamed of yourself? There's those that need it, while you and the others are playing practical jokes! May the Good Lord not punish you for it.

Aunt Piroska sometimes says things that make you want to lie down and die. But at least, there's silence. When it passed, Dorogi said, okay, that's enough! Let's head back. Then when they reached Sanyi Vida's place he yanked the reins. Halt! What's up, Jancsi Hesz asked. Nothing, Dorogi said. Who's coming in with me? Not me, said Jancsi, but Béres was game and so was Lajos Mérő, and Laci Veres, too. Just imagine, Jancsi Hesz later told Aunt Piroska, half the street wanted that wheelchair by then, especially the old people. Sanyi Harap cried, others offered money. Aunt Kiss promised a brood of young chicks, Pintér a barrel of wine. Any barrel. Or pálinka. But they'd brought that poor man outside by then to take him to Misi's. I'm referring to Uncle Vida's boy, the one that's got consumption. It's cancer, Aunt Piroska said. He looked like Jesus when they took him off the cross, Jancsi Hesz went on, but we weren't afraid of him, we picked him up and dragged him outside and held his hand so he shouldn't fall out, and he only fell out once. We went to Misi's with the horse and pointed things out to him, see, that's the bus stop, and that way the cemetery, and so and so lives over here & so and so over there, but he just kept his eye fixed on the horse, even though he hasn't been out of the house in years. When the horse, if you'll excuse the expression, farted, he laughed and Dorogi said, hear that? The ignition has just kicked in. His father cried as he walked behind us, but we laughed so hard, we bit our lips.

THE MAN WITH THE DOG

The sun's been going down sizzling white for months, lingering on the horizon at the end of the street, so when you go to Misi's, and why shouldn't you, you're practically blinded by the time you get there, and once you're inside, red & blue & yellow spots dance before your eyes, and you keep bumping into things. That small mangy dog, too, it nearly got stepped on. A good thing it can look after itself. The dog had a man with it; he was sitting at the second table, a stranger, no doubt, because the locals know that that's the card table. He's a withered little man with red, inflamed eyes and stubble, and he keeps clutching his stomach as if he meant to be sick any minute. No wonder that Esztike's been keeping an eye on him from behind the counter. Kindly take that dog outside, she says in an attempt to make him speak. But he just stares. The dog, Esztike says, her voice up a notch. Clearly, she can raise it even further if she wants. You mean this, the man says pointing to the small dog that's on this side of a kilo and a half, even among friends, & it may even be blind, because it just bumped its head against the foot of his chair. This here is a rat catcher. Great, says Esztike in the same tone of voice, and this here is a café, not some filthy dive. So get that animal out of here.

The place is empty except for Lajos Mérő standing despondently by the window, looking out, his eyes sad & bewildered, whereas he should be sitting; when he's in this state, he's usually sitting, which is a good thing. The window is filthy and so are the curtains, and Esztike is annoyed, why can't Lajos look out the door? It wouldn't kill him. It's bigger, too, and there's nothing to block the view. Lajos doesn't join in the conversation; he's got troubles of his own. When he was alone with Esztike just now, he bought up the prospect of a sexual encounter, to be conducted at his place, purely on a hygienic basis, of course. With you, Esztike inquired, choking back her wrath, whereupon Lajos Mérő informed her that he's got no shortage of volunteers, except it's Esztike he's taken a fancy to. She's clean and she looks healthy, and no halitosis, probably, because that's where he draws the line. Also, she's got good teeth and doesn't sweat, which is the other thing that makes his you know what go limp. Besides, he knows that Esztike's body also needs it, because by evening her husband is always drunk, and as for the rest, one can guess. With him it's the other way around, though, the more he drinks, the more he wants it. And if Esztike doesn't watch herself, she's gonna end up like an acquaintance of his who was also neglected, and by the time she got around to him, she was like Velcro inside. Enough already, Esztike cut in, exasperated, and regards to your mother. That's when the man with the dog walked in, ordered a small glass of rum, and sat down, even though nobody showed him any hospitality.

Later Jancsi Hesz also showed up, then Laci Veres, then Dorogi came in, blinking; he stopped short, looked around, then asked the man with the dog, who the hell are you? And he said he's Jurák & his dog's Arthur and he's a rat hound and they've just come from Adony. He had a sharp, bleating voice, strange yet somehow pleasant with drawn out vowels, at which Jancsi Hesz came out with it and said, you're not one of us. But that's not the problem. The problem is, you should get up from there because that there's the card table. As you wish, the withered little man said, he had a small green knitted cap on his head, then he said that he can drink half a liter of pálinka in one go, provided they let him. He did it the other day, too, then he went outside and hammered a guy that looked remarkably like Jancsi Hesz into the ground. In a minute, Jancsi Hesz said, soon as I finish this hand. Except, I haven't had my half a liter yet, the little man said demurely. Don't worry, Jancsi Hesz said. Esztike, give him what he wants. It's on me.

The man who called himself Jurák was a sorry sight in his small green knitted cap. But after Jancsi Hesz gave him two horrendous slaps outside in front of the place, he looked outright pathetic. He'd received the second on his way down. I didn't stand up yet, he said indignant, then once inside, he told everybody how they mustn't jump to no conclusions, because once he gets to know them, their strengths and weaknesses, they're putty in his hands. It happened the other day, too, when he beat a man the size of Dorogi to within an inch of his life.

The guy was on his knees, pleading for me not to strike him, and I just went like this, & he motioned with his hand. Swatted him like a fly. Into the dust and his own filth. Then he got up, went to the john, and pissed his pants. You're coming, Dorogi asked when he returned. Where? Just up front, Dorogi urged. It won't take a minute. Look here, the little man said, if I beat you up, you're gonna be a laughing stock. Is that what you want? Of course not, the large-size Dorogi said, his voice full of the milk of human kindness. Pour him another drink, Esztike, he's seeing things. I don't like this, Esztike said sulking, are you men gonna beat him up or not? Except for Esztike, by closing time they all had a go at the little man, and meanwhile they each consumed six shots of pálinka & two beers. Eh, that's nothing, the little man muttered, in Acsád the other day they measured it out in a bottle for me to take away, because I couldn't drink that much. He couldn't say how many slaps he'd had, though. You do what you gotta do to get by.

It got around that there were rats in the street or some other animal, weasels or hamsters, and though nobody actually saw them, by the time it got around, they did. Béres even said he'd been seeing them for some time scurrying round his feet at night and sneaking off with his chickens & hens. Jancsi Hesz said that others see them, too, provided they had as much drink in them as Béres, but the scare was on and something had to be done. The authorities sprang into action. Once again they put up signs by all the wells with a warning that the water is not safe for drinking, and another announcing that they've exterminated the rats in the street and people should beware of the poison and so on. Except it would've been no use looking for the poison, because there was no money for it, just for the signs. That's when somebody sent for Jurák to Adony to come and bring his rat hound. The little man traveled light. He didn't even have shoes on his feet, and he said that the scars on his hands were from the rats, because they get vicious when cornered. He came in the evening, let the dog out of his sack, then went into Misi's, where he soon got slapped around, then first thing in the morning, he set to work. There should be someone around at each house while he's working, he said, and they should pool their resources because he needs a kilo of bacon, two fistfuls of flat pasta, a big glass of pálinka, and salt, but no paprika. He always carries his own. Oh. And a bag of mentholated candy for the dog, because rats have a keen sense of smell. Nobody liked this, though, because the people in our street are a generous lot, but they don't like being asked. Why should they give him anything? And who asked him to come in the first place? And what if he doesn't catch anything? They're no fools. Then somebody said, let the grocer or Kocsis give Jurák what he wants. Kocsis has plenty of chickens, and Pintér's attic is bulging at the seams with last year's bacon. So what about it?

By nine they'd caught the first rat, because after a while Jurák's demands were met, they'd managed to pool their resources after all. Jurák and his dog got down to business in the dilapidated house at the far end of the street. The mangy little dog dug and scraped and scratched, Jurák kneeled by its side or lay down or sat up, encouraging and reviling the dog in turn, but he scraped with his hands and feet, too, and before long, they were covered in dirt, and then they moved on. It's probably further up the street, he said to the dog, and he spit on the ground, while the dog shaped its mug into a snarl, or maybe it was just laughing at the whole thing. It won't attack people, the little man said. He was covered in filth by then, then at the Kocsis house he had the woodpile knocked down, then he went inside the chicken coop; at the Kisses he had the haystack picked apart, and then suddenly, voilá!, half the street was standing by anxiously, with sticks and pitchforks at the ready, the women screamed & squealed, but then they all laughed, bravo!, the little guy sure knows his business! Then the men went to Misi's & Misi brought out a case of beer, though he knew as well as the rest of them that there were no rats in the street to begin with. The question was, how did the little man do it? They drank and generally made a lot of noise, then they took turns slapping Jurák around, because he kept insisting that once he has half a liter of anything to drink, nobody gets the better of him, because they fight like stupid peasants, it's a laugh. He could do better with one hand tied behind his back. He didn't get past six small glasses of pálinka now either, but he had four beers for a chaser, then he washed the blood off and told his dog that this here is a place to reckon with. His dog just snarled, or maybe it was just laughing at the whole thing.

Jurák liked our street and moved into that dilapidated, abandoned house at the far end, and every day he cooked himself chicken or hen in a bad cauldron, the poultry courtesy of Arthur. And he also had bacon and bread & even wine, because catching rats is no child's play. Admittedly, they only caught one, but where there's one, he said, there's bound to be another, a whole brood of them, and they gotta be caught, otherwise that one rat was in vain. In the meanwhile, the filthy little man went to all the houses and searched the rooms, the attics, the cellars, the chicken yards. At the Kisses he even opened the icebox, because the rat is a clever animal, and it doesn't mind the cold. As for Misi's, he gets beaten up there regularly now, for no reason, just force of habit, and because the people of the street are on to him. Sometimes even Arthur does a flip if he's near somebody's foot, and why not? It helps pass the time.

The nights, though, are another matter. The air, it hardly cools down at all, you boil in your bed, you stick to it, drenched in sweat, you twist and turn. At such times, Misi has to go outside to catch the breeze, then he has to go down to the cellar, because it's more than a body can take otherwise. It's also bad that you see fleeting shades in the dark, mice, rats, owls, monsters breath in your face and whisper in your ear, which is why he sent for Jurák in Adony in the first place. During the day it's better, but at night he carries a rubber stick with him, and he lashes out with it right, left, and even behind. On the way back he doesn't have to. Once he's had a drink in the cellar, things settle down. Now, too, he hears something, steps outside, waits, then lashes out in the dark. It's Lajos Mérő. He takes another step, lashes out again, and this time it's probably Jurák, because as he hits the ground, live rats come scooting from inside him. Only the dog sneaks away unharmed, a fat hen between its jaws, and this time he didn't hit Esztike either. And now he's at the cellar door, and not a moment too soon.

OUR VENIAL SINS

During the day our street is dull and lethargic, it may even be asleep, but at night it's restless, people shout, dogs bark, there's a dull surge of sound, doors, windows open and close quietly, a gray figure staggers along a fence, if there's a bang he's hit the bull's eye, not that it makes a difference. Our son Dezső disappears during the day, too, like the rest of them, which is all to the good, because when he's home, it's like a never-ending reproach. He's our son because nobody knows who his father is. Also, as ill luck would have it, he looks like his mother, a pretty, slightly creole face, dreamy gray eyes, small nose and ears and light brown hair; he looks so much like her, you don't know where to avert your eyes. If you're holding a glass of beer in your hand, it's easier, but a small glass is no good, it might spill if its owner gets overexcited and that wouldn't be worth it. Everybody had the hots for Rózsika, some may still do; we got her married off to a man from town, but he must've heard something and packed his bags. It happens, but it passes, worse things have been known to happen. The trouble is that Rózsika doesn't know the truth herself, she just smiles and loves her son.

As for Dezső, he goes into town, because he's a big boy now. He can even drink beer there because he's a tall young man, whereas he's just sixteen. He also lights a cigarette or two. He rides the bus for free, provided that Uncle Feri is the driver, because he used to live in our street. He tears off a stub for the boy, who stands by his side all the way to the last stop, telling stories, explaining things; Uncle Feri can't get a word in edgewise; he just presses the gas pedal, and his cheeks are on fire. No wonder. It's so hot, your face practically falls off. When the bus pulls in, they shake hands like adults *&* Dezső asks, when is your return trip, Uncle Feri? I'd like to go back when you do, alright? Alright, the driver says, and something else as well, but it doesn't matter, the boy will wait for him in any case, we've all got our cross to bear. Meanwhile, the boy walks off with a wide smile, he even waves, may the good Lord bless him for it, the driver thinks, touched to the quick, if only he'd get lost already, the passengers have been talking about the two of them behind his back.

When he's in Debrecen, Dezső always heads for the Union department store, a sad, blind man plays the violin on a corner, the violin case lies open on the sidewalk in front of him, and people throw him indulgence money. Except Dezső. He doesn't throw him anything, whereas he could use indulgence himself. Leaning against the glass pane he watches the nervous, teeming multitude; he doesn't speak to the blind man, and nobody bothers him either. Sometimes he squats down on the concrete and imagines that, for instance, he's loaded with money, a sack's worth of money, let's say, *&* there, in front of the gawking crowd, he slams a fistful of five-thousand forint bills into the violin case, will you open your eyes already and stop this intolerable scraping on the fiddle, because it's enough to drive a person bonkers. Then he slaps the old man on the neck, gives him a light kick in the ass, get lost, old man, he says, I never want to see you sitting here with that instrument of torture again. Aren't you ashamed of yourself? Then he scrapes out what's inside the violin case, like he always does, and walks off with it. He gets two scoops of ice cream for it, plus change.

Our boy is perky and fun loving, but he's got no friends here because he's coarse and rude to the other boys, even if afterwards he asks, are you mad? If the other takes offense or swings a fist at him, he might even cry, well, are you still, he yells into the other's face, are you still angry? He let Sanyi Harap's boys down the well one by one to bathe, and one time he had the dog pull the baby carriage with the baby inside and also a loaf of bread, so they could hardly catch up with him. While his mother works, he hangs around. Ever since they told him at school to stop attending because he's older and more mature & he's bad for the others, he's got nothing better to do. This happened after he pinched the skin on his knee together out in the yard in front of a bunch of kids and stuck his finger in so they'll understand what they were so eager to know. He got his diploma, he graduated, & now, since he's so smart, good riddance!

The clergyman had picked him out back when he was looking for old finds in the dugout for the water mains and the boys were making fun of him and Dezső felt sorry for him. He's probably mad at us, he thought, because that's what he read in the clergyman's eye, & in the evening he went to the rectory to see him. Uncle Minister, he asked, are you mad at us? It must have been around nine, the old man was about to retire, and he was suddenly at a loss, how could the boy have come in through the garden gate & stand there in the open door, when they were both locked? It's got to be hoisted up a bit, the boy explained. I can get inside anyplace I want.

And he did, about once a month, if he felt like it, the bus stop was right there. Then he loitered around the church until he spotted the clergyman, or else he walked right in and, for instance, came up with things like he'd like to join the congregation, and which is it? But he soon stopped listening to the clergyman and fixed his eye on the grayish blue jumpsuit he wore. He wanted it very badly. Other times he'd say that he's forgotten the Lord's Prayer again, but no, he just gets the lines mixed up, he can't manage to get it right, even though the minister recited it to him so many times, and then he knew, but then he forgot. I never get it right. Give us this day our daily bread, or lead us not into temptation. Which comes first? The clergyman was patient, and he was happy when the boy came to see him, Uncle Minister, I forgot again, dammit! Lord, the clergyman thought, could this be the Way? Is this what you want? He's recited the holy prayer for the boy thirty times at least, it can't be that he can't remember it, surely it's a sign from heaven that makes this hot tempered young child, who is constantly tempted by the Bad, but never the Good, come to him again and again. How is it, Father, the clergyman would ask the Almighty with a touch of malice, how is it that it's always the Bad that tempts us? The old clergyman has been discovering more & more quirks in this whole thing called Creation lately, but when the boy came to see him, he was always patient. He had plenty of time on his hands. People had stopped coming for evening prayers. But he was also afraid. Your eyes, he once said to the boy, flash like a cat's. Of course, the boy said. I can see in the dark. Then he asked for a loan of two-hundred forints, & by the time the clergyman had recovered, he was gone.

A man hardly notices when he's losing his right mind. On another occasion the minister was explaining the Bible, and the boy was tearing at his hair with a comb, because the minister had said to him that when he comes, he should at least wash his face & comb his hair. After all, the rectory is a church, too. Fine, the boy said, give me a rake. The clergyman grimaced and helped. That stack was full of straw and sand and ants crawled around inside, and it gave off tiny sparks whenever he touched it. Where on earth do you sleep, he asked the boy. In the straw, he said with pride. Come and see. You can sleep there if you like. There's plenty of room. Or you can sleep with my mother if you don't mind the smell of booze, he added and told him that Rozi, because that's what he calls her since they've become friends, in short, Rozi sleeps on a chaff bed in the back room, and he on one in the kitchen. The clergyman seemed to recall that a chaff bed was some sort of mat stuffed with straw and chaff. Is there no bed, he asked. A sofa or the like. No, the boy said, my father took everything. He just left me & the house. It's mine, he added. I can do with it whatever I want. Rozi can stay only as long as we're on good terms. During the day Rozi works in town cleaning the station, and in the evening she does overtime, manning the pumps in the basement. What is she doing, the clergyman asked, the blood rushing to his cheeks. What do you mean, the boy asked, and he looked at him so innocently with his child's eyes that the clergyman turned white from shame. Lord, he said to himself, and even so only softly, how can I have such a filthy mind? He then glanced at his watch and said, we had such a nice chat. The boy agreed. He said that he likes to talk to people, except he's got nobody to talk to, but when the clergyman marries his mother, things will be different. What will be different, the clergyman asked, because he'd let the rest go past his ear. So then are you coming, the boy asked, because he is. Where? To my place. I can't go alone, I'm scared, he added with a laugh. It's dark outside!

The clergyman was not an overly refined soul, but he knew that two people invariably affect each other, and so he was not particularly bothered that in our boy's company he inadvertently adopted his gestures, facial expressions, and at times could hardly stop himself from letting a juicy oath pass his lips. He saw nothing extraordinary in getting in his Trabant and taking the boy home either. It's service, even if he's reeling from the heady odor of the two filthy shoes on the boy's feet. I want a pair of white jeans, Dezső said in the car. And also the sweat suit you got on. Then he told the clergyman that he steals from a blind violinist when he's in town, but he knows, he asserted in lively tones, and doesn't mind! The other day, too, he rapped with his bow for me to take it. But I waited a bit, because there wasn't enough! The clergyman nodded, he wasn't paying much attention, these dirt roads are treacherous, and there's no lighting. Then Dezső touched his arm. We're here. Come in, otherwise Rozi's gonna think I was out whoring! So what's wrong with that, the clergyman asked, and was inordinately surprised that he was enjoying himself. When he got out of the car, tiny sparks flared up before him in the night and the pungent smell of incense assaulted his nostrils. The Lord will punish me, he thought with a tantalizing mix of excitement & anticipation. But not just yet.

SOMETIMES I JUST WANT TO GET AWAY

Lajos Woodchopper is called Lajos Woodchopper and not Lajos Wood, which is what most people think. This idiocy was the doing of his one time foreman (or over-seer, but never mind) back in the Tools Factory where for almost nine years Lajos Woodchopper was a sorter in the forge shop. The foreman was even intellectually incapable of remembering the names of his own men. For instance, he called Parker Porker, at other times Pork, and once he went to him with, now look here, Porkchop. But what he did with him was the most con-spicuous of all, giving him a new name practically every week, and he'd wrack his brain trying to figure out how the foreman came up with them. For instance, for a long time he called him Woody, then Pecker, then once after breakfast he suddenly yelled for him from his office, hey, Woodpecker! And that's just one ex-ample because, for instance, for a while he called him Zhivago,[16] which nobody could make heads or tails of, not just him. In that political regime the foreman (or overseer, but never mind) was a great poten-tate, but he went up to him, he's got a proper name, and would he kindly make an effort to remember it? And what might that be, the foreman (or overseer, but never mind) asked, whereupon he introduced himself.

Lajos Woodchopper. Well, isn't that interesting, the foreman said. Because, do you know what I hate most about you? Your name. And he laughed, whereas it wasn't funny at all.

How he came to be Lajos Wood after that he can't remember anymore, because he suffered a nervous breakdown & didn't have to go back to the forge shop, because they said that the constant noise and din was bad for his nerves. Just like Horvát. Except they drilled a hole in his head, and he's been pounding landscapes into copper plates ever since. They're disagreeable even to look at. He was transferred to the fire prevention brigade. He wore civilian clothes, a shirt, a tie, and he always had a pen or two stuck inside his breast pocket, which was a great step up from the hot forge shop. He'd go home like that, taking his date calendar and a couple of folders with him for good measure, but even this was not enough to make him forget that he's Lajos Wood, even though he was courteous by nature, even on the bus, where he gave his seat to others even if it was half empty, & once, when the driver swerved the bus into a ditch because of a dog, he gave everybody first aid and would not take no for an answer. No one was hurt, but by the time the police got there, the passengers were all lying in neat rows on the side of the ditch like corpses, though they did talk to each other in whispers.

His new line of work didn't give him much to do. His boss just told him to keep an eye on things for the time being, which lasted a couple of years, and in the meantime Woodchopper was hoping for a great big fire, though an earthquake might have done the trick as well and open his way to a promotion. Instead, just some people with bad souls badgered him, and wherever he showed up, cigarette lighters and matches appeared and were struck. Needless to say, he was above such things and couldn't have cared less, he just made sure to put their names down in his date calendar, and also the place & time, and the nature of the crime: Premeditated. He didn't even mind anymore that they also called him Lajos Wood, because here this thing carried a different weight. It had a serious ring to it. If, for instance, his boss said, Lajoswood, all in one, like this, you pump up my bicycle because I can't trust anybody else with it, he didn't laugh when he said it. Then a safety drill brought the decisive change. Woodchopper was entrusted with the intricate preparations because some big shot from the county was coming and the drill was for his benefit. And that's just it. Because the drill was set to start at seven in the morning, but the big shot showed up early, and kept laughing at everything. He asked if everything was set to go. Of course. Well then, let's get the show on the road! It was a quarter to seven. What's keeping you, his boss shouted at Woodchopper, and he looked around, but there was nobody there yet, and then, glancing at his own watch he said, I beg to report, it's not yet seven. The county big shot, who was just into another helping of pálinka, had a twinkle in his eye, and he laughed. That's all right. It's civil disobedience time, I take it. All the same, let's proceed.

In the course of these drills, just like in real life, nothing must be left to chance. Everything that would be needed had been loaded onto a diesel trolley the previous day; the men in the boiler house knew that the catastrophe was due to begin at seven, at which point they'll have to activate the steam whistle that nobody can hear five meters from the building because of the noise of the smithy machines, but that's alright, because everybody knows when they have to drop everything and run to their appointed spot anyway. And not till then. In this particular instance, this being a so-called complex drill, there were also a number of casualties who had to be given their belly and arm shots at six in the morning for the ten o'clock catastrophe. Those with fractures also had their broken bones by then and were in casts, and the gas poisoning casualties were sitting on stretchers in the isotope chamber, playing cards and, considering the circumstances, were in relatively high spirits. The little Woodchopper was not a stupid man, just unsightly, sunken eyes, low forehead, a narrow face, and in his eyes perpetual concern, as if he'd forgotten something; his grayish-black hair practically merged with his bushy brows & refused to be smoothed down. Being a lean man with a sprightly gait, he now hurried off, it didn't matter where as long as he was seeing to things, so he headed for his usual spot, the toilet of the toxic waste storeroom, where he sat down in one of the cubicles, and cried like a baby. It's the beginning of a nervous breakdown, he thought, relieved. He'll finally sleep to his heart's content. Then at seven o'clock sharp the steam whistle gave a hoarse moan, the rubber tires by the scrap storeroom burst into flames, the fire depot door flew open, and the diesel came out, roaring defiantly, with the men & whatever else was needed on top.

It all went off without a hitch, and the big shot from the county gave the drill an appraisal of "satisfactory," which could've been "excellent," if only there hadn't been that bit of uncertainty at the beginning. He and the others were drinking wine by then, and they hadn't seen anything of the drill, whereas there had been casualties, disinfection, preparations for a possible atomic catastrophe, radiation protection, and everyone knew when the fallout would be. Lajos was feeling better by then and he wanted to give a demonstration of crowd control with flying wedge formation, but he didn't get the chance, and next morning the head of surveillance called him to his office and said to him, Lajos, if there'd be something to drink around here now, I'd drink to your health, but I know that you'd be the first one to report me to myself, & that's commendable. You were the driving force behind everything here, he added after a brief pause. Except, you see, we've just invented fire prevention without a driving force.

Like the youngest son of the poor man in the tale, the little gypsy Woodchopper left home nearly thirty years ago with nothing, and he still has nothing, whereas he's been back for fifteen years. He was put on disability when he reached the best years of his life; it nearly killed his parents, and him as well. For a couple of years after that the city fire department paid him to be on call at public events, because he knew which windows to break in case of fire, but eventually that ended, too, and he's been home ever since. I go to the movies & the theater, he told everyone in the street who was willing to listen, but there weren't many of those. He didn't go to the pub, he didn't buy wine from Uncle Sarkadi, or only occasionally, and he didn't have credit at Pintér either, and nobody ever saw him drunk, so what does he expect? His father hailed from an old family of adobe makers. While he lived, he managed to put up a small room and kitchen out of sheer force of will and was waiting for Lajos to enlarge it. He was their only child. And then old Woodchopper went to his grave in wake of his wife, with no other prospect, except a thick rope of sufficient length.

People said that he had difficulty dying because his body was so small and puny it just hung on his neck, & he cursed. Some saw the doctor show up and Lajos standing around in the yard, because he refused to go inside until the body had been taken away. And then they said in Misi's that the doctor gave him a shot and he's going to be taken to the hospital, it's definite, they've already called the ambulance, and he's not likely to come back home anytime soon. The mood was bad, and at such times people drink hard liqueur, the beer is just for chasers, but even so, no amount of alcohol wants to go to your head. With the approach of evening, though, after the first wagon stopped, and then the second, and about ten more after that, there was a change in the air. They came asking for Lajos Woodchopper. Tarcsai was the first to pull himself together. He told them what happened, but they were only interested in where the house was. Handsome, plump women sat atop the wagons, budding girls and boys with audacious eyes, older men with big mustaches, and children making lots of noise, and the dogs under the wagons scratching themselves. One of the newcomers said they're from Palkonya, they're sedentary Roma, & they all had a bottle in their hand, have a drink, brother, they urged, then went on their way. They came back only after they've had two or three more shots of pálinka and a bottle or two of beer, and there was music, too, by then, and flowers hung from the sides of the wagons, and they sang & danced, and Lajos was sitting atop one of the dickeys like a king, laughing, and this slovenly bunch from Misi's, all they could do was stare their eyes out of their sockets, and then they went outside and Sudák was soon dancing up a storm with one of the women, then Sanyi Harap; they were all outside now, young and old, even the Vida boy in his wheelchair, and they lit colorful lamps, and

Laci Veres saw a rainbow in the sky and said that he'll go with them, and then Sudák said the same, & Lajos Mérő also managed to struggle to his feet, and we were all ready to go, the whole street, go anywhere, except for us it's too late.

GOD'S EYE

There's something in the air these days, or maybe it's the heat, because men and beasts alike feel that something is amiss. For instance, Dorogi's horse Palkó has taken to raising his tail lately when he drinks his beer, and Lajos Mérő lost his dentures, though he manages to drink his beer just the same, if a bit less of it. Or maybe the bartender Esztike doesn't put down as many notches. Also, Lajos got smacked on the head one stifling, restless night. The barkeep Esztike could tell you a thing or two about that, but she's no fool, and so could Misi, the proprietor, if he could only remember, though he can't help thinking that there are some as of yet undiscovered relationships here, because Esztike's been taking Lajos his beer to his table ever since. That's when that character from Adony that killed vermin with his own rat and liked to be slapped around disappeared. Yes, there's something definitely in the air ever since. Terka Papp, Jancsi Hesz's twenty-four-hour mother-in-law says that even Dorogi made up with his wife, and that Mancika has moved down from the attic for good and been sleeping downstairs with her husband. They don't even go to the outhouse, there's a bucket by the bed, and they do it into that, and in the morning they pour it out on the street, so that the smell of urine chases your dreams away. Terka Papp says it's the hand of God, all their lives will now take a turn for the better, and they'll stop drinking like animals, because the kingdom of heaven is just around the corner.

Something exceptional has happened to Terka Papp, too, not that she's made up with her son-in-law. On the contrary. Except she doesn't give a hoot now, because she bought herself a pair of binoculars from a Russian at the market, and it's brought her such peace of mind, she's got no words to describe it. She cut out the lilac shrub in front of her small house and replaced six shingles with glass up in the attic, and Laci Veres screwed the ladder into the wall, because Jancsi Hesz likes moving it when she's up there. It's his way of having a little fun. Terka's widow's pension is nine-thousand-three-hundred forints, of which she just spent two thousand on binoculars, it's not clear to her how, because she still has the two thousand forints. But this must also be God's doing, because He's everywhere. She'd have never thought of buying binoculars, but she was caught off balance in the heady bustle of the market. She doesn't know how it happened, but she practically swooned into the arms of that not bad looking foreigner who grabbed her from behind, raised the binoculars to her eyes, & she simply couldn't free herself, whereas her knees were trembling by then. And he kept murmuring into her ear, his hot breath practically stroking her round and round, hey, hey, what about it, but never mind, and he put his arm around her waist, too; she was holding the binoculars by then and felt that masculine man's breath issuing from his mouth, a manly mixture of vodka, tobacco, and beer, the rest she couldn't identify. Meanwhile the binoculars made the world go round with her, and also the noise, the shouting, the screeching, three shells and a pea, she could even see the pimple on somebody's nose, everything whirled around with her, and the Russian just pressed his thick belt pouch against her from behind, and his hands all over, my goodness. When she came to she was standing at the bus stop, panting like someone who's been running, & even back home, her heart pounded so bad, she had to have some white pálinka to calm it down.

There was the window to clean, of course, and an unobstructed view secured up in the attic, and she was now glad that she had had enough foresight to build the house in the back of the yard, on the slope, and not alongside the road, so that when she went up to the attic now, the whole street lay at her feet like an open book. Dear Lord, thank you, she prayed in gratitude, thank you. I won't have to go around so much anymore and can have a life of my own, humble as it may be. It's God's eye, she thought as her eyes filled with tears. I sing Your praises. And nobody knows, except for Him. And everything would have been just fine, if only she'd kept what she saw to herself, but after a while she couldn't stop herself from making snide remarks, if only up in the attic to begin with. She was a light sleeper, so she saw the drunks congregate in front of Aunt Sarkadi's house in the early morning, let them try and deny it. Her own son-in-law, no better than he should be, was among them, waiting impatiently with an empty bottle under his arm. As for Aunt Kiss, she throws the garbage out on the street, but first she looks around, ha-ha!, she thinks nobody sees, & Rózsi's son steals rolls from in front of the shop every morning, wonder if they know? Irénke, she said to Aunt Ács when she couldn't keep it to herself anymore, what beautiful skin you have, considering how you're no spring chicken anymore. You must drink a lot of milk! Aunt Ács was aghast, while she just smiled. And as for old man Ács, he's not averse to pulling a carton or two of milk out of the crate himself when the rest of humanity is still asleep. Another time she whispered to Pintér's wife that God's eye sees everything, and if I were you I wouldn't serve that soup to my husband. The flies were buzzing round it all morning! But she also assailed Uncle Kocsis, who squatted in the back of the stable in the morning, then shoveled the results out into the street. There's the dung heap, why not there? And the others, too, all of them. What did you talk about so long with that disreputable Dorogi, Esztike? What are those two hens doing in your yard, Marika? They must be newcomers, because the others can't abide them. Did they fly in over the fence?

How come she know so much, somebody asked at Misi's, possibly Lajos Mérő, or maybe Laci Veres;

this was already when people were afraid to fart in their own homes and drew the curtains if they wanted to scratch something down there. I always said she's a witch, Jancsi Hesz offered. In some places they set fire to the likes of her and good riddance! The night before his mother-in-law told him where he'd been, whom he talked to, & how many times he bumped into what. She also told Dorogi that a certain young woman is very nice, even though she's not from here, she must be from the village, because she lay down next to him in reverse, though it might work that way, too, for all she knows. As for Béres, his fly was open all day. Not the others', though. Laci Veres, who'd been in the Workers' Militia, now said that if he still had his service gun he'd know what was expected of him, and as for witches, he doesn't believe in them. There's gotta be a fly in the ointment. Then they all had another round of drinks, and the following day Dorogi stopped Terka on the street and asked, what's with your eye, old woman? My eye, Terka Papp asked with an edge to her voice, there's nothing wrong with my eye. I see sharp as nails with them, Pista! Tut-tut, barked Dorogi, I wouldn't be so sure. Not at your age. What do you mean? They look bigger than they used to, the big, hulking man said, & drove away. But Terka was headed for the shop & didn't think anymore about what Dorogi had said. She usually bought a kilo of bread, but now she also needed lard, that'll last a long time with tea. But when it was her turn, the proprietor Zsiga looked at her as if she were a ghost. Aunt Teri, he said, your face. It looks so strange. Or is it your eye? Gizi, he called to his wife, what do you see? Gizi didn't see anything, she just said possibly, and that that'll come to one-hundred & forty forints. But Terka didn't pay the one-hundred & forty forints, because she didn't take anything, she just turned on her heels and marched out the door.

She lived nearby, but she managed to run into Lajos Mérő all the same, who laughed when he saw her and said, you look great, Aunt Teri. What big eyes you have! That's what killed my grandmother! And what's your hurry? He said something else as well, but mostly, he just laughed. She laughed, too, but not like he did, and when she got home she took out the mirror, and the cognac, too, because enough is enough! She saw nothing out of the ordinary. So what were they on about? Not straining too much, neighbor Béres asked over the fence at four in the afternoon, just as she was about to go up to the attic. No, she shouted at him, how about yours? Then she remembered that she'd left the bread and the lard in the shop, whereas she'd have been wiser to leave it where it was, because the whole bunch of them were there drinking and laughing, and when she walked in, they fell silent. You left your purchase here, the proprietor Zsiga said with a sad shake of the head, then he called to the others, have you seen her eyes? Nobody said anything, but then Dorogi said that what she's got is a typical horse disease, but it can be corrected with glasses.

On the other hand, then it attacks the brain. And that alcohol is the only cure. Dorogi's got a high school diploma, and at the factory where he used to work, those that worked with a magnifying glass all ended up like this. Don't you use field glasses now and then? Because that can cause it, too! Laci Veres had a dog that ended up the same way, but they struck him with the back of a shovel, and that cured him. Terka Papp never got a word in edgewise, & she could still hear them once she was out the door. As she passed his place, Pintér said hello to her, then called to his wife in the back, come! This you gotta see!

And she was so damn stupid, she couldn't think of a better way to end the day but went and fell off the ladder; a good thing there were people around; Lajos Mérő tripped over her, then Béres pumped her breast to make her breathe, somebody ran to fetch the doctor, in case she dies, and the doctor shooed them all away. I see everything, she stammered, I see it all now. Drunk as a skunk. Then she told the doctor about the binoculars. The doctor looked at her the way he'd look at some plant, felt her leg and said, give them a rest, old woman. And don't go climbing that ladder unless absolutely necessary. He also said something double-barreled about her eye that made her turn red with shame. What a fool I was, she lamented, flinging it in the well! The scoundrels lied to me! When I built my flimsy little house my son-in-law said, go right ahead, it'll make a good outhouse once you're dead. They hate my guts, she said and grinned. Can you understand? But the doctor didn't, because he was no longer there, & then night came, too, like a shroud, the worst part of the day, but if she now reaches under the bed, Terka will find something left in the bottle. Nothing ever happens around here, ever.

BIRDWATCH

The Vida boy had been uneasy for days, he hardly got out of bed, ate next to nothing, and drank practically none of his wine, and then he said something to his father, the gist of which was that he sees a big black bird through the round window at night, it circles up above, and when it lands, he's going to die. Uncle Vida could have told him that there are no birds in the sky at night, only owls, and that the window is not round but square, and it must be his eyes, but he didn't say, he just made a scarecrow out of a broom and drew string around it so no bird could land. When people asked what it was for, first he demurred, then he told them. A couple of days later everybody knew that in our street birds were free to fly but not to land, whereas our street is not even superstitious. Béres swore at Misi's that he sees birds, too, day and night, but so what? Where, Lajos Mérő hastened to ask, because he'd been eating pigeons lately, but pigeons were now hard to find. People were in a bad mood and they were all secretly on the lookout for the bird, but only the Vida boy could see it on anguished nights. Then his father up and went to the minister, saying he needed to talk with him. Me?, the elderly clergyman asked. He sounded apprehensive. What have you got to talk to me about?

The minister was invariably apprehensive when people came to talk to him, especially from Crooked Street, where nobody went to church, not to speak of other things. If the person wasn't from Crooked Street the clergyman was still apprehensive, because it was so rare for anybody wanting to talk to him, that there had to be something terribly wrong. He was standing in the rectory garden now, because he'd already stood around, sat, or lay down inside more than enough during the course of the day. He'd also been over to the church, he'd looked out every window & door, and even though he was a bachelor, he couldn't imagine what the other clergymen did, year in & year out. In a garden you can hide even from yourself, he thought, because indolence is a sin, too, & what happens? This man shows up, wanting to talk to him. Sit down, he said to him grudgingly, then remembered that there was nowhere to sit. Or would you rather go inside? Uncle Vida said it made no difference to him, he wasn't going to impose on the minister for long, he just saw him outside and thought he'd ask. Ask me what, the clergyman said, putting up his guard.

The minister knew Uncle Vida by sight. At one time he'd been a frequent visitor to Crooked Street, but people of Vida's age looked pretty much alike there. Now, however, the question was not who this man was, but that he should say what he came to say and good riddance. He'll give him a Bible, the minister thought, though what's the use? Let's go inside after all, he said, because he could think of nothing else to say, but the old man didn't want to, he just wanted to ask if the minister saw God now and then. It was stifling hot. There was hardly a soul in the street, and the bus, too, wouldn't be coming for some time. There were no clouds in the sky, and, the air was still. The clergyman wiped his forehead, then with a weary sigh asked, you're joking, aren't you? I'm not joking, the old man said, the color rising to his cheeks, I'm not in a joking mood, believe me. If I asked the wrong question, kindly enlighten me and tell me how this thing works. Are you saying you never see him? Are you under the impression, the clergyman asked gingerly, that the Lord lives in the neighborhood? The old man said nothing. He just looked straight ahead and leaned on his bicycle as if he were afraid of falling. You're drunk old man, aren't you, the clergyman asked, trying to reconcile him. Let's go inside. You're not feeling well. No need, the old man said, and as a matter of fact, he wasn't about to faint. He was crying.

A rural clergyman's life is fairly monotonous, and the minister couldn't remember anything happening here except for the one time a young man with long hair showed up with the surprising news that he's Jesus Christ. The clergyman gave him some noodle soup that he accepted without having to be asked twice, then he asked the young man which bus he'd come by. Then later he suggested to him that Christ should be handled by a Catholic priest, and directed him, with due respect, to the other's parish. Afterwards he commented to the ubiquitous Mrs. Hüse that it's curious, the Redeemer traveling with a student pass, because you can't board the three o'clock bus without one. The constant presence of the widow Hüse, who was housekeeper at the rectory, reminded the clergyman of transience, and also that he could do worse than marry her, seeing how he's got nothing better to do. Now, however, there was no window Hüse & no noodle soup, only this man here who just said that his horse has wandered off somewhere and his son is in great pain and is about to die, and that he wanted to talk to God. Otherwise, there's silence.

Only later did the minister realize that he'd left his mouth open in surprise, in which case he should say something. Terrible, he said in sympathy, terrible. It is, Uncle Vida said, slightly more composed now, that's why I figured when I saw you that it's high time somebody told that certain someone that what he's doing is not right. Because, my wife died five years ago, granted, she was ill, and now my son, he's been ill for years, and then there's my horse. I never stole anything from anybody, I never robbed anybody, I never killed anybody, so what has he got against me? If my horse doesn't turn up, he might as well take me, too, because without him I'm nothing, and I can't even walk properly anymore, I can't even get on my bicycle, I just push it alongside to have something to lean on. So tell me. What has he got against Sándor Vida? The clergyman tried by saying, look, it's not that simple, and that one reaches the Lord through the path of faith, but Uncle Vida wasn't paying much attention to him anymore, though then he said, in that case, just tell him that it was a rotten trick he played on me. But no, he takes that back, he's going to tell him himself, because he's had all he can take. If he doesn't exist, fine, but if he does, he better lend an ear, and he'll find the way, in the other world, if need be. I told the foreman, too, when I didn't like something, he said. A man endures only so long. But everything's got its limits.

Uncle Vida was properly attired, clean pants, white shirt, a pair of old sandals on his feet, and he had even shaved. The clergyman saw that his speech was coherent, too, he didn't mutter under his breath like a drunkard, & yet there was something demented about the whole thing, and from time to time the old clergyman felt that his head was in a whirl, then later he asked, tell me, have you spoken to the doctor? Then he thought it best to go with him, just to get rid of him, because by then Uncle Vida was talking about the draught, the big cauldron that has a hole in it, and the hen's not laying enough eggs. Leave the bicycle here, he told the old man. You'll pick it up later. Just please. Let's get going. I'll take you by car. The old man was reluctant to get in the Trabant, & the doctor wasn't overjoyed either, it was past his office hours and he'd been drinking beer with pálinka, but then he put the remainder of the pálinka in his bag.

He hated being called to a dying man's bedside. Will these people never learn to die in the morning, he thought, but then he flushed with shame. I'm ready, he said, got in the car, and lay down in the back seat.

The clergyman was a poor driver, but only those coming towards him could've guessed, because there was never anybody behind him. Now, however, traffic was scant, just a couple of cyclists and people on foot staggering under the weight of the heat, generally in the middle of the road. The windows were rolled down and if he saw the need, the clergyman didn't honk his horn but called out, could you please! The old man started calling out himself after a while, then said that they might as well look for his horse along the way. Now that you're here with me, maybe the Lord will make an effort. Embarrassed for an answer, the clergyman looked over his shoulder to see what the doctor had to say, but the doctor had nothing to say, because he was fast asleep. Meanwhile, the old man told him where to turn, and by the time the clergyman realized what was up, they had left the village behind and were driving along a series of dirt roads and balks, between parched, sun-burned fields, fallow wastelands and pastures, but there was no sign of the horse. Okay, the clergyman said after a while, we will now turn around and take you and the doctor home to your place. The old man blew his nose into a rag then said that even God can't be counted on anymore.

Can't you do something, he asked after a while, but his voice lacked conviction. Like what, the clergyman asked tamely. Pray, the old man said. For my son. And my horse. I don't know how, the clergyman said, and I fear it's too late now for me to learn. Because I see now that it's the same with the Lord as with anything else.

Later he said, let's not turn around, it's shorter this way. Then they picked some plums from under a roadside tree, then some green grass for the hen, and even threw a large pumpkin they found by the side of the road into the car so that the drowsy doctor was soon covered with the stuff, then eventually he woke up, and they stopped so he could relieve himself. Is it far, he asked with a yawn. Now it is, the clergyman was about to say dismayed, because he didn't know where they were and why, & the gasoline was nearly gone, and besides, what is he doing here in this desolate landscape? Uncle Vida got out, too, and studied the horizon, then he looked up at the sky and said, there it is. What, the clergyman asked. He was thinking of the horse, but couldn't see anything. The bird, the old man said, his voice trailing off. My beloved son. Then after a while he asked, tell me please. Does the soul leave a man? What do you mean, the clergyman asked. Because if it does, there it is. That's superstition, the clergyman said, and he was aghast, because he now saw it too, there it was, circling dark and ominous in the sky. And then it landed.

QUIET, BURIAL

You'd think that death is something terrible, then when the doctor with the weary eyes listens to the body and turns it around, you find that it's barely more than anything else; it's a bit awkward when the knee cracks under the pressure; yes, the doctor says, he's dead. At the gate Jancsi Hesz is busy telling people that where he's from they break a toe and if the soul's still in him the individual will wake up. The soul that was circling high up in the sky and then landed, & then the Vida boy died. It was a jay, somebody says. A strange bird. It mimics the sound of the other birds, and when they come near, it swoops down on them. But what's even stranger, nobody can find the bird, and as for Lajos Mérő, who eats birds, he denies it. Was there one at all? The reverend had seen it when they were out looking for Uncle Vida's horse that morning, but he'd be loath to swear to it now. Still, when they reached home, the Vida boy was dead. The doctor busied himself writing out the documents, Uncle Vida put some wine on the table, the clergyman stood in the door. I should pray, he reflected. But what good would it do?

There's a dead man in our street. Uncle Vida's son has died. He suffered for years from some sort of lung disease, as a result of which people wouldn't even shake his father's hand, but then it turned out that it was cancer, not tuberculosis. A good thing, people said. At least that's not contagious. Uncle Vida's house is generally tidy, but now the gate is wide open because his horse Gypsy wandered off and when he returns he should be able to come in. God has it in for Uncle Vida. His wife died five years ago, and now it's his son, & everybody's taken aback a bit. This is not what Uncle Vida deserved. There's no justice in heaven or on earth. Jancsi Hesz says he could name two others in the street in place of the Vida boy, but everybody else says he's better dead, that was no life. And it's probably better for his father, too, though death is death, of course, no two ways about it. Still, he could've lived a bit longer, Terka Papp puts in, except nobody takes her seriously anymore.

The minister Márton Végső scheduled the funeral for two o'clock the following afternoon, but then the widow Hüse, housekeeper and symbol of permanence at the rectory, removed the announcement from the notice board. What are you thinking, reverend father, that's too early in the day. Too close to noon. Also, I'm busy. Not until three. Fine, the clergyman said, in that case, let's make it four. That's no good either. People are drunk, they can't hold off that long. Besides, a funeral like this lasts an hour at least, & by five she'll have other things to attend to. So it was agreed that they should ask Dorogi when he's available, because the dray has to be spruced up, decorated, & somebody's got to put the black plumes on Palkó, which he can't abide. The hearse is in the cabbage patch carting the cabbage. It'd make no sense having it idle in the Town Hall yard all day when it can be put to better use. Besides, Dorogi himself said that he wanted to take the Vida boy on his final journey.

The street fell silent, and the customers at Misi's fell silent, too, as they drank and played cards, because Uncle Vida's son was not really one of them, & yet maybe, just a little, after all. Terka Papp, who is Jancsi Hesz's twenty-four-hour mother-in-law, trekked up & down the street in her wide-legged rubber boots the entire afternoon, wearing the expression of one that knows everything, whereas that's past history. Béres, who had black circles under his eyes & was pale as a ghost, told everybody he's next. Then he asked for a shot of pálinka on credit, and also some beer, then he went outside the pub and stood there for a long time looking spellbound into the distance, beer in one hand, the other sunk in his pocket. He couldn't make up his mind if he should ask for one more, and if so, would he be able to make it home. Then he did. What will be will be. Lajos Mérő didn't speak to anyone, his feelings were hurt because Dorogi had accused him of eating the Vida boy's soul, so he had some beer, then went to the old locust tree that people call Béla and broke into a flood of tears. Lajos Mérő is unemployed, his wife has left him, he lingers by himself in a half finished house, & when there's nothing left to eat, he catches pigeons up in the attic with a clever contraption of his own design. Well, what of it?

You don't always know why, and then tears spring to your eyes.

Plastic palms in plastic soil graced the corridor of the Town Hall, & the windows wouldn't close. A distant relative in tow, Uncle Vida tried to find out what's to be done at a time like this, and where. They knew, of course, except it wasn't until Editke stamped DECEASED into his son's ID that the old man was shaken to the core. He knew it, of course he knew, except now it was official. They just stamped his son out of life. He had to sit down for a bit, then Editke said, that's it, Uncle Vida. You can go. Laci Veres and Jancsi Hesz were standing around in the corridor, Dorogi was talking to somebody out on the street, and Lajos Mérő was there, too, his feelings hurt from head to toe, except he refused to show it. The distant relative, an old man with sad eyes, took Uncle Vida's arm. Time to go, Sándor. He's got to be properly attired, and there's the coffin and what have you, and the grave digging's got to be seen to as well. Editke said she's sorry, but they can't provide gravediggers just now, but there's always two men by the entrance, they'll see to it. Also, the body must be kept in the funeral chapel until the funeral, that's the law. She'll talk to Dorogi about it.

It was Tuesday, a nothing sort of day, except somebody had died. With the distant relative by his side, Uncle Vida found the two men who said, two-thousand forints. Per head. Uncle Vida nodded, but Laci Veres couldn't help putting in that it won't do. What do you mean two-thousand forints? We'll dig the grave ourselves. That's how it was done for a hundred years, and people still got buried. Uncle Vida didn't know what to say, but Jancsi Hesz seconded Laci Veres, yes indeed. We'll dig the grave. No problem. The whole street will come and help, if that's what it takes. The two men with the disagreeable faces, who were sitting next to a bicycle on the sidewalk eating bacon & drinking beer, nodded. Fine. Have it your way. Then one of them offered that it's not such a good idea after all, because in that case they're not gonna carry the deceased out to the pit, and if they don't believe him, they can go ask Editke. Laci Veres, who had been in the Workers' Militia at one time, couldn't countenance such things. Who the hell are you anyhow that you're so well informed, he asked defiantly. Gravediggers, Editke said back in the office, because the two men didn't bother with an answer. Except, they're freelancing. More money in it. Also, what they told you is true, the carriers won't take the body out to the grave if they're not the ones to dig it, because it's gotta be done just so, the plank on top and the coffin on top of that, and she'd have gone on, except Laci Veres cut in with Editke, dear. We're going home now to fetch a gas tank. In the meantime everybody better leave the building, because once we're back with the tank, no two stones will remain where they are now. You do understand, don't you?

But then things got smoothed over because Dorogi showed up and pushed everybody out on the street where they grudgingly got up on the dray, and Palkó took care of the rest. Then at Misi's they milled over what's to be done, and Dezső, who has got as many fathers as there are men in the street, was sent running to fetch the women who would dress the deceased, lay him in the coffin, and even cry, and sprinkle the room with yellow sand. Then he'll go to the reverend and bring the obituary notices, & the Zeke boy will take them round where they need to be taken, Sanyi Harap will bring the coffin on his handcart, the sheet and a pillow inside, & a pretty cover on top, and then next day, the funeral. Uncle Vida mustn't do anything, just drink. He can pay what he owes later. He needn't even go home, he can sleep in the storeroom. Misi, the proprietor, brought out a case of beer, and then Sudák showed up, put his hand to his heart, and was about to make a speech, except they wouldn't let him. Then Jolán Árva also showed up, dressed in black from top to toe, and she had two cream puffs with her, she'd meant them for Uncle Vida, except she never got to him, because Lajos Mérő grabbed them and gulped them down. After that, nothing much happened till evening. Inside they sang halting, melancholy songs, outside the wind picked up and the sky cleared, then gradually night fell. It was going to rain. In which case, Gypsy, Uncle Vida's horse, was sure to come home. Provided nobody hitched him to a wagon, of course.

They were still singing at midnight, and some stayed even beyond, Uncle Vida was fast asleep in the store-room, and in the morning they all woke to an exception-ally beautiful October day. Then around nine the boy Dezső ran to fetch the minister. Uncle Minister, it's time. Dezső was a sixteen-year-old with a pleasant face, and he looked good in the clergyman's grayish-blue sweat suit, but the others were also properly attired. Neighbor Béres even managed to shave, with terrible scars to show for it. Sárika brought her husband Jenő Nagy on the bicycle, & the others came, too, the whole street, even some people from the village. A handsome corpse, Terka Papp said, but nobody paid her any heed. The Vida boy lay in his coffin dressed in his wedding clothes with a bedspread over him, then they placed the lid on the cof-fin and hoisted it on the dray decorated with wreaths. Even the wind forgot to stir. On the way they stopped at Misi's, because Tarcsai had also bought a wreath, and he also shoved two cases of beer next to the coffin. It'll come in handy. It did. By the time they sang all the songs and prayed all the prayers & arranged the grave, it was gone. As he headed back with Uncle Vida, the minister felt exceptionally gloomy. He didn't like funer-als. And just then they saw a young stallion standing by the gate, as black & gaunt as a ghost. It's Gypsy, Uncle Vida shouted for joy, and as for the clergyman, he had a peculiar, faraway look in his eyes, because he'd also seen that dark bird in the sky, except he was afraid to say so, & the widow Hüse, too, where was she? But the church bell, at least, was ringing.

MATTERS FOR GROWNUPS

One morning neighbor Kiss surprised Uncle Kocsis with the news that the fields are covered in hoar frost. That hapless man meant it as a joke, since every strand of hair on his head is gray, and as for Kocsis, there's barely anything under his cap, and the street, too, is white, the dry, stray weeds, the plank fences, as if dusted with refined flour. Kocsis didn't know what to say just then, and by the time he could've, the other had driven past him. He was out of sorts that morning anyway ever since he opened his eyes; he'd had some disturbing dream he couldn't even remember, try as he might, only the ragged feeling, the fear, the tightening in the chest remained. And then this foulmouthed man comes along and says it's covered in hoar. So what? Come winter, it'll be the snow. What's the big deal? He couldn't stand neighbor Kiss these days, nor the others, for that matter, though he couldn't have said why.

After his son died, Kocsis lived with his daughter-in-law out of the goodness of his heart, and also because when she walked, Margitka's ass pinched in her dress, and as everybody knows, that's the sign of a real come-hither woman, and he wasn't disappointed. He took his son's daughter Esztike under his wing, too, in his own way, and when he couldn't curb her nature anymore, his heart ached, but he married her off to Tarcsai, even though the dress on Esztike's ass also got pinched in, and that's not the only thing she knew. Except, Kocsis couldn't get Margit with child. He does his duty by her diligently, but nothing. When he thinks about it, he yells and even slaps her, but that doesn't help either. On the contrary. She's grumpier than ever, and at night she turns to the wall. He can remedy that with a single movement, of course. Margit can struggle all she wants, press her lips together, and her legs, she can't hold out for long. Kocsis sleeps without pants, and only an undershirt, and in summer not even that. His blood is so he's never cold. Besides, why wear all that stuff at night next to a woman, he likes to say when the subject comes up. And once he manages to slip in between Margit, the thing's decided, and her head goes banging against the headboard. Kocsis weighs ninety-one kilos, Margit sixty. She can't budge under that sort of weight, just sigh. Kocsis doesn't know that it takes such a long time, but it's no use even so, the life's gone out of him years ago. Then he leans over Margit's shoulder and wipes the sweat from his face on the pillow, and then it's better.

Margit was eighteen when she married the Kocsis boy, and they tried to love each other as they were supposed to. János was a fine man, gentle and soft spoken and prone to illness, like his mother, who was already in bed more than she was out of it when Margit went to live with them on the farm. This house here was their wedding gift; the parents remained on the farm with thirty holds of bad land. She used to go out there to help and this is how it happened that she found herself between her father-in-law's arms, then down in the hay, because he found the work monotonous, too, by then, and by the time she recovered, she thought that this is what being run over by a train must be like and that it must be good, because the last time she felt this strain in her abdomen was when she gave birth. Kocsis was still young, his face winsome, his bearing proud, his voice heavy, and he still didn't release her but panted obscenities in her ear, and she looked with awe at the raw, animal nakedness of this stubbornly sprawling man above her, like an animal in heat, she thought with a mixture of gratitude and joy in that mighty grasp. She'd never seen nor felt anything like it in all her life. Then they went at it again, and no wonder that in the next couple of days there was practically no time for anything else. Margit didn't even bother to go home. What for? Her husband worked in town, her mother-in-law lay sick in bed in the bake house most of the time, and before long they didn't even care if they got found out, just as they didn't care when poor János was dragged along for hundreds of meters over hill and dale by an unruly horse and broke every bone in his body, and they didn't care when her mother-in-law buckled under the weight of the heavy sheaves they threw down to her from the wagon and was more dead than alive when they pulled her from under the pile, just as they didn't care her standing behind the glass door while they were wrestling each other on the bed inside. Then at last János managed to die and the doctor yelled at them, why did they wait so long, he's been lying here a week, why didn't they fetch him in time? The cow was giving birth, Kocsis said. He couldn't very well leave her. Besides, people in the street don't go running for the doctor just because somebody falls. Then a month later her mother-in-law leaped into the well. They pulled her out in the evening when they were going to water the livestock and the bucket got caught on her. They burned her farewell note. They couldn't read it.

Kocsis was a man of prodigious strength, and people were afraid to say anything ill of him, but they whispered behind his back; he's living with his own daughter-in-law like man & wife and the child's there with them in that den of iniquity, in which other women also found what they were after, from time to time. I got plenty of reserves, Kocsis laughed if anybody brought it up, though Sanyi Harap's wife tried him only once and then said, never again. He's an animal. Once while they were at it, Rózsika swallowed the silver medal hanging round her neck, and they had to pull it out of her throat by the chain. They also said that at one time he saddle-broke his own granddaughter Esztike, no wonder she can't control herself. Kocsis had moved in with Margit by then, into our street, they worked hard and were well off. They were the first with a TV, a refrigerator. Everything one could wish for. Margit was quiet & she kept to herself,

she didn't go anywhere, *&* she made no friends, nor did
Kocsis; he'd have a drink or two in his son-in-law's pub
for free, then go on his way. They didn't like him there,
he was crude, he talked big, and he was rich. But what's
the use, when he's got no children, whereas one can tell
by just looking at Margit that they're trying. It shows
on her neck and her lips in the morning, and her walk
is like that, too. Terka Papp, Jancsi Hesz's twenty-four-
hour mother-in-law, says Margit can't conceive because
Kocsis's is too big, he always ruins what he's done before, and she's told Margit to grab hold of it at the base,
so it can't go in that far, and besides, she's a widow and
is lonely, and she wouldn't mind if Uncle Kocsis were
to practice on her. She's even told Mrs. Sarkadi, Aunt
Piroska, that there's just one man in the street whose
blanket she'd turn up, and that man is Kocsis. She was
drinking wine, three decis, like the men, because she felt
weak and hot waves all over, then it let up somewhat, and
after the second glass it was practically gone, and that's
when Kocsis having no children from Margit came up,
and so did the blanket. Terka Papp was counting on Mrs.
Sarkadi telling Kocsis, that's how it's done in our street,
and when she thought about all the things that might
happen next, she felt hot again and even her skin itched,
which called for more wine. That'll be too much, Terike,
Aunt Piroska tried. You'll end up doing something fool-
ish, and you don't need that. What do you mean, Terka
Papp said in full armor, then she played her trump card,

she's still got her monthlies, whether Aunt Piroska credits her or not. I was thinking of the wine when I said it'll be too much, the elderly woman offered with a sigh. As for the bleeding, if it's bleeding down there, have it checked. It's not normal.

Kocsis didn't actually marry Margit because part of the property would go to her, & after all, Margit was a stranger in the family, but this way, everything would go to Esztike. But he's regretted it long since, because his own granddaughter & her husband cheated so cleverly at Misi's that even he was impressed. By now they had more money than he, and Esztike is more Tarcsai's wife now than his, he's got nothing to do with her, so now he hasn't got anybody either. It's enough to give a man bad dreams. Because if a man's got another son, that's different. He can buy him a car, machines, a hundred hectares of land, and a house and everything. If only he could do it already! He wanted desperately to do it. And then, from time to time he'd stop by him on the street or the pub and put his hand on his shoulder and say to him, my son. He's tried it with that rascal Dezső, and Jóska Ács, but they just grinned and pulled away. No wonder. They're not his seed. Uncle Kocsis is not sentimental, but when he thinks about these things he feels such envy and yearning, he nearly falls off the wagon. He pushes his cap all the way back, his forehead is red & sweaty, and his face is white, he hears nothing, he sees nothing, he has no idea where the horse is taking him, and it's best not to talk to him. Terka Papp tried it, because somebody's got to try it, but she got no further than hey old man, where are you headed with that woebegone expression on your face? She even laughed. Kocsis looked down at her as if she were a reptile, then flicked his whip. Terka Papp had on a light, flower print housedress with a yellow cardigan over it, neither of which could be mended after that; they were in shreds because Uncle Kocsis reinforces the lash with thin wire. What a man, Terka said appreciatively when she got home, hissing as she applied a rag soaked in vinegar to her bony shoulder and the bluish, painful welts on her breast, good Lord, what a man.

Then Kocsis had an idea. Why don't they go out to the farm and do it like that first time in the hay. They were excited; they packed food and drink in case they can't stop, except, they couldn't even begin. There was rubbish everywhere, empty bottles, filth, excrement and stench, doors ripped off their hinges, and a vermin infested dog crawled out from someplace, too, with tears oozing out of his rheumy eyes. Kocsis kicked it aside so it shouldn't touch him. As for Margit, she found a soft, translucent something on the floor, like the finger of a rubber glove. A balloon, she said in surprise, but no. It had a hole in it and it was sticky, so she threw it away. The sick dog was whining in pain outside in the drizzling rain. Let's go, the old man said after a while. He was out of sorts. These kids come here to screw. Or should we wait? Except, for what?

IT'S AUTUMN, SAD

On our street everybody knows everything, and even more than that, but nobody knows what's ailing the minister. The minister doesn't live on our street, but he's been around more and more lately. The people here are friendly, & he's lucky that he comes in his old Trabant, because if he came on foot, he'd never make it to the end of the street sober. The minister Márton Végső says people here are like gypsies, said opinion having left his lips in the course of an unofficial exchange in front of Misi's when they were burying the Vida boy and the dray with the body stopped by the pub, because they always stop there. The clergyman was flustered, they really shouldn't, he spoke about piety, parental pain, lack of respect. That's when that certain something slipped out. The men were drinking, and anywhere else they'd have slugged him, but here they let it pass. After all, the clergyman might be right. We all got a wound to heal, Dorogi said. Maybe even you. No?

The clergyman sometimes drives this way in his Trabant & stops to talk to people. He'd like to get them to plant trees in their yards and also along the street, read the Bible, and go to church. They know him. He used to come round when they laid the water mains, and they wouldn't mind the trees either, even though there are two in the street already. But the Bible is an impediment.

The letters are too small, neighbor Béres explained, he tried it, he really did, but what's the use if he can't read them? As for church, most of them don't go because they don't have clothes. It took the clergyman quite a while until he understood because he had to wait for Béres to sober up sufficiently to put it into words. Neighbor Béres talks about everything sincerely, and very loud. What are we supposed to show up in, Bishop, he asked the clergyman. In these rubber boots? Nobody's got anything except what they're wearing. How would that come off with the other worshippers? You're saying people don't have Sunday clothes, the clergyman asked, dismayed. Those that had sold them the minute they were hard up. I did, & others did, too. Except, they won't say.

I'm not surprised, the clergyman thought, and suddenly, he felt sad. When will there be order and justice in the world, Lord? Because as he later saw for himself, the people here sell not only their Sunday best, but their furniture, too, piece by piece, along with anything else that finds takers. On the other side of the equation, though, stood the inconceivable amount of alcohol that some of them consumed at Misi's, or at the private dispensers, in the shop, and anywhere else they could get it. There seemed to be plenty of money for that. How come? Béres explained this, too, if a bit circuitously, because he couldn't manage the requisite complex movement of the lips by then, an explanation from which the clergyman drew certain conclusions only after he got home. Béres explained that it takes a lot of money to get drunk, no two ways about it. But if you're careful and don't sober up, not for a minute, you just gotta keep it flush, which doesn't take much, a beer or two or a shot or two of pálinka. Plus a little extra at night so you can sleep. What's so terrible about that? If they ever sobered up, the minister would have his hands full burying the dead. It's a bet. They'd all leap in front of the train, grab a rope, or jump in the well. People here are desperate, he concluded & grinned, because his lips unexpectedly curled that way of their own accord.

A while back, the clergyman had rummaged through pits and ditches for telltale signs of the village's pre-history, but today he's less and less interested in bones and ancient artifacts, which he couldn't find in the first place, and is held in check by the present. From time to time he stops at Misi's, then continues driving down the street, as if looking for something. It's got people baffled. Because granted that he comes to see Rózsika but doesn't want people to know. Still, why all the fuss? The way it's done around here is as follows. You throw something back at Misi's, with a chaser, then you arm yourself with twice three decis of cheap Othello, and by then it's dark outside, and inside, too, and you set off. Some people turn back from the door for just one more glass, then end up staying, because life is difficult. Besides, Rózsika doesn't need to be buttered up. Far as she's concerned, everybody starts off with a clean slate and leaves on his own two feet. Except, the minister's in love with her, & that doesn't happen every day.

Rózsika works in town. She cleans up all the rooms of the railroad station, from the attic to the basement, whereas she's not even on the payroll; the others put up the monthly six thousand forints, and she scrubs everything down, practically by herself. Meanwhile the others, four women from Hadház, busy themselves as movers, so to speak, just to pass the time. If people put down a bag or a suitcase, they hasten to move it away from its owner with the help of a broom, and then a bit further, then they remove it altogether, because it's in the way. A gawking child will also disappear from time to time only to reappear mysteriously soon after, except he's always missing something and his mouth is stuffed with granulated sugar so he can't cry. But at such times who cares? They bring him back, they even pant, out of breath, these four upright cleaning women, then with a show of reluctance take the couple of forints people offer. On the other hand, they always have reserved seats. Rózsika turns a blind eye. In the afternoon, when she finished work in the men's room, she places a broom crosswise in the door, and those in the know can go in. There are men of all sorts among them; Rózsika is squeamish only at home. In the evening she showers, gives her teeth a thorough brushing, changes, and heads home. She makes two to three thousand down there, more on holidays, but she's not particularly fond of the clergyman because, for one thing, he doesn't smoke, & around here women call the likes of him cold mouthed. Also, he's as shapeless as a plateful of noodles. He's not ugly and he hasn't got a beer belly, it's just that he's different somehow. Then when he said that he wants to marry her, she stroked his face and asked him not to come around anymore.

The reverend Márton Végső is unlucky with love, which wouldn't be so bad, except he's unlucky with Rózsika as well, even though after their first encounter, Rózsika's son Dezső kept hugging him and called him father, and gave him a loud smack of a kiss. The boy was wearing the clergyman's grayish-blue sweat suit, the clergyman wore almost nothing; all the same, this is not the kind of kiss he was hoping for, and demanded his clothes back. Dezső waved the demand aside; emotion had rendered him speechless, and he was in tears. Then he said that it's warm and nobody will see the clergyman in the car, & there's nobody on the street at dawn either, and offered to see him home. The boy was right. Except for Lajos Mérő, Sudák, and neighbor Béres, nobody saw him; as for Jancsi Hesz, he had his back to them. The four men were waiting in front of Aunt Sarkadi's wine dispensary and were not up to making comments, though not long afterwards Béres said, loud and clear, that it was high time that dear sweet Aunt Sarkadi opened her goddam fucking door, because if she doesn't, there's gonna be hell to pay. Just by way of an example, last night he had a dream in which Serbian troops were drinking watered down pálinka at Misi's. On credit. And just now he could've sworn he saw an armored truck pass by and the boy Dezső was the clergyman, and that he's been dreaming during the day, too, lately, which is why only half his face is shaved. The others hemmed and hawed, but Jancsi Hesz said, you're imagining things, neighbor. You should drink either less, or more. Which is why we're here. It was easy for Jancsi Hesz to talk because he didn't see anything, and as for the others, they kept silent, even though Sudák saw the vehicle, too, except nobody was inside, & how was he going to explain that to these people?

At this early hour, the rectory next to the church looked deserted. The clergyman stopped the car and told the boy it was high time he removed his arm from around his neck. Dezső hugged him warmly and shouted in his ear, when you have my mother take your name, Uncle Minister, you'll be my father, & I want to be in a pair of white jeans! Then after a while they managed to get out of the car and as a matter of fact, the street was deserted, only the widow Hüse was in the door, at her feet an armful of kindling, because she'd dropped it, and she was gaping, her mouth wide open like at the dentist. What she saw made her want to sit down, if only there were someplace to sit, a gypsy boy in the clergyman's clothes with his arm around the old man who, for his part, was wearing next to nothing, and this at the crack of dawn! My son, the clergyman said, then hurried into the house to put something on. The widow Hüse is forty-five years old and she's been in the clergyman's employ for eight years as his housekeeper, and now she felt cheated. What do you mean your son, she later asked the clergyman. This was not part of the deal! You should've married me. It would've been the decent thing to do. We could've had our own child by now, she added. Who's the woman? Because of a problem with her spine, Mrs. Hüse had a slight hump on her back, and she now jerked up a shoulder as if to prevent it sliding further down, then she reflected that though the Good Lord is with her, that's not nearly enough now. Meanwhile the clergyman went to stand by the window; he hadn't recovered yet, his head was buzzing and he might even be running a fever, he thought elated. So that's what it's like. Then he helped the naked Mrs. Hüse off the couch and handed her her clothes. What's wrong, he asked her with concern, because she was standing there in her slip. She felt that the rest was up to the man. Except, not this man. I'm leaving, she then said, now I understand about you and that boy. You should be ashamed of yourself! The clergyman, however, understood nothing. He just said that when she leaves, she should close the door. And lock it. Did you say something, he asked after a brief silence. No, screamed Mrs. Hüber and, crying her eyes out, stormed out the door into the big wide world.

It's been nearly a month now. Meanwhile the Vida boy died, autumn's come, and as for the clergyman, he still shows up in our street now & then, but that's about all.

THE NIGHT OF THE TRAIN

It felt good standing in the fresh air, gasping, even though the treacherous cold finds its way under your shirt & the icy wind pinches your cheeks, making your nose and eyes water, & each intake of breath is like the stroke of a hammer, from inside. Come on in, his wife shouts from the kitchen, Lajos, you hear? Lakatos hates this more than anything, that he hasn't got a moment's peace, no matter what he does, his wife yells at him, as if he'd done something wrong, goddammit, when he's just come out on the porch for a breath of air. Besides, he couldn't stay longer if he wanted, he's not dressed for it. And why are you holding your head like that, he hears his fat wife's barley-oats cry. She can't help herself. His head tilted to the side, Lakatos was testing the air, feeling the wind with his cheek. It's dry now, deceptive. At one time he could even tell how long it's strength would hold out, whether it would bring rain or not. He could feel the gusts, he could've made a sketch of them, the way they swept round everything before roaring past. If it throbbed, the scaffolding had to be reinforced with a cramp iron or two, trussed with a lath here or there, not everywhere, but he knew where, because in that case huge gusts were sure to follow. The scaffolding groaned, creaked, you had to hold on for dear life, & the chimney masons scrambled down, if he let them.

Just now, that good for nothing Lajos Mérő from the street went past in his paint-stained jeans, he even said hello to him, but he ignored it, he didn't feel like chatting with anybody just now. Lajos Mérő always walks down the street as if he were going about some important business, whereas if there's one thing he hasn't got, it's work. He, once he can walk again, is gonna show them what real work is like. He's gonna have work even when nobody else will. He'll board the train again and head for freedom.

Lakatos has just turned sixty-five. His bearing is straight, his face is ruddy & dry, his eyes narrow, hardly showing, because he's squinting all the time. But now he was wrong on two counts. Lajos Mérő was going around in paint-stained jeans because apart from what he was wearing, he had only a pair of tobacco colored cloth pants hanging on a nail back home that he didn't want to wear out, because what would they bury him in? And as for him, he'll never have his leg back. He should thank his lucky stars that Assistant Surgeon Nyíri didn't chop it off in the hospital, because that's what he wanted. The left. But he said to him, don't you chop it off, doc, because you won't live to regret it. Me, the doctor asked looking around in surprise, you'll be lucky if you pull through, my good man. See, Lakatos said, that's why you're not chopping it off. They gave him a stick (on deposit, the nurse joked, because she didn't get a penny from him, nor did the doctors), but it soon proved difficult for him to lift, because his other leg hurt, too, not very much, he must've pulled a muscle, not to mention all the sitting and shifting about. He then had an idea and fixed a small wheel to the end of the stick so he could push it, like a bicycle, and it won't even have to be picked up off the ground. He only fell twice, the second time off the porch, & then they took him to the hospital again, where they all had a good laugh over his stick. How did you think of it with that chicken brain of yours, Assistant Surgeon Nyíri asked after he'd stopped laughing. Wouldn't a scooter be better? Or a skateboard? What's your hurry, without legs?

He fared no better with his new crutches, he fell more than he walked, so they finally sent him home with this walker, you stand inside, then move it away from you, then take a step or two after it. Like children. Well, if they can learn to walk with it, so can he. And then he's gonna start by plucking Gizi like a goose. He might even trample her underfoot. He'll decide when the time comes. Then he'll head for freedom. Gizi, that's his wife. Gizi is difficult these days because instead of standing by him & giving him the encouragement he needs, she says things like, what do you need that for? We're gonna die soon anyhow. And instead of nursing him and helping him and taking him places like, for instance, Sárika, who takes that squeaker-faced man of hers by bike even to the pub, she pretends that her legs hurt, too. She can even get them to swell up. She says she can't walk or bend down, or cook, or do the wash and what have you. Instead, that fat Ukrainian cow comes five times a day. She brings them food, does the wash, cleans up and puts them through hell, & the council even pays her to do it. Well, he knows what he'd give her if he got the chance!

That Ukrainian cow, she says her name is Marika & that she's Hungarian, but Lakatos happens to know that that's not true. If you're Ukrainian, so is your name. But he didn't say anything to her. Let her talk. Marika was all cheers, this is what she said about herself when she fluttered in, hello there, I've brought you a bundle of cheer. She said this five times a day and never got tired of it. Then she laid out the food carriers, but Lakatos saw that one container had leftovers, and though he didn't see which container she ladled out the food from onto his plate, he suspected that the bone in front of him didn't lose the meat during cooking, somebody had tried to chew it off. She ate something, too, from a small plate, so her sick charge shouldn't have to eat all by himself, & also to help improve his appetite, at least, that's what she said wherever she went. She smiled, too, with those pink cheeks, when she ate the better part of the meat right in front of them, chatting and giggling. Lakatos hated her with a passion. Every time that slop was ladled into his plate he initially felt nauseous, but then thought of what he could fling at the head of this whore of a refugee from where he was sitting, and later still found comfort in thinking that if they were on a train now, like at one time, he'd have a go at her from behind so he wouldn't have to see her face, and then the others, all of them, long as they felt like it, and when they had enough, they'd bundle her out the window.

Lakatos and his wife lived at the far end of the street, and their house was just like its owners. It stood far back at the upper end of the plot, in the middle, mournfully hidden in the dark embrace of a huge, solitary linden, and in front of it wild shrubs and a vine arbor, so people couldn't see in. Lakatos never made friends with anybody. He never went to the pub even when he could afford it, and he never offered anybody of his own making either, whereas he had plenty of wine and pálinka, and if he wanted beer from the shop, or cognac or liqueur, depending on what they felt like, for half a glass of pálinka his neighbor would go to the shop to fetch it. His entire life he did everything himself, he wouldn't even take advice, and now a man hoes and sprays the vine stalks and steals the plums and apples and takes the mash to the distillery in secret, because that Ukrainian slut would never allow it. She won't allow anything. When she takes his arm, she pinches the skin between her fingers and laughs, in the afternoon she flings them into bed because she's run out of time, so kindly get in, and if you resist, she presses her knee into your thigh and she pushes his wife's face into her plate because she won't eat the piece of gauze that she says is peas. Meanwhile she has a grand old time, she jokes & laughs, if only I didn't love you so much, damn it, she says, & tears spring to her eyes, and she steals the sheets. Knives, forks. Everything. Eggs. Even the money, possibly, but they can't check, because it's in an envelope on top of the wardrobe and another is taped to the back of the mirror, but for all they know, it may all be gone. At times Lakatos thinks that he may yet grow to be afraid of this bitch.

At one time he worked on major constructions in Palkonya, Pentele, and Barcika, and wherever else they sent him. For a while he even went underground into the mines as a carpenter. He didn't like it, but he hung in there and persevered. They even built a bridge somewhere, and towers, and factory stacks, he can't even remember all the places now. He was strong and determined and was soon made a brigade leader, carpenters and scaffolders listened to him, and before long, his word was law on the whole construction site. The prisoners called him capo. They were afraid of him because only those he approved of got work, and on payday they all gave him a little something in appreciation, and if they didn't, well, then they didn't. In which case he didn't either. And this held true for everything. He was in command even on the workers' train. He said who was drunk and who was not, who could go work for him, who would man the furnace, and at which stations strangers could board. There was order on these trains, and no killings. On the other hand, there was drinking & also plenty of women that everybody could use equally, and if anybody objected, he got off at the first opportunity or fell out of the moving train. His son was twenty when he first dared argue with his father, who struck him in the face so hard, he got the light of his eyes back in the hospital. Gizi didn't say anything. She knew better. His daughter cried, but only until he wiped the back of his hand against her cheek, and then she stopped and peed in her pants. Then one morning she & her brother left home without a word. They boarded a train and were gone, God only knows where. Well, that's just fine with him!

He met Gizi on one of those trains, too. She was obedient, she took things in stride, and she didn't mind being slapped around. She carried bricks for the masons, but if need be, she also lay walls. Once when they reached Nyékládháza, Lakatos ordered everybody out of the compartment & said, from here on in Gizi is my wife, and don't anybody forget it. And that's when everything started going wrong. Though Gizi didn't stir up the waters, he was no longer a free man because of her. Because she was there. And she wouldn't leave him for anything, even though he'd repeatedly driven her away. She delivered her first child in the pigsty. Still, he built the house for her sake, & the children came for her sake, while he slaved like an animal, stealing the materials for the house by the wagon load, & the workers, his own men, came to help him raise this huge, dreary building, all the countless walls, the roof. This cold prison. Lakatos didn't like his own house because he had to live in it, &

he also hated his wife by now because he couldn't boss her around anymore. He hated the whole world and everybody in it, because he was sick and miserable. Only the wind remained his friend, clean and familiar like before, and so he didn't even realize that he was shivering with cold, that he was grabbing the iron of the walker with both hands, and that he was trembling with rage.

Droves of black crows settled on the linden, then swooped down on something now *&* then, competing, lightning-quick, merciless. Then Marika, this Ukrainian curse of God showed up and laughing playfully, ordered him back into the kitchen. Tut-tut, Uncle Feri, you should know better than to go outside in your shirtsleeves in this weather. Aren't you ashamed of yourself, making Marika worry about you? You are, aren't you? And she pressed down on Lakatos's thigh with one knee and she laughed, she gurgled like a child, I brought some cheer, isn't that nice? Aunt Gizi. Where in God's balls is she? You're drunk as usual, Lakatos said, just to get back at her, but she paid him no heed, she just took out the food carriers, including the one containing leftovers, and served them first from that. Old people don't have appetites these days, she mumbled under her breath. A shame. Two have tried eating this bit of rib already. As for the soup, they barely just stuck their tongue in it, when it's delicious! Have you any idea how much it costs the village? You do, don't you? Well, you'll eat it tomorrow, damn you. Or the day after.

Marika ate slowly because she had to entertain her charges in the meantime, and also because she wasn't hungry anymore. She said that she managed to find out the address of Uncle Lakatos's son and she's already written him to come home because his parents have one foot in the grave, but their daughter's whereabouts is still a mystery. Lakatos knew that she was lying, because his son had said that he won't come home until he's six feet under, and even then only so he can plough him up, and Lakatos believed him. Also, what's this about them having one foot in the grave? Meanwhile, Marika went on chatting, chewing, laughing, and he thought, from behind is not enough for the likes of her, her mouth's gotta be stuffed, too. To the base. Until the vomit comes out her nose. Except for the time being there was nothing he could do. One wrong move, and they'll be taken to the home because they can't look after themselves & they can't afford homecare either. And once there, they will kill the both of them, given time. Gizi doesn't say anything either, because she's drunk, but she mustn't let on, and so they endure the woman in silence. They have no choice. She'll be back again in the afternoon, but that won't last long because she combines it with her evening visit. She turns up the bed, turns on the TV, then leaves, and they'll finally be left in peace until the morning. The first thing Lakatos does is to pull the TV cord out of the socket above the bed, then he struggles to his feet and begins to walk with that iron. He will then stumble or fall and won't be able to get up, and Gizi is so dazed that in an effort to help him she's liable to fall on top of him, and then she won't be able to stand up either, and they'll end up lying on the stone floor until morning, when the Ukrainian woman shows up, and they'll say that they just fell, this very minute, because otherwise she'll call the ambulance, and then it's the hospital, or the home. It won't be the first time it'll happen like this. But not for long.

Lakatos never told anybody what was wrong with his legs, though the truth is, he doesn't know himself. Also, there was nobody to tell. Laci Veres, who lives in that horrible house next door, offered to fix the wheels to the iron walker so Uncle Feri could get around faster, while Jancsi Hesz, his other neighbor, suggested the wheelchair that the Vida boy used until he died out of it. Lakatos heard them out. It required the patience of a saint. Then he said that they should mind their own business, and haven't they got anything better to do? He knows what's gotta be done. He had a dream about it. They were lying on the stone floor again at the time, because the Swedish bitters bottle slipped out of his hand and landed on the doormat and he had to pick it up because it contained pálinka and was still intact. He even managed to reach it with his hand when that accursed walker tipped over with him, and it was only to be expected that Gizi would fall, too, when she tried to help him up, she's that awkward. Then they lay on the stone floor for a while, panting, then they drank the pálinka and talked about this and that, then around midnight Gizi told Lakatos that she loved him, except she could never get herself to call him Feri. Lakatos didn't tell Gizi that he loved her, too, that's why he married her, and that he never loved anybody else in his life, because these words could never leave his lips. He loved the children as well while they were small and didn't cry. But then they turned wicked and are wicked now, and when they got his gander up he grabbed them by the legs like a pair of chickens and as they hung head down, he beat their bottoms as long as his strength held out. Then they left home. But he's gonna leave, too, because he's had it. Towards sun-up Gizi began groaning, she's aching all over, this is no life, it'd be best if they died. Both of them. Although he wasn't sleeping either, he'd just nodded off a bit, Lakatos said nothing for a long while. Then he heard someone whisper. It was Gizi. Lakatos, she said, you hear? You got strong hands. Tell me. Have you ever killed a man? There's such a lot of talk about you, you can tell me. We're going to get better, Lakatos roared, you and me both! Understand? As you wish, Gizi said weakly. But I've had as much as I can take.

If only I can board a train just one more time, Lakatos thought, everything will be different. He'll get off someplace where there's work. The rest doesn't matter, just so long as he can get away. That Ukrainian woman locked them in every night and took the key, but

Lakatos found another in a drawer that he used when he wanted to go out on the porch. Or even further. It was cold, and that's good. The fresh air and the wind would put new life into him. If not, Beanstalk, who was a barber-surgeon in the army, would cure him. He'd made a doctor out of Beanstalk when there had been lots of accidents, but no doctor and no ambulance, but the work couldn't stop. When they called him over, he inspected the injured man & decided whether he'd live or not. If it wasn't worth bothering, they didn't bother, just pulled him out of the way and covered him. If it was, they called Beanstalk, who jabbed and cut and twisted and cracked and fixed him up. Some didn't make it, but that's bound to happen anyway. And if they died, they were nothing but trouble out on the puszta, under the open sky, far from everything. What to do? If a river ran past nearby, sometimes they'd drop the man in with his IDs and everything, somebody was bound to find him somewhere, and then he went and reported that so and so fell in the river and they couldn't reach him in time. Once, in an effort to entertain them, a group of folk dancers leapt up and down on the riverbank, because there was never a shortage of men to entertain the masses, with a dead man floating downstream behind them. He'll have Beanstalk cut his leg open to let out all the bad blood that's turning it practically black and making it throb with pain, so that it's nearly driving him mad. The very thought brought relief.

It was dark. He didn't switch on the light in the yard, but he made good progress all the same, he had the bottle in his pocket, and he managed to get down the steps, too, and then he knew he'd make it. He dragged his leg behind the walker slowly, carefully, but his thoughts were reckless, unrestrained, and before long he thought he could even see a light, he knew his mind was playing tricks on him, but still. Except, he'd forgotten to count the steps, what a shame, but now it was too late, and besides, the station's within easy reach now, he just has to go along the narrow path leading through the locust wood at the end of the street, and he's there. He must be going along the path already, because he can feel the soil beneath his feet. Stop, rest. Now go. The pálinka, too, hit the spot, and he wasn't cold anymore, and he knew that he was free at last, free.

His senses betrayed Lakatos just when neighbor Béres started shouting in the distance like he did every night when the mash went out of him and that's more than a body can take. Dogs were barking and howling in the night, and Lakatos thought he was already at the station and the train was in front of him, the one he'd been waiting for so bad, wrapped in darkness, and no wonder, they're all asleep, and his dog's in heat, and it's nice and warm in there, and a pungent smell and wheezing, but once he's up there, there'll be plenty of life! He felt a board under his hand in the dark and the door, too, and he was already pushing the walker up in front of him, but then he found he didn't even have to, and then he thought he could hear somebody yelling, and it sounded like somebody was yelling, Feri!, where're you going, Feri! And the light was on, too, now, but the yelling & screeching wouldn't let up, what're you doing by the gate? Where do you think you're climbing? Of course! It's Gizi, the woman he'd always loved and who comes after him even now, sick and miserable as she is, and who says, where do you think you're going, you fool, that's the garden gate. You're in your own yard. I can't believe it! And she takes his arm, whereas that's not a good idea because they'll trip and fall and lie prone on the ground till morning. Just so. And he couldn't help laughing at this even as he fell, & his wife laughed, too, what an idea, him thinking he was at the station when his hand just knocked against the fence and not the side of the wagon, my word! But even so, it's something. Slowly, very slowly, he raised an arm up to the wind. Next time I'll make it, he panted into his wife's ear, then he shook her. I love you, damn it! You hear? Kill me now, he cried, his voice deep & hollow, kill me soon.

AWAY, NO MATTER WHERE

Ocsenás also came to our street from town. He looked like a gentleman, he always pushed a bicycle alongside, and regardless of the weather, he wore trousers and oxfords and a small shoulder bag swung across his chest, and so for a while nobody would talk to him. Then it got around that he didn't have a family coming to join him because he was divorced, and also, he had no children; on the other hand, he owned a veritable palace in town furnished with all the worldly comforts, and he bought the empty, neglected house near the station not far from Lakatos with his share of the sale price, with plenty left over. It was no palace, not by a long shot, but he wasted no time letting people know that he'd be moving back to town soon anyway, he'll just rest up a bit here in the village. Money's no object, he's just waiting for passions to cool down. This was about five years ago, but definitely more than three, because he's been owing Dorogi a hundred-and-forty forints for exactly three years, and passions, too, have cooled down long since.

Then one quiet, early autumn afternoon, it came to light that he can't even ride a bike; on the other hand, it makes walking easier, and he's willing to make sacrifices for his comfort; money's no object, he told Mrs. Sarkadi, Aunt Piroska, then asked for another glass of wine on credit. This Ocsenás is a short, plump man, fortyish &

bandy legged, and he walks around in a loose, thread-bare pair of black pants. When weather permits he doesn't wear a hat & then people can see that he's practically bald, and he might even be Jewish, judging by the size of his nose; but when he puts on that black hat of his with the greasy brim, he couldn't deny he's a gypsy if he tried. Also, he's called Béla, which was a source of confusion at first, because that's what they call one of the two locust trees, the one that's standing by the pub, but people eventually learned that this Béla is not that Béla, even though he also stands around the vicinity of the pub most of the time, along with the rest of them. Ocsenás was an educated man. Over the years his bicycle was stolen four times, and each time he stole it back, whereas once they even painted it over. He didn't make a big deal out of it. At an opportune time he let drop a caustic remark or two in the pub about certain individuals who are too smart by half, and as for the opportune time, it always coincided with the presence of the individual in question, and then it was only natural that the individual in question should pay for beers and pálinka all around, because you can't be mad at a man like Ocsenás for long. Ocsenás also said that the bicycle, far as he's concerned, is not a vehicle for him to run around on but a vital health aid, which he then proceeded to explain. In short, he moved into our street straight from the clinic where he was an orderly, but here he's a no-body, like the rest of us.

He was quick to get the hang of things, not that anybody tried to stop him, and in a couple of days he was seen everywhere, along the full length of the street, and practically all the time. They saw him at Aunt Sarkadi's, who sold her own wine by the glass on credit, and they saw him in the shop, and also at Misi's; he got up early & stood outside in front of his house so he could greet the people taking the early morning bus, & by the time it opened, he was leaning against his bike in front of the pub, offering to help, if help was needed, to sweep up or scrub the stone floor, whereas just a couple of minutes before he was seen talking to Lajos Mérő at the far end of the street, who'd been suspecting for some time that there had to be several Ocsenáses, & all alike. He walked swiftly, with a nimble gait, he'd even run alongside his bike now and then, and when he was just sitting in the pub or leaning against the fence, even then he was doing something; he invariably had two ball bearings with him, and he'd roll them in his palm. And he still had time to listen to people, if called upon, untiring, for hours, rolling the balls around in his hand, occasionally helping the other out if stuck for words, and when neighbor Béres recounted to him the lamentable story of his life, even then he barely ever told him to keep his voice down, because Béres always talked too loud, even when he was told not to. Béres was under the weather these days, everybody could see, though he talked too loud even when he wasn't, except now he had stubble on his face that was several weeks old, and the hair on the back of his neck curled up, so that they even asked him what anti-shave he's using, because he looks just like the Messiah. Ocsenás even asked him, sir, why don't you shave? It was late afternoon, almost evening, Béres adroitly got around the answer, though his mood suddenly darkened, but then, after a couple of bottles of beer he said, why not indeed? His hand is still trembling too much when he wakes up, and the trembling won't stop until he sits on it, and by the afternoon it's unsteady again, and besides, he couldn't care less. Why do they call you Ocsenás, he then asked, what sort of name is that? Ocsenás also got around the answer because he didn't know himself, but he let on that when he was an orderly for about twenty-five years he shaved the patients before an operation, and for him it's child's play, he could shave Béres, too. He might even trim his hair, just a touch.

Béres didn't know what to make of it all because it was common knowledge by then that Ocsenás couldn't ride a bike, and also, he seemed to remember from somewhere that orderlies wear green smocks and their mouths are covered, but he figured that worse comes to worse he'll botch it up, and then what? Fine with me, he said, then gave a quick look around, but except for the two of them there was nobody in the place who could've talked him out of it. The next step was to get home somehow. But how? The big, tall man, when he walked out of Misi's, was suddenly afraid, as if he were standing on the brink of a precipice whose name he didn't know. He needed to sit down or hold on to something, but he knew that he'd be afraid even so, and that at such times he must drink either more, or less, and then everything would be alright. And so he quickly turned back from the door, because to drink less was no longer possible, but Ocsenás grabbed his arm and said, we'll come back when it's done, neighbor. You'll feel a whole lot better, you'll see. Fine, agreed Béres. He didn't have a penny in his pocket. Well, they could still go to Aunt Sarkadi, he thought with a resigned sigh as Ocsenás helped him up on the bicycle, and he grabbed the steering wheel with such force, the other could hardly steer the bicycle at all. Life is difficult, he later breathed despondently to no one in particular. So where are we going? To my place, Ocsenás said, but Béres said that that won't do, because how would he get home from there? Though Ocsenás swore he'd take him back himself, Béres held his ground. His place is closer, he said, & he's got everything, soap, brush, a blade. Also, Aunt Sarkadi lives practically across the street, and come to think of it, they might as well go in right now and drink to all the excitement. Except Ocsenás should tell him when they're there, because he's not opening his eyes till then.

This Ocsenás was really an orderly at one time, and not your run of the mill orderly either. As he wheeled her ladyship Mrs. Pásztori along the corridor to the op-

erating room he sang to her, ain't it grand, to be bloomin'
well dead, it being her favorite music hall ditty, though
she never found out how Ocsenás could have known,
because soon after her successful operation she expired,
and only the new pacemaker went on ticking inside her,
even in her coffin. As for old man Osvát, he had his leg
amputated, first just under the knee, but when the nice
young orderly came to fetch him, he didn't mind, the one
that knew arise, ye workers from your slumber, arise, ye
prisoners of want, singing the last refrain at the top of
his lungs as they reached the treatment room, so come,
rally round us, comrades, the Internationale unites the
human race! Uncle Osvát was a communist way before
most of the others and was still a communist when it
was no longer fashionable, but that didn't save him from
getting vascular constriction. He survived Albania and
Recsk,[17] but he never learned to walk with a crutch,
which was no problem as long as Ocsenás was on duty,
because Ocsenás picked Uncle Osvát up along with two
or three others like him, put them in wheelchairs, and
off they went. He pushed two in front and pulled two
or three behind and they rolled down the long, wide,
deserted corridor into the elevator, and weather per-
mitting, from there out to the yard, all of them singing
and laughing and having a grand old time of it in the
meantime. Needless to say, he could do this only in the
afternoon because, for instance, if Assistant Erdei, the
respected laryngologist, heard Ocsenás in the morning,

he immediately wanted to sign him up for septal surgery, though he'd have preferred laryngotomy, it always comes to that anyway.

The assistant physician had no ear for music, but he loved surgery, just as Ocsenás loved singing, or acted as if he did, and the patients loved him for it. As for the laryngotomy, he didn't fall victim to it because Assistant Erdei got him to agree to a cursory examination first, which indicated excessive and continual consumption of alcohol; Ocsenás made vodka from ethanol with the addition of distilled water, both of which he acquired from the storeroom, and consequently it was difficult to decide if they should fire him because of this, or because he offered the concoction to the patients as well. Repeatedly. He wouldn't take money for it, but something had to be done, and done quickly, and though there seemed to be nothing wrong with his throat, the cardiologist detected suspicious cardiac noises, and then the orderly's blood pressure shot up and his joints began to ache, then the lymphatic glands under his armpits began to swell, so by the time he went through the hospital gates for the last time, he had at least three incurable diseases, as a result of which the hospital had no choice but to send him into early retirement.

They all liked Ocsenás, the doctors, the nurses, the patients, because he liked to do good deeds, whether called upon or not. He was born that way. Now, too, he supported neighbor Béres's scrawny back on the bicycle with a gentle hand as he hummed something like the sheep's in the meadow, the cow's in the corn, at which the heady smell of grass on a dewy morning assailed Béres's nostrils, gentle bells droned in his ears, and before long, he was fast asleep.

It wasn't real sleep, though, he'd just dozed off, because when they reached Aunt Sarkadi's house he took one whiff of the air and was wide awake, except he couldn't turn the steering wheel in that direction because Ocsenás also had a grip on it as he went on humming, so Béres's heartfelt cry, we're here!, stop the bike!, fell on deaf ears. He even said that in that case he's gonna jump off, but his threat couldn't be taken seriously. Ocsenás knew where the tall, scrawny man lived, just as he knew which house belonged to whom all along the street, how you could get inside, and also whether the owner lived up front or in the back annex, or the bake house; he knew how each of them lived, he may have even known what each of them ate, what and when, and what his bowel movement was like. In short, everything. They passed through the small garden gate into the yard with some difficulty, then Ocsenás gently leaned the bike to one side in front of the door and Béres slid off like a bag of potatœs. See, said the former orderly, that wasn't so bad, was it? When was the last time somebody brought your lordship home like this, practically by cab? You mean me, Béres asked, in some confusion, because Ocsenás was not always easy to understand. He talked funny, maybe because of the hospital. Let's not stand on ceremony, he told the other because he was lost for an answer and also, he didn't want the other to know that this wasn't the first time he'd been brought home, supported under the armpit or pulled by the arm as his heels dug a furrow along the length of the street. It was still there the following day.

Ocsenás had seen and heard many things in the hospital, and so was not easily shocked. When they entered the house his nostrils picked up a familiar smell, the pungent mixture of urine, medicine, sweat, and old age characteristic of the chronic ward, the acrid, sour smell of transience or, as they said amongst themselves, the smell of death. Béres's wife Magdika was sitting on the bed laughing. She laughed at everything. Magdika had suffered two seizures years back, & she's been lying or sitting on the bed ever since, and a couple of months later, Béres took to the bottle. I'm sorry, he told everybody, I can't bear it otherwise. Then he was sent into retirement so he could care for his wife; other than that, nothing out of the ordinary happened. Ocsenás saw right away that this patient would live a long time, as long as they feed her and give her drink and don't take her to the hospital, but until then, she'll be the undoing of everything & everyone around her. How do you do, he said to the woman, raising his voice, how are you feeling? You're in the pink of health little lady, he went on, because he got no answer, were you out in the sun?

Magdika's face was white and pale, practically translucent. Stop it, Béres grunted, she doesn't understand you. Didn't I say? Then he yelled, lie down!, lie down!, and Magdika broke into heartfelt laughter & leaned back on the bed. Sit, Béres now yelled, sit! I said sit! His wife had a good laugh at this, too, then she sat up. See, Béres said, that's the only language she understands. Like a dog. She knows other things, too. You'll see. This was nothing new to Ocsenás either, but he didn't say anything; an old, filthy textile splash guard ran along the side of the bed, he was taking that in, then the dirty dishes on the table, the stove, then he looked at Magdika again, queening it on the rumpled, yellowish-gray bed linen. Somebody had gathered her graying hair in the back and secured it with string, but she was beautiful even so, like a cheerful, overgrown, unruly child, with wounds on her hands, bruises on her neck, and saliva glistening on her lips and under her nose in the poor electric light. Oh my God, Ocsenás thought, profoundly moved. Scratch!, he now heard Béres's cry again, and the woman began scratching the tattered comforter with both hands, and when she leaned forward, a wet, massive, brownish stain showed under her, and a small washbowl tipped on its side, its contents all over the blanket. You peed and shit in bed again, Béres said. This is what she does until I thrash her to within an inch of her life. It was hot and there were lots of flies. Magdika laughed, she even said something, but what it was they couldn't make out, because just then the shaggy black dog started barking outside and was soon joined by all the others.

The shaving might have gone off without a hitch if only Béres could've sat up straight and not move his mouth all the time. Also, the blade was a thousand years old, if one, and the edge had to be sharpened on a piece of glass, but then everything turned out just fine. You know what, neighbor, Ocsenás said after a struggle, why don't you lie down on the other bed. Lie down, Béres asked incredulously. Yes, said Ocsenás, that'll be the best. I shaved plenty of patients lying down, not to mention the dead. The dead, repeated Béres as his voice suddenly faltered when with a swift, sure hand Ocsenás pressed his head against the mattress, then proceeded to make lather in a pottery bowl; then he pulled the shirt off the tall, skinny man and pushed it under his head. That's so the lather won't stain the sheets, he said. There were no sheets. He worked swiftly, skillfully, swaying in front of Béres with slightly bent knees while Béres pinned his eyes on the ceiling stained with fly poop, his ears picking up the light crackle of the skin. Careful around the mouth, he said, because I got just four teeth. It's caved in. My mouth. Don't worry, Ocsenás said breezily, and when it was time he shoved a spoon in Béres's mouth to make the skin taut, while he helped out under the nose with his fingers, and by the time Béres started retching and was about to throw up, he was done. We're done, Ocsenás said, kindly pay the cashier. Then with an old pair of pruning sheers he clipped off his nails and cut his hair with the naked blade held between his fingers. They couldn't find the scissors. Wash up, Ocsenás said, because the skin was bleeding in spots; I'm dizzy, mumbled Béres, everything's turning round & round. That's not from shaving, Ocsenás offered. Sit up! Sit! At this Magdika gave a laugh on the other bed and sat up, then she pulled a dirty towel out from among the rags around her, placed it between her legs, then reaching behind her with one hand, began pulling it back and forth, the way it's done after bathing; Béres looked on for a while, then yelled at her, put it down! Down I said! And then, now lie down! Down! Who is my mare, he then asked, his expression gentle but firm and, going up to her, he forced a finger between his wife's thighs. Magdika said nothing, just smiled, closed her eyes, and bit her fist. Hey ho, soldier boy, ride your horse until she's sore, two on a pony and three on a mare, sang Béres into her face, at which Magdika laughed again, thrashing about with her waist, hell's bells, said Beres when he stood up from beside the bed, I love this piece of trash. Even like this, he added later with a sad shake of the head, and the color rose to his cheeks. She's become part of me. She & I, we're one festering wound. Can you believe that? Ocsenás nodded. He could. He really and truly could.

You can't imagine what this woman has suffered in life along with me, Béres explained later, and his brow darkened. Nobody can! They just run off at the mouth!

And see? This is what life gives her! Where's justice? Can you tell me that? Where? He hadn't washed his face; it felt good sitting like this, freshly shaved, and the bed wasn't turning round with him now either. Meanwhile, Ocsenás rolled Magdika there and back, pulled that filthy, tattered sheet from under her, and changed the bed linen. You told me already, he now called to Béres over his shoulder as he pushed Magdika to one side. We even worked the threshing machine, Béres went on, his voice gritty with indignation. That, too, Ocsenás said. And in Palkonya she worked on the construction, even though she's a woman, Béres added. I know, neighbor, Ocsenás said. I know everything. Even I don't know everything, Béres said. He was sad, and getting more and more drunk by the minute. I sometimes think I do, he yelled, except, the trouble is, I forget. Ocsenás switched on the light. I gotta wash her down. Is there a washbowl or a tub? There's nothing of the sort, Béres lied, then he said that that's not what she needs. If you don't mind, Ocsenás shot back, I think I know better. Don't delude yourself, Béres said, because this is the Lord's gift to her, this illness. At least she gets to rest in her old age. You should take her for a walk sometime, Ocsenás advised, it'd do her good. Her leg muscles will atrophy. He stood in front of Béres and showed him where, and Béres looked, then grabbed the other's groin, this is what she needs, he said. And wine. Take my word for it.

I can get her wine, but this other doesn't make her happy anymore, it's always at half-mast. That's my great sorrow. See, he added when he released his grip on Ocsenás, you don't know everything, do you?

All the same, they managed to wash Magdika down in a big pot as she continued to laugh and giggle, and in the meanwhile Ocsenás explained what had to be done and how, talcum powder, he asked when they were done, but there wasn't any. And these will have to be laundered, he added. Where are the clean sheets? Nowhere, Béres said, she sleeps without sheets until they're dry. She's ripped three sets apart. When we were still sleeping together. Then they went to Aunt Sarkadi's for a quick drink and Béres also asked for two liters in a plastic bottle to take away, & out on the street he dropped it, it didn't break, just cracked, & they drank it so it shouldn't go to waste. Then they went back to Aunt Sarkadi's, possibly even more than once, then back to Béres, but they may have also gone to Ocsenás's place, because as long as Béres had his wine, he never argued, he just sat quietly on a chair or a bed or the bicycle frame and listened, while the other talked and talked; they even laughed, then each lay down somewhere, then around dawn Ocsenás asked for Magdika's hand. They went out to the well to take a leak, the second time it dripped on the dog, and that's when Ocsenás told Béres that he loved Magdika. I love her, too, Béres said, then they lay back down under a blanket in the shed, & didn't mention Magdika again.

Later Béres got up one more time, started yelling out in the yard, then in the shed, too, beating his head against the planks, like he always did when the mash went out of him, and then he feels like he's going out of his mind, but Ocsenás didn't hear, and in the morning neither of them could remember anything.

Ocsenás loved ailing women because their infirmity made them delicate, illness & fever smoothed out their faces and skin, they were weak, helpless, their movements enervated, soft, femininely beautiful as they lay back on the damp sheets, these capriciously wrinkled draperies, their bodies prostrate on the warm pillows, like on those old sepia photographs. Or translucent catheter tubes slithered from their spent & weary bodies into bags under their bed, filling up with mysterious liquids. Ocsenás had also loved a handsome, sulky youth with almond eyes whom he used to carry to the numerous painful examinations in his arms, despite the fact that he'd known for some time that he wasn't a girl. He was fifteen and a diabetic, his blond hair was curly and his cheeks like velvet, this is what had misled the innocent orderly, who knew that the boy would soon need glasses for those resentful eyes, thicker and thicker, his life would be bad in this healthy world, & he wouldn't have children either, just as Ocsenás had none, whereas there's nothing wrong with his sugar. Csaba was a petulant, highly excitable young beauty, a nervous and undisciplined boy hiding behind the face of a dreamy girl;

he got hefty doses of shots in his stomach, and jerked off in the women's washroom when nobody saw. Ocsenás supplied him with cigarettes, occasionally even vodka, whereas that was also off limits to the boy, and at night hid a couple of sugar cubes in his locker. He had favorites among the women patients as well, especially the weak and the post-operatives, or those who were just brought in, prey to fear and anxiety, but who, after a dose of tranquilizers, veritably gave themselves up to the hospital. Ocsenás couldn't remember his wife ever having been ill; epidemics, the cold, the heat, fog, rain or snow storms had no hold on her; she never even had a cold, not even a fever, ever. Except she refused to have children. She said she can't because she used to work in radiation therapy, but Ocsenás was sure that it was because his wife was incapable of loving anyone in the world except for herself. And maybe her cat.

Edith worked in another hospital boiling disposable needles after use, which called for concentration and expertise as well as daring, because only she and the head nurse could know about it. She was a strong woman, when she vacuumed she moved the furniture around on her own, and she vacuumed every day. She rolled up her sleeves and her cheeks were ruddy with work, she talked to Captain, the fat, shaggy, long haired tomcat, who at such times leaped lazily up into the armchair & nestled in, waiting for Edith to put him on the narrow ledge of the prefab window, so he shouldn't have to leap over the twenty-centimeter distance himself. In warm weather he sat there in the sun with a happy, satisfied expression, while Ocsenás, if he happened to be at home, sat in the kitchen. But he was rarely at home. Even at first it took a veritable siege to get Edith into bed, and later she wouldn't even let him, or only on rare occasions; she considered the whole thing unclean, even filthy; she turned her head away and smoked or covered herself with her arms, and it was written all over her how much she hated it. When it was over she rushed off to take a bath and cleaned the bathroom after herself, and she even washed the floor & scrubbed the tub, and when she was back in the room, she opened the window to let out the smell, and first thing the next morning, she laundered the sheets. By the second or third week they slept in separate beds. Ocsenás tried everything he could think of, then gave up. He'd brought her flowers for her name day then, too, like always. He could've guessed that when he opened the door his wife would be vacuuming, cleaning, dusting the top of the wall unit, but it never occurred to him that the draught would shut all the doors and windows and that a gust would push Captain off the sill into the depths below. From the ninth floor, because that's where they lived, though after the cat fell off the ledge, only him, because his wife wouldn't go home anymore if Ocsenás was there.

At the time, Ocsenás was in love with Mrs. Bátonyi, molded into a fine china thinness by cancer. He didn't trouble himself much with the stretcher or wheelchair, he carried her to the complex treatments in his arms while he pushed the chair in front of him, and Mrs. Bátonyi wrapped her soft arms around his neck and leaned her head on his shoulder. But Vera Ács, who was suffering from a variety of ills, was also beautiful, and so was Mrs. Bimbó, whose illness none of the doctors could diagnose, and who was grateful when Ocsenás sneaked her a drink, and there was also Aranka Jármi, whose intestines adhered, and who had already undergone two operations, but to no avail. And there were always some who were dying, and Ocsenás would look in on them through the open door several times a day to see when he could take them to the morgue. There was no separate ward at the hospital, they put up some sheets around the person's bed and waited. Ocsenás thought how good it would be to shield Magdika from the outside world like that, with a light veil, from its noise and filth, and most of all from her husband, so she could live in her own enchanted fairy tale world for many years to come under the wings of an individual as loving and caring as himself. The minute he laid eyes on her he knew he'd found her, and he felt infinitely at peace, though infinitely excited, too.

Béres, on the other hand, remembered nothing, and the next morning he was surprised that his face was so smooth, and no stubble, and that there was an ugly man lying in the shed near him, of whom everybody knew

that his name was Ocsenás and that he sticks his nose
into everybody's business until somebody comes and
breaks it for him. Béres was always wrought up in the
morning, impatient; now, too, he started a frantic search
for the empty bottle in the hay; it took him some time
before he found it under Ocsenás's hat, but he found it,
which was lucky for Ocsenás, because this way he could
go on sleeping, and as for Béres, he resolved to make it
to Mrs. Sarkadi, Aunt Piroska, across the street, come
hell or high water. It took some doing, but he got there.
He had to wait, though, because the old woman hadn't
opened her door yet; she hadn't been feeling well lately,
& half the street prayed that she shouldn't die, or if she
did, she shouldn't do it the morning but sometime during the day, when both Misi's & the shop are open and
Pintér also starts selling his wine. Misi opened at six, the
shop at seven, and Pintér pulled the bolt aside around
eight, after he'd fed the animals and he & his wife had
breakfast. Except Pintér didn't like selling anything on
credit, a shame, considering that he sold pálinka, too;
and you couldn't ask for credit at the shop either; but
even at Misi's only a couple of customers could drink
on trust, and Béres was not one of them, because the
credit relationship is based on trust, and Béres talked
too much, and he talked too loud. Mrs. Sarkadi, Aunt
Piroska, on the other hand, entertained no such preju-
dices, & before long Béres was done with his first three
decis, then as Aunt Piroska filled up the plastic bottle,

he drank another glassful, and then he stopped for a bit outside by the fence because he felt sick; he was nauseous and broke out in a sweat, but he knew that this was actually a good thing and that life is beautiful, even though the day is just beginning.

This street, it's like a garbage dump, or a cemetery, Dorogi once said in the pub, at one time those that could left here, & now they're trooping back, even strangers from town, penniless downers on the ragged edge, like Sudák, Jenő Nagy, and now this Ocsenás. Dorogi knew what he was talking about because he finished high school and his diploma was all A's, he's pinned it to the stable wall with a roofing nail. By the horse's ass, the big, ruddy-faced man says with a smile when he's in a good mood, but that wasn't the case now. The mood was bad all around because that crackbrained Béres, as people called him, scolded and abused everybody these days and tried picking a fight, & though they wouldn't hurt him, nobody would buy him a drink either, and since he couldn't buy his own, he grew more and more cantankerous by the minute. You're back, too, he now turned on Dorogi, because they kicked your ass out in the cold! Then it was Jancsi Hesz's turn, who's such an expert, he eats shit with a fork, but at Aunt Piroska's, he drinks on credit. Which was another lie. Aunt Piroska's house was not the only place where Jancsi Hesz drank on credit, except they weren't concerned with Béres now, whose pale face, covered in sweat, was distorted by rage.

He's got one of his crazy fits again, Lajos Mérő said, pointing to his forehead. These days even Ocsenás couldn't reason with Béres anymore, whereas he went to see him every morning to help. Morning? It was more like the crack of dawn; there was hardly anybody up and about, the cows lowed in the barns, piglets squealed, & Béres sat on the cot drinking his wine, watching what Ocsenás was doing to his wife, and when will he get the hell out already?

On the other hand, he was a great help because he cleaned her up and dumped the dirty clothes in the big metal pot, and he even made breakfast. Something was cooking on the stove now, too. But still. Béres wanted to lie back down next to his wife because it's better there than on the hard, narrow cot, & he'd have also liked to play with her a bit, the way only they knew how. After a while Ocsenás went home for a bit but was soon back and he said something, but Béres was not interested, he still had some wine, and that's why. But when Ocsenás said, okay, let's take her out for a short walk, he said he'd help. Fine, the big, somber looking man said. But where? The outhouse, of course, Ocsenás said. Maybe she'll get used to it. Never, Béres said, not her, then he yelled at his wife, stand! Stand up!, at which Magdika started searching for the towel on the bed, except it'd been put in order, & she couldn't find it. Ocsenás slid her off the bed like a pro, then said, stand up, Magdika, but she just looked at him & laughed, her merry, mischievous eyes devoid of sense. Lean on me, Ocsenás said as he wrapped his arm around her waist, then he dragged her outside, where there was more room to maneuver. Out in the open Magdika gasped for breath as if she were drowning, but she liked it, then she started scratching with her hand, then she tried to sit down, gimme, hungry, she shouted as Ocsenás dragged her alongside, meanwhile Béres stood in the door, and he was very drunk.

This scene out in the neglected, shabby yard was repeated for days, sometimes with Béres's help, sometimes without, because the big bony man was at Misi's or at Aunt Sarkadi's, yelling at the top of his lungs how they're all gonna be struck dumb with wonder, because that Ocsenás, he's gonna make Magdika all right, take it from him. Meanwhile, Jancsi Hesz next door was full of concern, because at times there was no telling who's carrying whom on his back, or who's taking whom and where, or who's lying on the ground again, while at other times there'd be a horrendous crashing noise against the fence and the shaggy black dog would go scurrying behind the shed, because if Béres was around, he'd holler, walk!, walk! Left! Right! Then Ocsenás had an idea, and he tied Magdika's leg to his so they could take a step together and he'd pull the other leg after, but they hardly ever got beyond the threshold, and went crashing to the floor like nobody's business. Terka Papp, Jancsi Hesz's twenty-four-hour mother-in-law, was even thinking of going to see the mayor, because enough's enough, torturing that sick woman like this! Because after their walk Ocsenás massaged the soles of her feet and made her do exercises, pulled, tugged, and stretched, and Magdika put up with it for a while, but then she started moaning, then crying, then she turned on her stomach and sulked and refused to do anything even when they shouted at her, lie down! Sit up! Scratch! At which point Béres threw her her favorite towel and slapped Ocsenás. That's enough, he yelled. Get out!

Then the two of them went to Misi's, because Béres needed Ocsenás's bicycle, & Ocsenás, too, to get there, and at Misi's the orderly told him about lots of things as he rolled the ball bearings round in his hand, but Béres wasn't paying attention, he just sat at one of the tables drinking, and then it occurred to him that actually, he wouldn't mind if he could remember everything he can't remember that has to do with Magdika, because it's not true what people say, that his wife's an invalid because she worked like an animal, & he didn't stop her.

They had worked as hired hands together, he ate and drank the same thing as his wife, and he never rushed or pressed her, not so much as with a word, though he couldn't be so sure anymore. And also, that his wife shouldn't've had to hoe as much as he, or gut the earth, and why did they compete, when looking after the household and the animals should've been enough, because they said that, too, except nobody said how they were supposed to put up that small room and kitchen next to the old one otherwise. Talk comes cheap. No matter how he wracked his brain, he couldn't fault himself. Back then, whoever was in the same shoes as him worked like an animal, otherwise they'd have starved to death. Except from time to time it also occurred to Béres that if he had done things differently, maybe things wouldn't've turned out so bad. But how? It was bad thinking about these things, because it made you want another drink, and that just made things worse, and then something spoke from inside him, and by the time he realized, he heard himself whisper to Ocsenás, go, lie down with my wife. Let her enjoy herself at least one last time in her life. The voice came faintly from him, he wasn't yelling this time, & so Ocsenás, who was just talking with Lajos Mérő, didn't hear, but Béres grabbed him by the shoulder and pulled him close. Did you hear what I said? No, admitted Ocsenás without guile, but then he did. Neighbor, he began after a while, his eyes round with gratitude, but Béres pasted a hand over his lips. Come back for me when it's over, he said, his voice strange & husky. You'll find me here. Or someplace else.

Béres had been very strong at one time, there were small tubers on his arms and back and even his legs, protuberances caused by the strain, because his hands grabbed more than his body could bear, and which should've been excised because they hurt whenever there was a change in the weather, though sometimes they just burned and itched. When he was young, he'd jump a ditch with a sack of stolen wheat on his back if there was a field guard nearby, he heaved up the sheaves by twos to feed the thresher, his hoe & spade were always bigger than the others', and he picked up half a shock at once with his pitchfork. True, the dipper he ate from was the size of a trowel, and when he was thirsty, he drank half a tin of water. But the slap he now got from Dorogi sent him reeling over the table. The second one he didn't even feel anymore. He must've said something to the big man, except he didn't know what, nor did he care, because they were holding him down by then, beating him and yelling, what's got into you old man, have you lost your mind, then they pushed him out to Béla, the locust tree that stood in front of the pub. The sky was speckled with stars, he remembered this for a long time, & also that Ocsenás didn't come to get him. But by holding on to the fences, crawling, creeping along the ground he managed to reach home and even got inside the house thanks to that short piece of wire, then for what seemed like ages, he stood panting in the dark. Where are you, my mare, he muttered, though he thought he was yelling, then suddenly it was light, and Magdika was on the bed fumbling with the towel and Ocsenás was leaning against the door; he was filthy, his face bloodstained, marked up with scratches and tears, his lips split open; she won't let me, he grunted with exhaustion, & threw up his hand. She got filth all over me, but she wouldn't let me. The shaggy black dog sneaked inside, crouching, whimpering, Béres kicked out but missed, then he wanted to laugh at this bewildered & pitiful Ocsenás with urine all over his pants, laugh long and hard, but only his lip cracked open and no sound came, just the lukewarm vapor of a staggering sigh.

THE SILVER COIN

When she comes home, Rózsika lights the lamp because
it's late, then she extinguishes it, because it's time for bed.
Her son sleeps in the kitchen, she in the back room, each
on a chaff bed. The door between them is always open;
for all they know they couldn't close it anymore even if
they tried, but why should they? We'll soon have furniture now, she tells him for the hundredth time. The electricity's been turned off long ago, not that they couldn't
afford it, but it's better this way; they burn the lamp for a
bit, then lie down. Rózsika works in town, Dezső's home
all day, he's a big boy, he's finished school, but nobody
wants to talk to him, or make friends, though he stops
to talk to everybody, except the children, they're too
young, they trip and fall & break their bones, and the
adults drink and then can't talk, except for the same old
tune, so how's things? Or whasup? This means what's
up, but they don't expect an answer. Sometimes he'll
grab hold of somebody when they're about to fall and
they stroke his face, which is as much as he can hope for.

Dezső also goes into town now and then when he's
really bored, he's got a friend there, a blind violinist who
wouldn't mind talking to him, except he's busy, he has
to play his violin all day even though he gets practically
nothing for his pains, and even that nothing he gives
him. The other day he asked, are you an orphan, & he

said no, but the man didn't believe him, he even had the nerve and said you're lying, I can tell by your smell. He yanked the bow out of his hand and yelled at him, say you're sorry! I'm sorry, the man said. Then Dezső asked, how do you know I'm the same as yesterday if you can't see? The old man said, nobody stops to talk to a beggar except another beggar. And also, there's such a thing as inner vision. At other times he goes to the movies, or Kati Sós and him, they bite each other's lips, but she won't lie down with him on the chaff bed, some other time she says, just like the others, & then it's really bad. He'll have to wait till his mother gets home.

We'll have furniture, his mother says from inside. When? When we have the money. Why don't we have the money? Because the kind I want costs a lot. What kind is that? A white wall unit. And a bed. For two. A table, two arm chairs. Maybe three. A bourbon palm in front of the window. An aquarium. Are you sleeping? No. Well, sleep. You always say something different. You just saw this at somebody's place. Place? What place? Where you went whoring today. Watch your mouth! How much money do we have? Not much. I want a pair of white jeans. I don't need furniture. How many times must I tell you? Well, I do. Don't fight me, Rozi, the boy says, you know how quickly my hand moves if you're bad. And three bads is one stroke on your behind. And three strokes on your behind is one slap in the face. And three slaps is one whiplash on your back. Alright?

Yes, Rózsika says in a sleepy haze & they laugh, because they haven't even got a whip. Rózsika wants to sleep, but the boy wants to go on with the game. Or three bads could be one kiss. Three kisses, one feel-up. Three feel-ups one finger job. And after three finger jobs? Well? What's next? There's no answer, but the boy's body is still wide awake, his hand moving, stroking. A screw job!, he groans as his head sinks into the pillow.

Rózsika's got a silver coin hanging on a chain around her neck, but you can hardly make out the writing anymore, just the two-headed bird on the other side, and nothing else. She got it where all the girls wore one of these coins around the neck, it was eternal summer and the sun was always shining. There were seven of them, siblings, the boys slept on the right, the girls on the left. They called the space between the beds the ditch, that's where they swung their legs when they were eating, and the fire was there, too, and above it the pot. They were not allowed to go over to the other side, only mother and father, but they did anyway when they were alone. If mother went over, the boys grumbled, if father, then the girls, because there wasn't enough room. Then they giggled, because they all knew what was going on. There were three sisters, Rozi was the middle one, and when she turned thirteen, her older brother said to her, come. I have something to say to you. They went over to Árpi's house and her brother said, I sold you to Árpi in exchange for his little sister. You stay here. Viola is coming with me. During the day people were out in their yard or scattered throughout the village, they were working, so nobody bothered them. The boy was already fifteen, like her own brother, except handsome, with soft lips and sweet saliva, his face like the moon, the smell of smoke and elder blossoms issuing from his shiny, curly hair, and his eyes were like lanterns. Come, he said to Rózsika, let me look at you, then he placed a coin between her lips to stop her from crying out. Here! Bite it!

In the evening she went home, and after a couple of weeks she didn't need the coin between her lips anymore, and a year later she was so beautiful, everybody tried to palm her, the older ones sweet talked her, the younger ones held her down, just so their little balls could touch her, and she laughed, and so did Árpi. By the time they're ten or twelve, girls around here know that the first time it hurts and it bleeds, eyes upturned, the mothers scare their young daughters, and so the wedding night, as they imagine it, is a veritable bloodbath, gore and violence, while the boy waiting outside is pure ecstasy, and not for the first time either. Sanyi hurt Rozi, but only because he didn't take off his leather belt, but nobody else. Then Árpi had an eye knocked out in prison and he didn't come back, and Rózsika ran away with a woodchopper, then a merchant stole her from him, then somebody else, and so it went. Her path was strewn with passion, strife, and fire, some wanted to marry her, others to kill her.

SÁNDOR TAR

When Rózsika came to our street with the circus, she was already like a queen. The show was long and interesting, and she and her mates were eager to make the humblest man feel like a real man in the back of the caravans, and it cost almost nothing, a bit of money, a duck, or a hen. Two days later none of the men from the village wanted to go to work. This is where she met the robust truck driver Illés Molnár, who'd heard about the circus three villages away, but couldn't catch up with it till now. Illés had a house in Adony & Gelse, and in our street, too, and people were happy when he married Rózsika, because she would now live among us. He had furniture brought here, and rugs and drapes and many other things besides that we didn't even know what they were for. Flowers. Then those that could manage it had a look inside for themselves, and what they saw made them gape in wonder as they lay on the wide bed, under the veils. The truck driver was away a great deal, while here there was always somebody with time on their hands, and afterwards they told the others what they'd seen and experienced, that there's soft music playing, and scented incense sticks, and oh, those pictures on the wall! And that Rozi's got a coin round her neck that she puts between her lips when it's time and bites down on it, but she won't give it to anybody for anything. Dorogi tried to bite it off but couldn't do it, somebody else wanted to steal it, but it was good even so. Those that was there were in a daze for days, and kept bumping into things.

261

But it wasn't until a couple of years later, when Illés stripped the house bare with his own to hands, that people's jaws dropped in earnest, down to the last nail; he knocked everything off the wall, too, and threw the whole lot on the bonfire in the yard, and before he left for good, he hitched the dog down the well, and good riddance. Rózsika found herself in the stripped house with her son, like two sparrows. Then she got two chaff beds somewhere and crates for a table and chair, knocked some nails into the wall to hang their clothes on, and said that everything will be just fine. That was a year ago. The men were shaken by what happened, but the women smiled, which gave rise to the general suspicion that one of them must've let on to Molnár that the boy's not even his. And then for a while many of the men beat their wives, but after a while that passed, too.

Rózsika's eyes were like two gray, glittering teardrops in obscure shade, two mountain lakes, said Lakeview, who was the physician at the time, and who couldn't wrest himself free of those eyes, though eventually he had to, because by then he just drank, while Rózsika sat next to him on the chaff bed, the coin between her lips, and the two of them doing nothing. After a while the doctor was taken to the hospital because he refused to go home, and he wouldn't go anywhere else either; also, he wouldn't eat, and before long he looked just like everybody else in our street, and people even started calling him by his first name. She's a she devil, Terka Papp, who knows about these things, whispered confidentially in Mrs. Sarkadi's ear, she casts a spell on them with that coin. It's got magic in it. When she puts it between her lips, she's overwhelmed by love like nobody's business. And that boy, he sees everything. He watches. What's to become of him? To which Aunt Piroska offered the observation that there are certain women in the neighborhood who could put anything between their lips, & still nothing would happen. As far as that goes, she then added, I envy her myself. You're not the only one.

Dezső goes to Misi's, too, when he's got the time, but there's nobody there now & it's no use asking Esztike for a Coke, so he contends himself with a quick hello, then goes out to the yard, but Misi, the proprietor, calls after him, hey, boy! Whasup? Nice day, the boy says, adding that he was thirsty, but he's not so thirsty anymore. What would you like, the obese, ruddy-faced man asks from the cellar door. A Coke, the boy says. Come, the other says, then lowering his voice he adds, if you need anything, don't go in there. Come to me in the cellar, come to your Uncle Misi. The others do, too. Dezső is the spitting image of his mother, that rusty hair, his face, the gray eyes, just looking at him makes a man's heart skip a beat. The boy drinks one Coke after another, stuffs himself with cream puffs from off a tray, and listens to what Misi has to say, the gist of which is that he should bring him the medal from round his mother's neck. He says he'll pay for it. He begs. He implores. Or he'll just have a look and give it right back. Then he draws the boy to him and kisses his cheek and weeps. Dezső doesn't know why, but he's close to tears himself, which doesn't prevent him from eating some minced meat patties, and some chocolate, too, and he also tries some of the liqueur. The beer tastes too bitter. He later vomits it all up in front of the pub by the locust tree that people around here call Béla, and since it's getting dark, a voice comes praising him in the twilight. Then he feels he's ruined more than just his stomach, & besides, he's fed up. With everything.

Rozi, he says to his mother back home, I'm fed up with everything. Give me my inheritance. I'm leaving. He says this whenever he's fed up with everything. His mother is sitting on the chaff bed inside. She says nothing. I'm hungry, the boy says. Is there anything to eat? In my bag, his mother says. By the door. One bad, says the boy, you didn't cook. I never cook this late, Rózsika says. Two bads, the boy says. What did you bring? Cold cuts. Three bads, he says. You know how I hate cold cuts. His mother laughs softly in the half-light inside. You should've been born a count, she says after a while. Four bads. Why didn't you make sure I'm born one? Besides, who's my father, anyway? That's so many bads, I can't even count them! He's getting ready for bed, too, now, and they will soon turn on the lamp, or not even bother. Where's the furniture? Where's the money? Where are my white jeans? Rozi's in a good mood; she probably had something to drink. You'll get your surprise tomorrow, she says. But I want my surprise today, the boy insists. You can wait for yours until tomorrow if you want! Then they chat for a while, then Dezső goes to the back room with a bottle. Want a drink? Where did you get it? I got it. The boy drinks a little, too, but it doesn't feel good. You shouldn't drink, his mother says. Neither should you, he says, that's so many bads, I'd be inside you so far, I couldn't see out of you if I tried!

His mother is not afraid of him, she knows he'd never hurt her, not even if he shouts or yells or bangs his fist on the chaff bed or holds a knife on her. Then she continues her tale, a trickle of hushed tones about the twilight, the sun, the fire, the poplars in the field where the girls bathed in the buff, and where a little boy brought her the water, then sat down a ways off and watched. Her son listens, there's hardly anything left in the small bottle when she nods off, then he goes to bed, too, no need to rush, he thinks, his hand is still awake, but his head is asleep, and as he dips into the night's slumber he sees his father, they're like two peas in a pod and they love each other very much and tears spring to his eyes and then he dies and nobody mourns for him. He wakes up sniveling, lights the lamp, and goes to his mother. In the light, from close up, she's nearly ugly, like an old hag, her face puffed up and wrinkled, her neck, too, around it the necklace, he pulls it out from under her clothes & yanks off the coin. It's in the palm of his hand. It's his.

From now on everyone will love him, and not her. He runs out to the yard with it & holds it up to the light of the moon, on one side the two-headed bird, on the other, etched in clumsy letters, MY LIFE. He puts it between his teeth, but feels nothing.

ENDNOTES

1. Endre Ságvári (1913–1944): A Jew, chief organizer of the left-wing youth movement and active opponent of the fascist Arrow Cross. He died in a gunfight on July 27, 1944, when the police tried to arrest him and he pulled a gun on them.

2. Miklós Radnóti (1909–1944): Jewish poet, scholar, and literary translator, called into forced labor in May 1944. Too sick and exhausted to continue his forced march through northern Hungary, he was shot, along with 21 others, in early November 1944 on orders of lieutenant-colonel Ede Marányi.

3. The co-op: The cooperative movement became a major priority of the newly established Communist government in 1948. The object was the large-scale, socialist industrialization of Hungarian agriculture. Forced into producers' cooperatives, the peasants, left without land and livestock (they were allowed to keep only two pigs and one cow), began to troop into the towns in search of livelihood.

4. They signed a contract: During the Kádár years (1956–1989) couples could obtain low interest loans for housing by signing a promissory contract to have at least two children.

5. Diósgyőr: During the Kádár years Diósgyőr was a major center of heavy industry, a Communist showcase with a huge steel factory.

6. I'm an Antall boy: After the democratic changeover of 1989, when József Antall (1932–1993) became Prime Minister, major socialist plants were privatized or shut down, leaving many people without jobs.

7. The co-op is falling apart at the seams: As part of the post-89 privatization scheme, the farmers' and producers' cooperatives were bought up by the "highest bidder," usually former managers or government insiders, leaving the farmers who had worked there without land to cultivate.

8. It can't be given away as compensation land anymore: As part of the post-1989 privatization scheme, farmers whose land had been nationalized or given to the farmers' cooperatives after World War II could apply for compensation in the form of land made available by disbanding the cooperatives. However, in the meantime, many such cooperatives were bought up by insiders.

9. Getting ready for Parliament?: Prominent members of the conservative MDF (Hungarian Democratic Forum), which formed the first post-Communist government, grew a mustache to look more authentically Hungarian, i.e., patriotic & a true "Magyar."

10. Workers' Militia: a paramilitary organization created after the failed revolution of 1956. Under strict Party control, it was meant to support the Communist regime — an easily mobilized irregular "working people's" army.

11. Brigade diary: A Communist invention, Workers' Brigades had to keep a diary of their activities in and out of the workplace. There were regular "work achievement contests," too, and if a brigade could demonstrate that it had achieved its work directives or, better yet, had overachieved them, as evidenced by the brigade diary, it was awarded the Socialist Brigade distinction. The award generally came with extra money as well.

12. Zaporozhets: Manufactured between 1959 & 1994, the Zaporozhets was the "people's car" of the Soviet Union and most of its satellite states. With its rear wheel drive, it was both sturdy and affordable, but after the demise of Communism, lost its popular appeal.

13. How did these people get hold of so much money in four years?: Presenting the cost to human lives of the years immediately following the democratic changeover of 1989–1990, the stories in *Our Street* span the years between 1990 & 1994.

14. He was recruited into the state security forces in '56: In 1956, the Communist government set up a special military task force independent of the army with the express purpose of helping the Soviet forces put down the revolution by force of arms.

15. The local chapter of MDF: The conservative Hungarian Democratic Forum, or MDF, was one of the main forces behind the democratic changes of 1989–1990. In 1990 it won the popular elections and for eight years was the leading party of the coalition. It was known for handing out foodstuff like potatoes to people in the countryside for free, especially around Christmas time.

16. For a while he called him Zhivago: In the novel (Boris Pasternak, 1957) as well as in the film (David Lean, 1965), the first part of which plays out during the Russian revolutionary period, Doctor Zhivago was a doctor by profession, but a poet at heart.

17. He survived Albania and Recsk: Between 1950 & 1953, the Secret Police, or ÁVH, operated a labor camp near the town of Recsk. Because of the extreme conditions at the camp, it became known as the Hungarian gulag. Similar camps were in operation in other Soviet satellite states, including Albania.

COLOPHON

OUR STREET

was typeset in InDesign CC.

The text *&* page numbers are set in *Adobe Jenson Pro*.
The titles are set in *Dirty Ego*.

Book design *&* typesetting: Alessandro Segalini
Cover design: Contra Mundum Press
Image credit: "Bacedasco Alto 2014" by Alessandro Segalini

OUR STREET

is published by Contra Mundum Press.
Its printer has received Chain of Custody certification from:
The Forest Stewardship Council,
The Programme for the Endorsement of Forest Certification,
& The Sustainable Forestry Initiative.

Contra Mundum Press   New York · London · Melbourne

CONTRA MUNDUM PRESS

Dedicated to the value & the indispensable importance of the individual voice, to works that test the boundaries of thought & experience.

The primary aim of Contra Mundum is to publish translations of writers who in their use of form and style are *à rebours*, or who deviate significantly from more programmatic & spurious forms of experimentation. Such writing attests to the volatile nature of modernism. Our preference is for works that have not yet been translated into English, are out of print, or are poorly translated, for writers whose thinking & æsthetics are in opposition to timely or mainstream currents of thought, value systems, or moralities. We also reprint obscure and out-of-print works we consider significant but which have been forgotten, neglected, or overshadowed.

There are many works of fundamental significance to *Weltliteratur* (& *Weltkultur*) that still remain in relative oblivion, works that alter and disrupt standard circuits of thought — these warrant being encountered by the world at large. It is our aim to render them more visible.

For the complete list of forthcoming publications, please visit our website. To be added to our mailing list, send your name and email address to: info@contramundum.net

Contra Mundum Press
P.O. Box 1326
New York, NY 10276
USA

SÁNDOR TAR (1941-2005)

JUDITH SOLLOSY

Judith Sollosy is the translator of Sándor Tar's contemporaries Péter Esterházy, Mihály Kornis, & Lajos Parti Nagy.